The PIRATE

The PIRATE

THE SAVAGE SEVEN

KATHERINE GARBERA

KENSINGTON PUBLISHING CORP.
www.kensingtonbooks.com

BRAVA BOOKS are published by

Kensington Publishing Corp.
119 West 40th Street
New York, NY 10018

All Kensington titles, imprints and distributed lines are available at special quantity discounts for bulk purchases for sales promotion, premiums, fund-raising, educational or institutional use.

Special book excerpts or customized printings can also be created to fit specific needs. For details, write or phone the office of the Kensington Special Sales Manager: Kensington Publishing Corp., 119 West 40th Street, New York, NY 10018. Attn. Special Sales Department. Phone: 1-800-221-2647.

ISBN-13: 978-0-7582-3212-0
ISBN-10: 0-7582-3212-8

First Kensington Trade Paperback Printing: July 2010

10 9 8 7 6 5 4 3 2 1

Printed in the United States of America

Chapter One

A warrior must only take care that his spirit
is not broken.
—Carlos Castaneda

The full moon hung over the Indian Ocean like something out of a fairy tale. Daphne Bennett walked along the deck of the oil tanker *Maersk Angus* enjoying the sight. The winds were light and the temperature warm on this night in mid-June. A moment of unreality struck her as she paced near the railing.

This was so different from the affluent suburbs of Washington, D.C., and her life as the ex-wife of a prominent U.S. Senator. A part of her couldn't believe she was really here. But another part relished the start of her adventure.

"It's a little late for a stroll," a deep masculine voice said.

She stopped and glanced toward the stern of the ship where the glow of a cigarette could be seen in the deep shadows. The voice was American, and she knew immediately it was the captain of the *Maersk Angus* who spoke to her.

"I couldn't sleep, Captain Lazarus," she said.

Her group had met the crew when they'd boarded the *Maersk Angus* two days ago.

"Call me Laz," he said.

"I'm Daphne," she said, unsure he remembered her. Her group, Doctors Across Waters, or DAW, wasn't that large, but they'd been a last-minute addition to his tanker. They'd caught the ship in Lisbon when the flight they were scheduled to take had been canceled due to renewed violence in Somalia. She flinched inwardly as she remembered that the violence had been the terrorist bombing of another humanitarian group's chartered plane.

Daphne thought about turning back when she realized that Africa was just as violent as she'd always heard. The news stories she'd read were about to have a direct impact on her life. But she'd spent the last few years living in a kind of stasis and she was tired of never doing anything other than her job. She needed an adventure.

"Excited about your trip?" he asked, stepping out of the shadows.

He was a rough-looking man but still attractive. A light beard shadowed his strong, square jaw. His dark hair was shorn close to his head, revealing a scar twisting up the left side of his neck.

As a surgeon, she could tell that whoever had stitched up what she guessed to be a knife wound hadn't been to medical school. As a woman, she guessed that Laz hadn't minded, since if the wound hadn't been stitched up he probably would have died.

She'd been single for almost two years now, but this man wasn't like any of the men she'd dated. An aura of danger hovered about him. It might be due to the fact that he led a crew of men who looked like they'd be better suited to crew Johnny Depp's *Black Pearl* in Disney's *Pirates of the Caribbean*. Or maybe it was due to the fact that when he looked at her, she had the feeling that he looked past the confines of her profession and saw the woman underneath.

"A little nervous, actually."

He laughed, a rough sound that carried on the wind. "Somalia—hell, all of Africa—has that effect on people."

The sea around the tanker seemed calm, and on this moonlit night with no one else on deck, she felt like . . . like they were alone in the world.

"On you?" she asked. She couldn't imagine this man being nervous in any situation. He radiated the calmness she always experienced when she was in the operating room. It was a calmness born of the fact that he knew what he was doing.

"Nah. I've been around this part of the world for a long time."

"Why is that? You're American, right?"

"Yes, I am. But I was never one for staying put. I wanted to see the world." There was a note in his voice that she easily recognized. It said that he was searching for something that he hadn't found. Something that he might never find. She understood that now.

It was funny, but before her divorce she would have thought he was unfocused or didn't know himself well. But now she understood that sometimes life threw a curve and dreams changed and your way was lost. Hers had been. She'd been drifting without a focus, and she hoped this summer in Africa would help her to find her way back to who she had been.

Did this rough-looking man have dreams? Dreams that she'd be able to relate to? At one point in her not-so-distant past she would have seen Laz as a man she had nothing in common with—a man whose dreams would make absolutely no sense to her. She no longer looked at the world in the black-and-white terms she used to, and she guessed she had to thank Paul and his philandering ways for that.

"Well, you are certainly seeing parts of it that are off the beaten path," Daphne said.

She'd spent all of her life taking the safe route. College followed by medical school. Marriage to an up-and-coming lawyer who morphed his successful career into a successful

Senate bid. She'd had two children with Paul Maxwell and raised them to be very successful teenagers before Paul decided that it was time to trade her in for a newer model. A microbiologist named Cyndy who didn't have stretch marks.

She shook her head. She wasn't bitter.

Really.

It was just that when Paul had walked away from their marriage he'd broken something that she'd always claimed as her destiny. He'd broken her dreams of a fifty-year wedding anniversary party. Her dreams of being married to the same man for her entire life. And she was still trying to figure out who she was if she wasn't going to be Mrs. Paul Maxwell.

She realized she'd let the conversation lag while she'd been lost in her thoughts of her ruined marriage. She looked over at Laz.

"Our group goes to the places that really need aid," she said.

He gave her a half-smile that showed her the dangerous-looking man could also be sexy in a rough-hewn sort of way.

"Good for you."

She glanced over at him; it was hard to see much of his features in the dim lighting. "Are you being sarcastic?"

He shrugged. "Not really. I admire people who walk the walk."

She had no idea if he was sincere or not. But she'd always tried to be honest about who she was and what she wanted. She heard the sound of another engine. "Did you hear that?"

"Yes, ma'am. I think you should go below," Laz said, standing up straighter. He tossed his cigarette over the railing.

"Why?"

"Pirates operate in these waters, and Americans are some of their favorite targets. Go below where I know you'll be safe."

She hesitated for a moment but then saw him draw out a handgun. Moonlight glinted off the well-polished steel of his weapon. His entire demeanor changed. He no longer wore an aura of danger. He was danger. She'd think twice about talking to this man if she saw him on the street back home. In fact she'd do her best to avoid him.

She turned and headed for the stairs, stopping when she heard a voice call out in the dark.

"*Bonjour, le bateau.*"

"*Bonjour. Arrêt. Ne parlez pas encore.*" Laz said. He spoke French like a native, she realized, as he continued conversing with someone she couldn't see. Telling them to hold until he gave them the signal.

She was a little rusty on her French since she'd last lived in Paris during her college career, but she knew enough to make out what he was saying. She hesitated, knowing she shouldn't eavesdrop but wanting to make sure he was okay and not in any danger.

She knew she should get belowdecks to her quarters, but waited to see if there was anything she could do to help. The captain certainly looked like he could take care of himself, but her conscience wouldn't let her leave him alone up there with a potential threat.

Another man joined Laz on the deck. She recognized him as Hammond Macintyre, the second in command. "What's going on?"

"Someone was just up on the deck and I don't want anyone to know what we are doing," Laz said.

"That's fine but Savage has radioed twice."

"I know that," Laz said, turning toward his second in command.

"Why haven't you responded?"

"Don't question me, Hamm," Laz said.

"Are you ready for them to come aboard?"

Laz turned back to where she'd disappeared and she felt like he could see her. She huddled close to the wall of the stairwell, trying to keep still and avoid being seen. What was going on with Captain Lazarus? Was he a pirate?

"Yes," Laz said.

Daphne stayed where she was on the gangway. A part of her wanted to just go back to her sleeping quarters but another part demanded that she see what was going on. She was one of the more senior members of their group.

Although this was her first trip with Doctors Across Waters, she'd served on the board of directors for the last fourteen years.

Who were they trying to let on board? She didn't want to believe that Captain Lazarus—Laz—would betray them but . . . to be honest she didn't trust men. Paul had taken that from her as well when he'd left her.

It made her a little sad but lately she believed the worst of men all the time. Even her sons. That was the main reason she knew she had to get away.

She crept back up the stairs and hid in the shadows watching as Laz used a flashlight to signal someone. She saw the answering flashes of light and then heard nothing but the gentle *thwap* of waves against the hull of their boat.

Was her imagination getting the better of her? She walked carefully toward the shadow cast by one of the containers that were on the deck. She crouched there in the shadows and watched as Laz lowered a rope over the side of the deck. Two minutes later four men had climbed up and stood in a circle around Laz.

Daphne knew that this wasn't a good thing. Each of the men wore camouflage face paint and dark clothing, but that wasn't what really disturbed her. No, what bothered her was the fact that they were all carrying semiautomatic weapons, and Laz seemed perfectly at ease with them. No wonder the captain had tried to hurry her off the deck; she stayed where she was.

What was he up to?

Crouched in the shadows she listened intently to the men as they talked. Their voices were little more than a whisper, and she couldn't make out the conversation. The men moved away from the gangway and she was tempted to follow them.

She heard footsteps on the stairs behind her and stood up as a crew member walked around the corner. He was a tall man, probably about six feet. His jeans had seen better days and the T-shirt he wore had a hole near the shoulder. He apparently hadn't shaved since they'd left Lisbon three days ago, and he smelled a bit sweaty.

"What are you doing here?" he asked in heavily accented English.

"I couldn't sleep," she said. His accent sounded Dutch to her, which made sense given that this was a Danish ship with an international crew that was mostly comprised of men from along the North Sea.

She'd learned a long time ago that lies didn't serve her well. Was this man part of the group with Laz or someone she should notify of the captain's moves? But she suspected if she said she was spying on the captain this man might not like it.

"The seas aren't that rough tonight," he said.

"No, they aren't. I'm Daphne," she said.

"I'm Fridjtof," he said. "You should go back to your quarters now."

She wasn't ready to leave yet—not until she saw more of the men that the captain had been talking to, and got some of her questions answered. She knew that this part of the world wasn't exactly the safest. If there was a problem she wanted all the information she could lay her hands on.

"Why isn't your captain a Dane?" she asked, trying to keep him talking and hoping he'd reveal if he was in league with the captain.

Fridjtof shrugged. "We're a multinational crew. He came over on a boat from Alaska over a year ago and stayed."

"How long have you been working with him?" she asked.

"Just this voyage. Why you ask?"

"No reason. Just curious. I decided when I signed up for this summer trip to learn as much as I could about the people and cultures I encountered."

"Good for you. Now head back to your quarters so that you will be rested when we make berth in Somalia."

She realized Fridjtof was done with her and was on his way somewhere else.

"Good night," she said, walking down the stairs to the corridor that led to her room.

She thought of just letting it go, but that didn't seem like a good idea. She'd watched CNN and Sky TV. She'd seen all the news reports about the pirates that operated in this area and Laz talking to those armed men alarmed her.

The one thing that didn't quite make sense to her was the fact that everything she'd seen or read about the piracy here in the Indian Ocean had indicated that the perpetrators were Somali. And Laz was definitely American.

She started back toward the gangway, but stopped when two of the men she'd seen on deck came down. They turned right without seeing her. She stayed where she was for a minute and then followed them.

This was silly.

She was a doctor, not a detective. But she'd been around people long enough to be able to read danger when she saw it. And she knew something about this situation just wasn't right.

She started to go after them but then stopped. What was she going to do? They had weapons and she had none. Was she just borrowing trouble?

Maybe the men were just crew members . . . like a security staff to keep them safe. But if that were the case, why had Laz asked her to leave when the men came on board?

Maybe she was looking for something more than this really was, she thought. She didn't follow the men. No matter how many bicycle circuits of her neighborhood she'd made as a preteen, she hadn't been Nancy Drew then and she wasn't about to become a girl detective now.

She heard the sound of voices in the galley and recognized them as two of the other members of her group. She entered the dining area, where a long table was bolted to the floor with two solid teak benches on either side.

Bob Dickerson and Franny Milanese sat close together quietly talking. They had both been on this trip before and were well aware of what was in store for their group.

"Hello, Daphne. Restless?" Bob asked. He stood as she entered the room.

She smiled to herself, touched by his old-fashioned manners. Bob was the leader of their team. His experience was a given and he was very good at putting their group at ease. Of the five of them he was the one they all seemed to look toward as the leader. "A little. I was talking to the captain up on deck."

"You shouldn't be on deck at night," Franny said.

"So I've heard."

"Pirates operate in this area and it's too dangerous."

"If they spot foreigners they will target this ship," Bob said.

"If they target this ship it will be because it's a tanker and its cargo is worth more money each day. Besides, everyone in the crew is foreign," said Daphne.

"That is true," Franny said. "But foreign—European or American—hostages fetch more money."

"I didn't realize that," she said. "I'm sorry. I should have stayed down here, but it feels so closed off."

"Yes, it does," Bob agreed. "You'll have a little more freedom when we arrive in Somalia."

"I'm looking forward to that. And doing work for people who need us. I haven't done this since I was in my first-year residency."

Bob smiled at her. "We are so glad you decided to join us this summer. What made you change your mind?"

She shrugged. She didn't want to talk about her personal life with Bob or Franny. "The timing seemed right. Can I ask you both about the Captain?"

"Sure, what's up?"

"When I was on deck we heard an engine approaching and he told me to come downstairs. I did but waited to see if he would need help, and . . ."

She wasn't sure if she should say any more. What could Franny or Bob do to help the situation?

"Did he?"

"No. He knew the men who came on board. But he was speaking to them quietly and . . . they were all armed."

Bob stood up. "I'll go up there and see what's going on. Daphne, you go with Franny back to our quarters. Make sure all of our group is awake. If there is a situation I want everyone ready to move."

"Move? Move where?" she asked.

"Out of harm's way," Bob said.

Franny led the way out of the galley. "Do you want me to come with you, Bob?"

He shook his head.

"No, stay with the others. I think that if there are too many of us—"

"My husband—ex-husband—is a Senator. I'm pretty good in tense situations."

"I know that, Daphne. But in this part of the world sometimes just the fact that you are a woman will work against you."

She nodded. There was a lot of truth to what Bob was saying. She followed Franny down the lit hallway to the bunks where the rest of their team was. Rudy was already waiting for them. When she entered they were all awake and waiting.

"What's going on? I heard a speedboat approaching on the port side." Rudy asked.

Rudy was a nurse with their group who had been working for the last few years in South America. He said he was ready for a change of locale and had signed up to go to Africa with this group after rebels in the South American jungle had killed his girlfriend of eight years.

"I don't like this," he said.

"No one does. Do we have any weapons with us?" Jerry asked.

"Bob always carries a handgun in his med bag," Franny said.

She left them to go and retrieve it.

"Where is Bob?"

"I . . . was up on deck and overheard the captain talking to some men. Bob went to investigate."

"Fucking hell," Jerry said. "I was hoping for a little adventure on this trip but not this much."

She shook her head. Jerry was her age and from California. He was fit and tan and according to Franny was on wife number four. Daphne knew Jerry by reputation only. He was an excellent surgeon, but she'd heard he was a bit of an asshole when he wasn't in the operating room.

Bob reentered the room. "There was no one on deck when I got up there, but I did walk the deck and saw a boat moored off the stern."

"One of the rescue craft for this tanker?" Jerry asked.

"No. A speedboat. The captain was on the bridge talking with two men. But to be honest, at that distance I couldn't make out if they were crew members or not."

"Did you confront the captain?" Franny asked as she rejoined them. She handed the weapon she had to Bob. He took it and then squeezed her shoulder as if to reassure her.

"No. Listen, folks, I'm not sure what's going on up there, but I think we need to stay alert," Bob said.

"I agree," Jerry said.

"Me too," Daphne said. "But we're not armed nor are we trained to take on pirates. I think we need a backup plan."

"I agree," Franny said. "We need to send a message to the DAW home office in Manhattan. They will contact the UN and send forces to protect us."

"How will we do that?" Jerry asked. "My cell phone signal has been spotty for the last twelve hours."

"Mine too," Rudy said.

"We'll have to go to the radio room and send a message," Bob said. "Daphne, would you feel comfortable sending the message to your ex-husband? I feel like we need the U.S. State Department on this as well."

She didn't like the thought of turning to Paul for anything, but dying or being held hostage wasn't like asking him to come over and help her figure out how to work the security system on her house. "Yes, I will do that."

"But when?"

"Tomorrow," Bob said.

They all went to their quarters. She and Franny were sharing accommodations that would have been for the first mate. There were bunk-style beds against one wall and a two-drawer dresser bolted to the floor.

"This is proving to be an exciting trip," Franny said.

"It definitely is," Daphne said. "I really wanted to do something different this summer."

"Me too. I've been traveling to Africa for a while with our group but the restlessness in Somalia and seeing all those children with gunshot wounds and missing limbs . . . they need the help that our organization can provide."

"Yes, they do," Daphne said. "It was the kids that motivated me to come."

That and the fact that her own life had become kind of pitiful. A boring routine where she did nothing but try to figure out what she'd done to drive Paul away. What she'd done to make him turn to another woman.

And that kind of thinking was making her crazy. Even her kids had suggested she do something this summer instead of staying home by herself, which had proven to her that it was beyond time that she started living again.

Lucas had summed it up nicely when he'd reminded her that he and his brother would be in college in less than two years' time and she'd be all alone in that big house.

Chapter Two

A warrior never worries about his fear.
—CARLOS CASTANEDA

J.P. "Laz" Lazarus had reinvented himself more times than he could count. Captain of a Danish tanker wasn't too far of a stretch from who he really was. He loved the ocean and had grown up in the warm waters of Florida's Gulf Coast.

He used his given name—J.P.—with each incarnation to remind him of the family he'd left behind eons ago. His last alias had been J.P. Crosby. But some things—like his love of the sea—had stayed with him.

He'd been an idealistic eighteen-year-old when he enlisted in the U.S. Navy and signed up for Navy SEALS. He'd become a SEAL, one of a team of men he considered closer than brothers. Losing them had forced him onto this path. He was a mercenary, a gun for hire, and that didn't cause him to lose any sleep.

He did what he was good at because frankly at his age—thirty-eight—it was too late for him to go back and try a new career. He wasn't exactly qualified to do much more than this.

And on a night like this, with the warm breeze stirring over the Indian Ocean and his team at his back, he didn't want to be anywhere else.

But talking to Daphne got him thinking about home. He

had a place in the States that he went back to when he had some downtime. It wasn't much. Just an old Florida coquina home on a remote stretch of unspoiled Gulf Coast in south Florida where he could just hang out and fish all day and then drive across Alligator Alley to Miami when he wanted to taste a bit of the nightlife.

The Savage Seven had become his life and his family. The jobs they took working for different clients around the world had validated who he was in a way that nothing else ever had. The differences between Daphne and him were more pronounced than she could guess. He made his living taking lives; she saved them.

"What are you doing? Savage and the team are ready to come on board," Hamm said joining him on deck.

"Quiet. I told Savage to hold because Daphne was just up on deck."

"Daphne? Do you mean one of the doctors?"

"Yes," Laz said, glancing over toward the gangway where she'd disappeared when he'd told her to go below.

He hadn't been sending her away only because he didn't want her to know that his team was coming on board; he needed to keep the deck clear until they found out what they were up against.

"We look clear. Savage, you're okay to come aboard," Laz said. He lowered the rope ladder over the side. The first man over the side was Jack Savage.

He was their leader, and he was every inch the savage he was named after. He was as tough as nails and didn't back down for anyone except maybe his sweet British wife. But even that didn't happen too often.

"Boss," Laz said.

"Romeo."

Laz laughed. "I'm not romancing anyone."

"Yeah, right. Just stay focused on the job."

"I am. Let me show you the passive system I've added to the bridge."

"Great. Hamm, show the rest of the men where to hide the weapons. We heard some chatter on the radio earlier. I think you should expect some action tonight or early tomorrow morning."

Laz led the way to the bridge and showed Savage all the systems he'd been able to put into place.

"Since we are allowing the pirates to take the ship, I've added two recording devices here—one is video and audio, the other is just audio. The audio only is built into the radio and will allow you to monitor the frequency they are broadcasting on."

"That sounds good. I'll need you to show Wenz how to handle the scrambler. We have had some problems with all of our communications."

"The salt air will do it every time. I will show him how to maintain all the radios," Laz said. He was the team's communications guy, as well as their transport expert. There wasn't a machine that Laz couldn't make work.

"As long as we can keep the lines open, I'm happy. Do you need me to leave another man on the tanker?"

"No. Hamm and I have it covered. Besides, at this point, if we had another man I think the crew and our passengers would question it."

"I agree. Who are the passengers? Your message was a bit garbled . . . you said doctors?"

"Yes. They are going to Somalia, so we are going to take them close to the shore and they will take one of the speedboats there."

"Who came up with that plan?"

"Their group. The plane they'd chartered was sabotaged."

"Why didn't they turn back?" Savage asked.

Laz shrugged. "I didn't ask. But the fax I got from Maersk

said that they were needed in Somalia to relieve the group of doctors who are already there."

"Will they get in the way?"

"I don't know. I'm hoping we can deliver them before we lure the pirates to the tanker." Maersk was a shipping line and not a passenger fleet.

Savage shook his head. "We can't count on that. I'd recommend locking them up at the first sign of trouble so that we can keep them all alive."

"Yes, sir."

"Laz? You here?" Hamm said through the wireless earpieces they all wore.

"Yes, what do you need?"

"One of the men is up on deck."

"On my way. Savage, do you need anything else from me?"

Savage shook his head. "Mann?"

Laz heard the conversation via his earpiece.

"We're done. As soon as the deck is clear, we'll meet you on the boat."

"Sounds good. We're running silent now," Savage said.

Laz left his team leader and went back down to the deck to see what his crew member was doing at this time of night.

The ship was always active and this time of night was no different. It had taken a lot of careful planning to make sure the deck would be empty when Savage and the team arrived.

He wasn't bothered that Daphne had been up on the deck tonight. He remembered his first time on the Indian Ocean and the Gulf of Aden. He'd been anxious to see how these seas were different than the ones back home.

And he had found that for all that he was on the other side of the world there was sameness to the oceans. A feeling of home that came to him only when he was on the seas.

And like that feeling of home there was now the familiarity of having to deal with a fractious member of his crew. Since they'd left port in Madrid, Fridjtof had been running around making trouble.

Laz knew it was past time that he stopped it.

Tankers were like a city at sea and he was the man in charge. Laz hated the bureaucracy that went along with being the captain. He wasn't sure how Savage put up with it. Laz laughed to himself. Savage put up with it by ruling with a iron fist.

More than once the Savage Seven had had a knock-down, drag-out fight to settle differences of opinion. Violence was its own kind of peacekeeping method for their team. And right now Laz was running high on testosterone. He needed to get rid of his excess energy. He couldn't take it out on the small crew they had on the tanker, though.

They were running with a small crew on this trip because of the recent piracy. Maersk and their clients wanted the pirates stopped, which was why they'd agreed to allow Hamm and Laz to infiltrate the crew. The rest of the *Maersk Angus* crew totaled ten men.

Fridjtof was the one man who made Laz uneasy. He was always poking around where he shouldn't be. And twice Laz had caught him coming out of the radio room. The crewman was a loader so he had no business in the radio room.

Laz had already had a run-in with the man once before when Fridjtof was bullying one of the rookie crewmen. He was a tough man who only respected brawn. He wasn't the type of man that you could talk around—fists worked best for him.

Laz rubbed the back of his neck. Or was that his wishful thinking coming into play? He needed the release and sparring with Fridjtof that would do that.

And now he was on deck in the middle of the night when everyone else was sleeping. Well that wasn't true, Laz thought. Daphne had been up here but somehow he didn't think she might be working a double-cross on the tanker crew. To be honest he did believe that Fridjtof had two bosses.

"Fridjtof? What have I told you about being on deck after hours?"

"Ah, sorry about that, Captain. Just needed to get out of my bunk for a few minutes."

The night was calm and clear and not the type of weather for the men to stay belowdecks, but the dangers of the waters they were traveling through had made the "no deck" rule that Laz had put into place viable to the men.

"No exceptions," Laz said.

"I thought I saw a woman up here. Was she an exception?"

"She's none of your damned business. You will do what you're told," Laz said, pointing his finger at Fridjtof's chest.

The other man took a deep drag on his cigarette and blew smoke back in Laz's eyes. "I guess if I had boobs you'd feel different."

Laz punched the other man on the shoulder. "Watch it. Our guests will be treated with respect."

"Yeah, I know. They are off limits as well but not for you, eh, Captain?"

Laz narrowed his eyes on the other man. What had he seen? Maybe it would be simpler to simply take Fridjtof captive and send him with Savage and the rest of their team.

Daphne? How long had Fridjtof been up here? He didn't really like the thought of this man talking about Daphne.

"She isn't used to life at sea the way a seasoned crewman like yourself is."

"I just think if I were curvy you'd be treating me differently."

Laz shook his head. "Regardless, get below."

Fridjtof looked like he was going to argue and Laz took a step toward the man. His command had to be absolute; there was no time to argue or run the ship like a democracy. "Or I can put you in lockup."

Fridjtof held his hands up. "I'm going, Cap."

Laz watched the other man disappear.

"Damn it, I don't like that guy," Hamm said, joining Laz at the railing.

"I don't trust him," Laz admitted.

"With the women?" Hamm asked.

"With anyone. Is the rest of the deck clear?"

"Affirmative," Hamm said.

"Team, you are clear to retreat." Laz spoke softly and knew that his message had been received when the other four members of the Savage Seven appeared on the deck. Aside from Savage, there was Kirk Mann, who was the second in command for their team. He had been a marine sniper before joining their unit. No one shot with more accuracy than Mann. Wenz was their medic and Van was the team's computer expert. He was the one they were all relying on to track Samatan's ship when it surfaced.

Samatan was the leader of a particularly bloodthirsty group of pirates. The Savage Seven had been hired to capture him. The general belief was that if the head of the viper was cut off it would lead to the nest of the pirates. Then the attacks would launch.

Hamm took up a post near the gangway so that they wouldn't have any more surprise visitors. Slowly the men departed over the side railing.

"We're not going far. Just out of sight of the ship. We'll be in radio contact if you need us," Savage said.

"I'll alert you the minute we see anything suspicious."

"Good. Once you let them on board don't fight. Their MO is that they take the ship with a show of force but usually don't kill their captives."

"You're telling me stuff I already know, boss."

Savage put his hand on Laz's shoulder. "I don't like having those civilians on here. The tanker crew knows how to handle this kind of thing."

"I'll take care of them," Laz said.

"You do that. I'm going to have Wenz dig up what he can on the doctors' group. I'll send you back what we find. Good luck."

"Thanks, boss."

Though everything was in place Laz didn't relax. Experience had taught him there was no such thing as an easy mission, especially with all the variables they were dealing with here. The added passengers and stopping to deliver them to their destination was not going to be an easy matter. But their schedule did have the time for a one-day stopover.

He almost wondered if someone knew that the Savage Seven was watching over this ship and that's why they'd arranged for the Doctors Across Waters group to travel with them.

Laz would keep the group safe. Savage would want them protected as well. He was keen on keeping as many civilians alive as possible on their missions. That was one of the things Laz liked about working for Savage. That and the fact that he was a valued member of the team. Despite the fact that Savage was their leader, the group respected everyone's opinion and skills.

Laz couldn't ask for a better life, he thought while standing on the deck and looking out over the moonlit ocean. So what if sometimes when he was at home he felt lonely?

This was the best job in the world for him, and he knew that nothing and no one would ever make him give it up.

"The deck is busy tonight," Hamm said.

"Damn straight. I got an itchy feeling on the back of my neck that something is going to happen."

"Having Fridjtof up here was odd. That man is always creeping around."

"I agree. Keep a close eye on him."

"I am."

Hamm and Laz had been in some tight situations together but they always came out the victors. Their current mission was working secretly for the allied nations to stop the threat of piracy in these waters.

Their group's aim was to be offensive instead of defensive. Instead of waiting until a ship was taken hostage, they were proactively in the area to thwart and capture the pirates.

One of their own men—Kirk Mann—had been working in Somalia to infiltrate the pirates. It was Mann's lead that had brought them here to the *Angus.* Kirk was the best at disguising himself, and he had a soulless attitude that made it easy for him to fit right in with lawless men.

Laz had seen a different side to Kirk last year when he'd fallen in love with Olivia Pontuf. Laz had thought it would change Kirk but it hadn't. He still worked with them and was just as lethal as before.

Laz didn't know if he'd stay in this business if he had a woman like Olivia waiting at home for him.

"Laz?" Savage said through the wireless earpiece.

"Here."

"We just got word that the pirate group is moving to attack tonight. They are looking for Americans and they had some intel on our doctors. Someone in that group has a connection to a U.S. Senator."

"Nice. Who is it?"

"It's the woman . . . Daphne Bennett, she's the ex-wife of Senator Paul Maxell," Savage said.

"Fucking hell. That's all we need," Hamm said.

"Thanks, Savage, we will handle her protection here," Laz said. "Tanker out."

"Why did they let her come here? Don't they know what kind of hotbed this is?" Hamm asked

Laz had no idea what motivated anyone to do anything. He only knew that he and Hamm and the rest of the Savage Seven would do their damnedest to protect Daphne and the other doctors in their group.

"I guess it doesn't matter," Hamm said.

"Not really. She's the kind of bait that could draw Samatan out of hiding."

"Indeed. She'll make nice bait but I'm not sure she'll agree. And capturing Samatan is our goal," Hamm said.

Getting Samatan—the leader and possible trainer of most of the pirate groups that operated in this area—was their ultimate goal. The man was elusive and deadly. And, Laz suspected, smart. Samatan had been operating in this area for over three years and had never been caught. He was very good at raking in the dough.

"We'll do it without using the woman," Laz said. "We always get our man."

"Yes, we do. I'm not sure I like this setup with the civilians."

"No one does. It's really the wrong place and wrong time for them to be here."

"Damned straight," Hamm said.

"What do you need me to do?"

"Check the radio room and the communications that have gone out. I want to know if they found out about the doctor from someone onboard this tanker."

"Will do."

"Let me know as soon as you find anything. I want to keep a low profile on the radio waves if we can. Not contact Savage again or have him back on the ship."

"I think we can manage that," Hamm said, walking away.

Laz stayed where he was—staring out over the sea. One of

the reasons he'd always liked being on the water was the sense of isolation. That feeling of being alone in the world. He rubbed the back of his neck. No doubt a therapist would have a field day exploring why he needed to be alone.

But he didn't give a crap. He liked it. And tonight in the quiet before the storm that he knew would be coming he felt at home with his place and purpose and that was enough for him.

Lately he'd felt . . . empty. Unsure of his reasons for always moving on. Maybe it was the fact that both Savage and Mann had married. It made him aware of the fact that he was closing in on forty and still alone.

He checked his weapon and walked across the deck. Laz pulled his night-vision goggles out of his pocket and put them on. He skimmed the horizon around the boat and saw . . . nothing. Maybe the faint shadow of something but nothing concrete.

Damn, he was restless. He really wished that Fridjtof had given him an excuse to fight. He needed the physical release of sparring with someone.

He sent a wordless message to Savage using clicks on his wireless mike and earpiece to be on alert that the pirates may have been signaled and continued about the business of running the ship on alert for an attack from pirates.

Laz tried not to think of the lovely doctor who might be risking her neck by just being on this mission, but it was hard not to. She had captured his attention whether or not he wanted the distraction of her. His secret fantasy woman had dropped in his lap—here of all places.

He had combed bars and bowling alleys back home looking for a woman like Daphne . . . hell, that was probably why he hadn't found her. She wasn't a honky-tonk barfly but a real sophisticated woman.

He didn't waste time worrying about the class differences between them. He knew that he could overcome any of those superficial differences. Talking to her tonight had made him realize that he wanted to overcome them. He wanted to have something with Daphne. If it turned out to be a fling, well he knew he'd be better for it.

Damn, maybe it had been too long since he'd had some R&R. Maybe what he should have done before they'd left Madrid was found a lovely Spanish señorita and spent a few days in her bed.

But somehow he suspected no matter how many women he'd had, Daphne still would have affected him the way she did. If the threat of pirates wasn't imminent, he knew he'd have found a way to seduce her tonight.

"Laz, you there?" Savage said in his ear.

"Go ahead," Laz said.

"Wenz has picked up an unmonitored call coming from fifty nautical miles from your location. This beacon sounds like it might be a distress call."

"Do you think it's the pirates?" Laz asked.

He crossed the deck quickly and took the stairs leading to the bridge two at a time.

"Thor, take a break. I've got the bridge," he said to the crewman working in the bridge.

"Yes, sir. I've been dying for a cigarette," Thor said.

"Enjoy," Laz said. Once the man was gone, he pulled up the navigation maps on the computer.

"Go ahead with the coordinates, Savage," Laz said.

Savage gave him the coordinates and Laz logged them into the computer program. "We don't have a history of attacks in that area."

"Affirmative. Check your logs and let me know if any previous captains experienced distress calls before being attacked."

"Will do," Laz said. That was one way to get his mind off Daphne and back on the job, he thought ruefully.

It wasn't usual for him to woo a woman, and he'd never been tempted before this. The job—this mission—was the most important thing in his life. Like all the missions before this one. And the ones that would come after.

The lovely doctor was just a woman, and he knew he'd do well to remember that. She was someone he could enjoy for the length of this mission but beyond that she was from a different world.

And a man who changed his name and his persona every few months wasn't the kind of man who could offer her anything more than a few hours' pleasure in bed.

And he did want that. She was sweet yet sexy at the same time. She was smart and sassy and everything he wanted in a woman.

He shook his head. The job, he thought. He needed to stay focused on the job. Men who didn't often ended up dead.

And he sure as hell wasn't ready to check out of the game yet.

Chapter Three

The way of the warrior is resolute acceptance of death.
—Miyamoto Musashi

Daphne was a bit unsure of herself this morning. Her "alarm" last night had been for naught and she felt very foolish. The rest of the team didn't censure her and they all still remained on guard. Daphne and Bob were still planning to send a message to Paul as soon as they received permission from the captain.

Bob was seasick and asked her to wait a few hours before they went to use the radio and contact Paul. She wondered if he was having second thoughts now that it was daylight. She was. With the heat of the sun on her shoulders and the fresh air in her hair, she didn't believe there was any threat to them.

This trip, which had seemed the answer to so many of her problems, now just seemed foolish. Her intent to help impoverished children didn't feel silly to her. Even at home she had always done that by making sure her practice treated kids from all income levels. What worried her was the desire to have an adventure so she wouldn't feel like the left-behind woman anymore.

No matter that they hadn't been attacked by pirates last night, she knew that Laz was up to something. And this morning, as she jogged through the crates lining the deck of the tanker, she tried to clear her mind. Her iPod Shuffle was cranking out Black Sabbath and Trick Daddy but her mind wasn't going any further than the bridge of the ship.

She was tired of being lied to by men. And though Laz didn't come right out and lie to her, he hadn't exactly been honest with any of them either. He was a pirate. That was the only explanation that she could come up with. Why else would he be beckoning men onto the tanker in the middle of the night?

She slowed to a walk to do her warm down and sensed someone behind her. She glanced over her shoulder to see Laz. She turned off her iPod as he approached.

"Mind if I join you?"

"I guess not."

"That's not very gracious. I must have made a bad impression last night. How about I make it up to you?"

She shook her head. How could she admit to him that his impression had been fine until she'd spied on him from the gangway? "You were charming, as I'm sure you know."

"Charming?" he asked, arching one eyebrow at her. "Well, that's promising."

"It's your tanker so I guess you can do what you want," she said, not wanting him to read too much into her allowing him to join her.

"But I still want to respect your space," Laz said.

"Please sit down," she said.

He sat down next to her and the first thing she noticed was that he smelled good—a mixture of soap and mint. She took a deep breath.

"How many more days until we arrive at our destination?"

"Maybe a day," Laz said. "The seas have been calm and we are making good time."

"That'll be great," she said.

"Anxious to get to doctoring?" he asked.

"Yes, I am," she said. "I don't know if I can really explain it without sounding stupid but I feel like I'm half-alive when I'm not working."

"That makes sense. Being a doctor is more than a job—it's a calling. Not many people are lucky enough to find that."

"Did you?"

He shrugged. "I think so. What I do is a necessary evil but I'm very good at it."

"What you do? Captaining a tanker isn't evil, Laz."

"Nah, I guess you're right. It's just that compared to being a doctor captaining a tanker isn't all that glamorous a calling."

Daphne looked at him. He still had that aura of danger that surrounded him, but there was sincerity to his words.

"We are all called to do something different. All those different parts make up the whole."

"Very wise."

She started laughing. "My son said that to me before I left."

"So he's smart like you?"

"And lazy too," Daphne said. "He was trying to convince me to let him play video games all summer instead of going to the academic camp I signed him up for."

Laz arched an eyebrow at her, "Did it work?"

"No," she said. "I want my boys to have every opportunity and only a good education can ensure that."

She just shook her head at him. He was charming and that was a big part of her problem. She didn't want to like this man, because she didn't trust him.

"Fight!"

Another man yelled something she didn't understand but she recognized the telltale sounds of a crashing chair. She looked over at the tables behind her in time to see two men fighting.

Laz stood and reached the men in two long running strides. He didn't reach into the fighting men but just stood next to them.

"Break it up."

His voice was a bellow that made her ears ring. The command was clear, but the men he spoke to weren't fazed at all and didn't pause in their fighting. She didn't know what Laz was going to do but he waded into the mess and slammed the men's heads together. They both fell to the deck but continued fighting.

Laz kicked the back of one man's knee and he fell to the floor moaning. He grabbed the other man and punched him in the gut. They were both on the floor. The tall African man whose name she couldn't remember was bleeding.

Daphne walked over to the crowd of men on the deck. The coppery smell of blood brought back memories of her residency days when she'd worked in the ER. She'd enjoyed that time and the adrenaline rush that came from treating patients who had critical needs. There was a lot to be said about doctoring like that. Though she did enjoy her pediatric practice she'd always liked ER medicine.

"Stay where you are," Laz ordered.

She shook her head. "That man is bleeding profusely, and I can help him. In fact, that's what I'm trained to do, Captain. So let me do my job."

"In a minute," he said. "I doubt that Renault's wound is critical. He can wait until I get to the bottom of this ruckus."

Renault said something in a language that Daphne didn't understand. But Laz nodded and spoke back to the man. How many languages did he speak?

It was another facet of the man she was starting to know, and she realized that the more she learned about him the more questions she had.

Why would a sea captain speak that many different languages? She guessed fluency came from traveling. She was looking for suspicious behavior and kept finding it.

She didn't know if she liked this side of Laz but she did find comfort in the fact that he knew how to handle himself. She felt just a little safer knowing that he wasn't a man who'd run away from a fight.

Laz signaled to Hamm and another crew member to take Renault and Fridjtof down below. They had a small first-aid room, which is where he ordered Renault taken. He really needed to bash some heads together to get rid of the excess anger that was riding him.

The tension of waiting for the pirates to attack and of hoping that their plan would work was getting to him. Having his men act like teenagers with no discipline also pissed him off. He needed his men to behave like grown-ups. There was enough tension on this tanker without adding testosterone posturing into the mix.

"Is it safe for me to go with the injured man?" Daphne asked.

"Yes," Laz said. He didn't want her alone with any of his men. "Hamm, stay with her. I need to talk to Fridjtof."

Daphne followed Hamm down the gangway. Laz didn't like the trouble that Fridjtof had caused. What was going on with that man?

Laz entered the hold—a rather large room that was used to transport private containers that weren't large enough to make the trip on deck like most of the containers they hauled. Fridjtof was led to a chair and sat down.

"Thanks, Rick," Laz said. "Go back to your duties."

"Yes, Captain."

Fridjtof looked up at Laz with contempt in his eyes.

"What happened?"

Fridjtof shrugged. "It's nothing that you need to worry

about. He just gets on my nerves. I can't have someone always watching my every move."

His accent was stronger now that he was aggravated. Laz noticed that the other man's eyes were bloodshot and sunken.

"Are you ill?" He hoped that Fridjtof wasn't using drugs. But if he was that might explain his erratic behavior both today and last night. He had never met the man before this voyage, so Laz had no idea what to expect from him.

"What?" Fridjtof asked. "Nah, just didn't get any sleep last night."

"Why don't you go to your bunk for a few hours and catch up on some sleep?"

"Nah—"

"That's an order."

Fridjtof stood up and paced around the room. Laz watched the other man, waiting to see if he was going to attack. Fridjtof was moving like a caged tiger. And Laz was more than ready for whatever the other man decided to do.

"Hell. I'm not a boy to be ordered about."

"On this ship you are," Laz said.

"Whatever."

"You can cool off here or in your bunk. It's up to you."

"My bunk." The other man stood and stretched. "I get itchy being out to sea for this long."

"I thought this was your normal run," Laz said.

"It is. I still get restless. And having women on board . . ."

Laz wasn't sure what the other man was getting at. "In the old days they used to think women brought bad luck at sea."

"That's what I mean, man."

Laz realized the more they talked the more Fridjtof settled down, so he leaned back against the door and thought about the other man's point. "Some curses still are in effect."

"Yeah, I know. Red sky in morning, sailor take warning."

"But that's a weather warning system."

"Women are a distraction, Captain, which you seem to be experiencing firsthand."

Laz didn't bow to anyone and wasn't about to stop talking to Daphne. "I'm not distracted."

"We'll see."

Laz shrugged. He didn't like Fridjtof's attitude but there was little that could be done for it now. "No more fighting or else I'll lock you in the storage closet until we get to port."

"Yes, Captain."

"Cool off at your bunk for a few hours. I don't want to see you until mealtime."

Fridjtof nodded and Laz opened the door to let the other man go.

Laz watched until he disappeared down the long gray hallway. Then he started to return to the bridge.

"Savage?"

There was no sound in his earpiece, not even the crackle of an open comm. "Damn it."

Laz walked down the hallway toward the gangway. "Savage?"

"Here, Laz, what do you need?" The signal was weak and Savage's words faded in and out.

Laz walked farther away from the hold and the sound got better. "Damn, the hold is a blackout zone for communication."

"Is that a problem?" Savage asked.

"It could be, if the pirates attack while we are down there. I don't know all the scenarios but I'd prefer to be able to talk to you from the entire ship."

"How'd we miss that?" Savage asked.

"I don't know. I'm going to have Hamm see if he can fix this."

"Roger that. What did you need from me?"

"Can Wenz do a background check on Fridjtof?"

"We already screened the crew," Savage said.

"I just feel like we missed something. Last night he was on deck and this morning fighting with another crew member."

"Not a problem. Wenz will radio if he finds anything. Any sign of trouble yet?"

"Nothing other than the tension on the ship. I think having passengers is making the crew antsy." Laz hadn't captained the crew of a tanker before. His small sailing yacht back home was just right for himself to crew. He had no problems giving orders, but a part of him was leery of having all these men under his command because he just didn't know them. He trusted Hamm but beyond that he wasn't sure of any of the other men.

"Makes sense," Savage said. "They are used to being themselves without witnesses."

"True."

"You doing okay?" Savage asked.

Laz thought about it for a minute before answering. He didn't want to admit that seeing Savage and then Mann marry had him thinking about his future and whether he'd ever find a girl to settle down with. He especially didn't want to say that now when he was in the middle of a tense mission.

"Yes. I like being at sea and making sure the ship is in top shape. To be honest I could almost see myself doing this."

"Uh oh, thinking of leaving our group?"

"Never. But this is a glimpse at what my life could have been."

"I know the feeling."

"I've got to get back to work. I'll look forward to hearing from Wenz. Laz out."

"Savage out."

* * *

The first-aid office was really all that the medical facility was. It had a battered desk that was bolted to the floor, as was all furniture on the ship. A cabinet held rudimentary medical supplies.

"Does this kind of fighting take place often on board?" Daphne asked Hamm after Renault was patched up and had left to talk to the Captain.

Hamm was the second in command on the ship and had a friendly next-door kind of face. She realized that he had a way of moving that was completely silent.

"Sometimes. Depends on the crew. Tankers are a world of their own for the length of the cruise so we tend to just do our own thing. I'm not sure what those boys were fighting over."

"Men can be that way," she said, thinking of her own boys, who just got testy sometimes with each other, and needed to slug it out to get back to normal. She'd been surprised at first at that type of behavior in her boys. She'd done everything to discourage violence, but she'd noticed from a young age that their play involved more physicality.

"Boys can be that way," Hamm said. "Men learn to control themselves."

She tilted her head to the side. "I'm sorry. I was only thinking of my boys, who can be that way sometimes. I didn't mean to offend you."

"You didn't. I just wanted to make sure you knew that men can control their tempers," Hamm said.

"I've never been in a situation like this," she said.

"Why are you here?" he asked. "Pardon me for asking but this seems about out of your milieu."

She smiled at the way he said it. He was trying to be polite but being here wasn't her thing. Serving on the board for Doctors Across Waters—that was her thing. Traveling across the world on a tanker . . . that was not like her.

But she'd changed. Been forced to realize that her life wasn't on one set path. She had choices. And she'd made this one because she was tired of always wanting to make a difference in lives but never leaving her practice or her office.

She wanted to be an adventurous person, she thought. Part of it was because of Paul and the way her marriage had ended, but a bigger part had been when her youngest son Lucas had declined to go on a scouting trip because he didn't want to risk being out of the city.

She realized her reluctance to face her own fears had been passed on to her boys. And she wanted—no, needed—to be a positive influence on them. They were the one thing she was proud to say came from her marriage.

"I needed a change," she said. "This is a bit more adventurous then I originally anticipated. But being out here on sea has been interesting."

"In what way?" he asked.

"Just seeing the way the crew and the captain interact. Have you known the captain for long?" she asked. She really wanted to know if Laz was a man she could trust. Every instinct she had said she could, but her instincts weren't always on target when it came to men.

"For a while."

"Do you trust him?" she asked.

"With my life," Hamm said. "Why do you ask?"

She shrugged. Now what was she going to say, that she'd seen the captain on deck last night doing something suspicious? That would make her sound . . . silly.

"We're all depending on him to get us safely through these waters. The attacks on ships in this area have been up and naturally I'm concerned."

Hamm nodded. "Laz will deliver you to your destinations. He's reliable and dependable."

"Ah, Hamm, you're making me sound like a Boy Scout," Laz drawled from the doorway.

"You are," Hamm said.

Daphne hated the way her pulse speeded up just because Laz had entered the room.

"How's Renault?"

"Good. The cuts were superficial. I bandaged them and he's fine now."

"Back at work?" Laz asked Hamm.

"Yeah. How's Fridjtof?"

"Cooling off some. He's edgy. I was hoping you could keep an eye on him," Laz said.

Daphne cleaned up the papers from the bandages and tried to look busy. There was no need for her to stay, except she didn't want to have to try to squeeze by Laz to get out of the room.

"No problem. Do you need anything else?"

"Yes, but we can discuss it later."

Hamm nodded.

"Thanks for your help, Daphne. If you hadn't been here—"

"You would have handled it fine. This wasn't a real medical emergency," she said.

"No, it wasn't, but it's always nice to have an expert around," Hamm said, as he walked out the door.

Daphne started to follow him but Laz stopped her with his hand on her arm.

"There is something I'm dying to know," he said.

"What?"

"How your lips feel under mine," he said, lowering his head and brushing his lips over hers.

She surrendered completely to the embrace. The doubts she had about Laz were slowly melting away. Though she knew her instincts had been wrong before when it came to trusting a man, this time she thought that maybe she'd found a man she could rely on.

She realized as he tunneled his hands through her hair and tipped her head backward to give him greater access to her mouth that whether this was wise or foolish she didn't want to miss out on a moment of this experience with Laz.

He was exactly what she needed.

And for once she knew what she wanted. It had been a long time since she'd felt this decisive. She wanted to experience everything she could with this strong, sexy, mysterious man. She wasn't about to let him slip through her fingers.

She wrapped her own arms around his lean waist and leaned up into the kiss. His tongue felt smooth and tasted wonderful against hers. She forgot to breathe, forgot everything except the feel of his hands on her body.

She'd never felt an enflaming attraction like this before. It wiped out all her other thoughts. All she wanted—no, needed—was to get closer to Laz.

She slid her hands down his back and cupped his firm butt, pulling him closer to her. She rocked her center over the side of his hard-on. A moan escaped her.

"Damn, Daph, you are one sexy woman," he said, his voice gruff with passion.

Ten minutes ago she would have argued that she wasn't sexy. That she was just a nice girl. A girl-next-door-kind-of-girl. But in his arms she felt like the most beautiful woman in the world.

She was the sexiest of creatures, and she knew she could tempt him. And that was a very powerful feeling.

"Yes, I am," she said, with a half-smile.

Laz pulled her back into the first-aid room and closed the door. He lifted her up on the exam desk and then stepped forward between her legs.

Daphne reached for him, drawing him even closer, wrapping her arms around his lean waist, and resting her head on his chest.

She took comfort from this man. From the way he moved and the way he wanted her. He made her feel like she wasn't just a divorced woman with stretch marks, but as sexy to him as a Victoria's Secret cover model. It was a heady feeling and she was almost drunk from the sensation.

She wanted Laz. The sea captain that she wasn't sure she trusted. But that was her mind talking. Her body knew that he could be trusted to bring her pleasure. To make her feel like she was a woman again.

He could bring back the feelings she'd lost two years ago when the words "another woman" had left her husband's mouth—the words that had stripped away the very heart of who she was and how she thought of herself as a woman.

She lifted her head and saw him looking down at her. There was desire, lust, and passion in his gaze, and she shook from the power those feelings evoked in her.

She reached down and drew him even closer to her, afraid that he'd change his mind; she didn't want to take a chance on that.

Chapter Four

A warrior takes responsibility for his acts. An average man acts out his thoughts, and never takes responsibility.
—Carlos Castaneda

Laz didn't question his instincts. This time they were telling him that everything he wanted and needed was here in his arms. Daphne felt so damned right. Later he might find that she regretted this moment, but right now, he knew she didn't.

Her taste was addicting; he couldn't get enough of her mouth. Her lips were wide and full and when he kissed her, he felt consumed by her. His blood flowed heavier in his veins and his cock hardened against the front of his pants.

She rested her head against his chest right over his heart and he ran his hands up and down her back, wondering briefly if he should slow this down. Was it too soon for Daphne to be intimate with him? But then she tipped her head up and twined her arms around his neck, drawing his mouth back to hers.

She arched her back and he felt the brush of her breasts against his chest. The skimpy running top she wore was little barrier between them. He loved the feel of her body against his.

He traced his forefinger over the neckline, feeling the residue of sweat on her skin. She was so earthy and sensual.

He had sensed there was more to Daphne than the woman she presented to the world.

And having her in his arms showed him that he had been right. Every touch of her mouth against his, his hands against her body, and her breasts against his chest just inflamed him more.

He pulled her top up and felt the bare skin of her back. She was so delicately built. He stroked his finger down the line of her spine. She arched against him again as he again drew his fingernail down her spine. She shivered and pulled her mouth from his. "That feels . . ."

"Good?" he asked, speaking into her ear.

"Ooh, yes!" she said.

She reached for the hem of his T-shirt and drew it up over his body. He pulled back from her so she didn't discover the gun he had tucked into his jeans at the small of his back. He pulled her hands around to his front so that she could touch his chest.

Then he pulled her shirt over her head and tossed it on the floor next to them. She wore a plain white bra underneath her T-shirt. There was a ring of sweat around her nipples, and for some reason seeing that mark made him groan.

He unclasped her bra and drew it down her arms, exposing her breasts to his gaze. He leaned down and sucked her right nipple into his mouth. She gasped as his lips closed around her flesh.

She tasted of sweat and woman. The scents of her, the tastes of her were intoxicating and went straight to his head.

He cupped her other breast in his hand, rotating his palm over her skin, stimulating the nipple. He felt her hands on his shoulders and then in his hair. He liked the feel of her clutching at him. Felt the rise of her passion as she held him more tightly.

Daphne loved the feel of his stubbled jaw against her skin.

She'd never felt so alive. For the first time she was making love to a man and not thinking about errands that had to be run or chores that still needed doing. She wasn't sure if it was the fact that her life wasn't just routine anymore or if it was this man.

His touch was electric and for the first time in ages she felt truly alive, not like she'd become zombie mom and woman. So disconnected from being alive until this moment when Laz kissed her.

His lips on her breasts made her feel voluptuous though she wasn't near that. Every inch of skin was sensitized and she couldn't help moving against him. She wanted to feel his naked chest against hers. She wanted his large hands skimming over her body.

She put her hands on his back, hating the T-shirt that was in her way; she tunneled her fingers under the cloth to touch his bare skin.

She felt rippled flesh on his back—scarring—and she wondered what it was from. Her experienced fingers were telling her it was a burn mark. She wanted to ask him more questions about it but right now all she could think about was the pulsing ache in her center and how good his mouth felt on her nipple.

He pulled back to look at her. His eyes were glazed over with desire and his mouth looked full and so damned tempting. She leaned up to kiss him and he bent to take her mouth. She tipped her head back as he plundered it. She felt completely conquered by him and enjoyed every second of it.

The tepid air in the room stimulated her breasts as the moisture from his mouth dried on her. She closed her eyes because the feelings were too intense. She shouldn't be feeling like this, not with a man who was for all intents and purposes a stranger, yet he was exactly the man she needed.

Laz felt familiar enough that she was comfortable with his

arms around her. His hands slid down her back and into the waistband of her running shorts. She felt his fingers sprawled on the full globes of her ass.

"Damn, Daphne, why did you have to come into my life now?"

She shook her head. "Do you want me to leave?"

"Hell, no," he said. "I want you naked."

The sounds of crewmen on deck outside reached the first-aid room and she felt scandalized at what she was doing. Not enough to stop, though.

"I want you naked too," she said.

"Not yet."

He traced his finger over her lips. The touch made them tingle and she wasn't sure what else she could do except suck the tip of his finger into her mouth and run her tongue around it.

He groaned her name and that was exactly what she needed to hear to know she wasn't alone in a one-sided passion. Despite the fact that she was the topless one, Laz was just as vulnerable as her.

His desire for her was a powerful aphrodisiac. She pulled his finger from her mouth and put it in his own, then traced circles around both of her nipples with his damp finger. She shivered. She'd never wanted a man more than she wanted him.

She needed to touch him and reached for his shirt again. But he shook his head.

"Put your hands behind you and lean back," he said.

She shook her head but he leaned down and took her mouth with his. Rubbing his lips over hers until she forgot why she hadn't wanted to give in to him.

The passion he called forth so effortlessly in her was drawing her down a path that promised pleasure. He took her wrists in his hands and brought them together behind her back. Placing her palms on the flat surface of the desk, he then skimmed his hands up her arms to her shoulders.

Every touch of his big rough palms on her skin made her squirm. She ached in her center. She was creamy and pulsing and needed his cock inside her and she needed it now.

This was nothing at all like the polite couplings she'd had in the past. This was full-on lust and passion and it was overwhelming her, especially when Laz put his hand between her legs and rotated his palm against her mound. She clamped her legs on his hand but he still managed to move it.

His other hand was on her breast, pinching her nipple and driving her out of her mind. "Laz . . ."

He leaned down and took her mouth. His tongue slid over hers, sucking her bottom lip into his mouth before biting it. She felt so vulnerable with her hands behind her back but she couldn't move. He had leaned over her and she had to use her own arms to keep from falling back on the desk.

Finally he wrapped one arm around her and she lifted herself into his chest. He felt . . . so damned good, she thought. He stepped closer until she felt his cock at the center of her aching pussy. She rotated her hips against him.

It had been so long since she'd had an orgasm it wasn't going to take much to send her over the edge. But she wanted . . . hell, she wanted Laz.

Now.

She clung to his shoulders with one arm and caressed his chest with her other hand. She slipped it on a path straight down his body until she found his cock waiting. He strained against her fingers. His hips jerked as she stroked him through his clothing.

She struggled to unbutton the fastening of his jeans and moaned out loud when his cock finally came free. He continued to toy with her mouth, sucking and biting gently until she thought of nothing else but the final penetration from him.

She needed his hot hard length inside her. She slowly lowered his zipper and found that he wore briefs. She stroked her finger around the tip of his penis, knowing from experience that the area was very sensitive.

He pulled his mouth from hers and moved his hands between their bodies. He freed his cock. She wrapped both hands around him. He was hot and silky smooth and as she stroked her hands over his erection she felt a drip of pre-cum on the tip.

She rubbed her finger over it, smoothing it into his cock. Rubbing one hand down his length, she reached even lower to cup his ball sack with her other hand. She liked the feel of his balls in her hands as she let her fingers roll them.

He groaned her name and it was like nothing she'd heard before.

He wrapped his arm around her waist and lifted her off the desk just high enough so he could pull her shorts and underwear down her legs. They got stuck at her knees but Laz didn't seem to care. He just shoved his cock up tight against her pussy.

"Damn it, woman, I have got to get inside you," he said.

"Yes," she said, not objecting at all. She just wanted her pants all the way off so she could wrap her legs around him.

She shifted her legs but it was hard to get the shorts to move.

"What are you doing?"

"My shorts . . . take them off so I can put my legs around you," she said.

He pushed them down and then stepped back between her legs. The feel of the tip of his naked cock at her entrance made her realize she knew little about this man. "Are you clean?"

"Hell, yes. You?"

"Yes," she said.

"Protection?" he asked.

"Birth control."

"Sweet Daphne, can I come inside your body?" he asked.

She looked up into his sea-colored eyes and nodded. But then she didn't want to be passive about this. She needed to live her life full-on.

She lifted herself up and took his mouth with hers, plunging her tongue deep inside. The tip of his cock stayed right at her entrance and then she bit his lower lip before meeting his gaze.

"Yes, Laz . . . come inside me."

He slipped the tip of his cock inside her slowly. Drawing out the moment when he'd drive himself home. She shifted, trying to make him take her faster, but he wouldn't be hurried no matter how she gyrated her hips or grasped his buttocks.

Laz took his time with her and she then realized how much she needed that. She didn't want a hurried coupling with this man. She wanted to experience everything she could. Lord knew this might be the only time she held him like this.

She wrapped her arms around his waist and lifted her hips toward his. She shifted until she was able to gain another inch of his shaft inside her.

"Do you want all of my cock?" he asked.

"Yessss," she hissed.

He slid home in one long driving thrust and she felt him deep inside her. It was almost too much as she felt her body tighten and her orgasm washed over her. Laz kept thrusting, which made the orgasm keep on spasming.

She grabbed the back of his head and lifted her body again, needing to feel his mouth against hers, but he turned his head at the last second and she felt the brush of his stubble against her cheek.

There was no pretending she was with another man. She knew that it was Laz who was taking her, and she loved every second of it.

It was hot and earthy and everything that she'd never been before. She rubbed her hands through his hair, wishing it was longer so she could tunnel through it.

She loved the powerful feeling of his hips driving between her legs. He suckled her neck right at her pulse point. She knew he had to feel the staccato beating of her heart.

Daphne felt his heart racing under her own fingers when she touched his neck. His neck muscles strained as he swiveled his hips.

"Come for me again," he said.

She did. Just like that. Just hearing the rough, sensual timbre of his voice drove her over the edge.

She dug her heels into the back of his thighs and lifted herself higher on his cock, grinding her clit against the lean hard muscles of his lower stomach.

Laz bent her legs back toward her body, exposing her even further as he thrust into her. His hips hammered faster and faster, and as he leaned over her, he took her right nipple into his mouth, sucking her deeply as he came. She felt the warm jetting of his cum inside her as she tightened around him one more time. Her third orgasm.

He fell heavily against her and she just lay sprawled beneath him. He licked her nipple as he lifted his head and then kissed both breasts before looking down at her. Bracing himself on his arms above her, he leaned down and kissed her mouth.

This kiss was as tender as the earlier ones had been passionate. "Daphne."

"Laz . . . what is your first name?" she asked.

"J.P. Jean-Pierre after both of my granddaddies," he said.

"Jean-Pierre. I like it," she said, "It suits you."

"You suit me. Thank you, Daphne."

Tipping her head to the side she looked up at him in question.

"For reminding what the good life feels like," he said.

That made no sense but he gave her no chance to ask any questions. "I'm going to need to clean up and get you cleaned up."

He pulled out of her body and she realized just how vulnerable she really was as she lay there completely naked when all that he'd bared was his penis. It had shriveled, and as he turned toward the sink she realized she wasn't ready for him to leave but there was no way she was going to ask him to stay with her.

She sat up and was about to hop off the table when he came back with a wet cloth in hand. "Lay back."

She hesitated but there was something soft in his eyes, something she'd never seen in him before, so she did what he asked. He gently wiped between her legs, cleaning away all the residue from his semen.

"You are a beautiful woman," he said.

"Not really," she said. She looked in the mirror every day and though she wasn't a dog, she knew "beauty" wasn't a term that anyone would use to describe her.

He held his hand out to her and helped her to sit back up. He bent over, handing her shirt to her. She pulled it back on, feeling a bit awkward as she slowly redressed herself. She still had her running shoes on, she realized, as she struggled to get her shorts and underwear on over them.

Laz didn't do anything but lean against the door and watch her and she did take a certain comfort from that. No matter that she wasn't Angelina Jolie. When Lazarus looked at her, he saw a woman who was beautiful.

She finally had her clothes to rights and went over to where he was. She put her head against his chest and stole a little strength from him, because Laz had already proven that he wasn't the kind of man who could be intimidated or scared and she wanted that. She hoped that their lovemaking had meant something to him. It had to her. It was another stage in her metamorphosis from half-living to fully alive.

"I've got to get back to the bridge," Laz said.

Daphne straightened away from him. "Bob and I are going to try to radio our families. Our cell phones aren't working very well. Is that okay?"

"Why do you need to radio them?"

What could she say? That she suspected him of being in league with the pirates who plagued the sea here? No, of course not. Besides she didn't know what she thought about Laz anymore. She just knew that she needed to talk to her boys.

"I miss my sons," she said.

"How many do you have?" he asked.

"Two. They aren't babies but still I am used to checking in with them every day. And I want to make sure they are okay."

Laz rubbed his hand over his chest right where her head had been resting a minute ago. "I guess I can't say no to that. You have my permission."

"Thanks, Captain."

"You're welcome."

He opened the door and she watched him walk down the hallway. She wondered if this was the last time they'd be alone. This was a big tanker and he had a lot of responsibilities on the ship.

She wanted his mind on the safety of the ship. Did that mean she trusted him?

Given her track record with men, trusting Laz was a pretty big deal. She had no idea if she could trust him or not, but she did know that she was no longer uneasy about what he was doing last night. Still she had questions.

And she knew she'd get answers from him soon enough.

"Daphne, there you are," Bob said, coming up behind her. "Are you okay?"

"Yes, why do you ask?"

"You look like you have a rash on your neck. I have some special soap that should help. "

She flushed even more deeply, realizing that the marks on her neck had to have been left by Laz. "Thanks, but I'm fine. When I run my skin gets splotchy. It should be back to normal soon."

"Glad to hear it. Are you ready for the radio room or do you want to clean up first?"

Considering she could still smell Laz on herself, she opted for a shower, telling Bob she'd meet him in a few minutes in the galley. It was where their team had taken to hanging out. Being up on the deck of a tanker was different than being up on a cruise ship's deck.

Daphne took her time in the shower and then dressed slowly. She stared at herself in the mirror as she finger combed her thick curly hair. Brushes and combs just made her look like Medusa, according to her kids.

She didn't know what she was searching for in the mirror. It was still her face. She looked the same. Not like a woman who was on the cusp of a huge change.

Changing was something she thought she was past. For the longest time she'd looked in the mirror and saw a woman who had it all. A successful career in a growing practice. Two children who were on the honor roll at school and the stars of their respective sports teams. A husband . . . that was the one that had changed her, she thought.

She'd always wanted to be a wife and mother and now she was an ex-wife and a mother and those words just didn't sit right with her. No matter how she tried to change them in her head she'd been feeling like she was living someone else's life. That this life wasn't the one that she'd written for herself.

And now she knew she was right. Because of the encounter—that raw sex—she'd had with Laz in the infirmary she knew that her life had changed. The change she'd been seeking was a new direction for her dreams.

She wasn't just a wife and mother anymore; she had feared without those labels she'd be nothing. Today she realized that she was still someone. In fact she was probably getting closer to her real self than she'd ever been before. Because she'd had her kids when she was young she'd never had a chance to figure out who the real Daphne Bennett was but in Laz's arms she'd had a glimpse.

Chapter Five

Nobody is born a warrior.
—Carlos Castaneda

Daphne left her room and found Bob waiting for her in the galley. She was infinitely glad that Laz wasn't there, but then she hadn't expected to see him again. Not now. He'd be busy doing whatever it was that captains did. And she had her own job to do.

Right now she really missed her kids and her familiar world. She couldn't wait to hear their voices and to talk to them.

"Ready to go?" Bob asked.

He patted Franny on the shoulder and walked over to her. Daphne smiled and tried to be her usually sunny self but inside she didn't feel it. Instead she felt . . . broken. No, she thought, that wasn't right. She wasn't broken. She just wasn't herself.

She followed Bob down the hallway to the radio room. It was empty.

"This is odd," she said. "This seems like the one place they should always have a man."

"I agree. But the Captain did say they had a smaller crew than normal."

"Yes, he did."

"Do you know how to operate this?" Daphne asked Bob.

"Ah, no, not this type of radio. I've never seen a room like this one before. Give me a minute to figure it out."

Bob sat down at the chair and analyzed the communications board. For an older tanker this room appeared state of the art. There were all kinds of buttons and switches. She imagined that with the threat of piracy in this area communications was one place that the tankers didn't scrimp.

The door opened behind them and she turned around with a smile as she heard Bob stand up from his chair.

It was one of the crew members, Hamm. Laz's second in command. She didn't know why but she blushed when she saw him. "Hello."

"What are you two doing in here?" Hamm asked. "This room is off limits to everyone."

"Sorry, Hamm. I asked Laz earlier if it would be all right if we used the radio and he okayed it. My cell phone isn't working. In fact no one in our group has coverage out here, and I need to check in with my sons."

Hamm gave her a sideways look and she wondered if she should have just kept quiet.

Hamm was a serious looking man with a crew cut and silver-colored eyes. There was an aura of danger around him and Daphne took a step backward so she was closer to Bob.

"Well, if the boss said it's okay, then it must be fine."

"Thanks," she said.

Bob was looking at her as well and she suspected later he was going to inquire about her talking to the captain before they'd come down here.

Bob put his hand on her shoulder. "Her youngest son is an asthmatic. The only way I convinced her to come on this trip was the promise she could talk to him every day."

"Well I guess I can help out," Hamm said.

He walked over to the console and Daphne watched as he turned the large dial in the middle and then pushed a series of buttons on the computer keyboard. She carefully watched the sequence. She didn't know if Hamm could be trusted or not. She felt better knowing how to operate the radio system.

"What's the number you are trying to reach?" he asked.

She quickly gave him Paul's home phone number. Hamm entered it on the keypad and then she heard the sound of the phone ringing on the other end. She glanced over at Bob and he smiled at her.

"Hello."

"Lucas?"

"Hello, Mom."

"How are you? I was worried about both you and Joshua. Is your breathing okay?"

He sighed in a way that only a teenage boy could. "Yes, Mom. I told you not to worry about me. How's Somalia? Did you hear the news that Dad is traveling to New York to talk to the UN about the pirate situation there?"

"No, I didn't hear that. When is he going?"

"He's there now. Josh and I are old enough to stay here alone."

"If you say so. Are you behaving?"

"Of course," Lucas said. At fifteen he was clever, witty, and at times a bit of a prankster. Despite the maturity of his age and his brother who was sixteen, Daphne knew her boys could find trouble anywhere and at any time.

"Be good," she said.

"We will, Mom. Love you. Do you want to talk to Josh?"

"Yes, please. Love you too."

"What's up, Mom?" Josh asked a minute later.

"Just checking on you two. Is Lucas doing okay with his breathing?"

"Peachy. I can make him sit down for a while if you think I should."

"No, that won't be necessary. Just stay out of trouble."

"We will."

"Love you, kiddo."

"You too, Mom."

Josh hung up the phone. She handed the handset back to Hamm. "He's okay. Paul is flying to New York this week to speak at the UN."

"That's good to know," Bob said.

She thought so too. "Hamm, will it be okay if I call my kids back in the morning? I'm not sure I trust two teenagers."

Hamm laughed. "Definitely. I was a teenager once so I know what kind of trouble boys that age can get into."

Hamm didn't know the half of it. Lucas and Joshua were good boys most of the time, but they were easily bored and often came up with elaborate schemes to amuse themselves. They were only eleven months apart and sometimes were almost like twins with the crazy stuff they did.

"Thanks," she said.

She and Bob left the radio room and walked back to their quarters, where the rest of the staff was assembled. "Did you get in touch with the Senator?"

"No," Daphne said.

"But we did see how to operate the radio, which we never would have figured out on our own," Bob said. "I think we should stay close together and on our guard. I'm not sure what is going on with the crew and until we can talk to the Captain I think we should be cautious."

"Agreed," Franny said.

They all went to the quarters and Daphne tried to go to sleep but she couldn't. Her mind was full of worry for her sons . . . not because of any mischief they might get into but because of the danger she'd put herself in by coming on this trip.

Still Daphne didn't regret coming on this trip, because she knew her boys would be better for it and right now she felt better for it. Really, she did.

* * *

A loud explosion followed by gunfire brought Laz down to the deck from the bridge. He'd been keeping an eye out as the speedboat approached. He picked up the loudspeaker radio. "Unfriendlies inbound. Arm the water hoses."

He watched as his men ran about the deck. Some of them grabbed the hoses and others manned the water. They sprayed the boats as they got within range, but there were four boats and only two working hoses. Daphne came up on deck with her group and he barked an order for them to go back below.

He left the bridge and drew his weapon as one of the boats got close enough to throw an anchor overboard. It dug into the deck of the tanker, scraping it until purchase was found.

"Damn it, Savage. This is real and we are being taken."

"Affirmative, Laz. Just make a good show. We are on our way."

Four men came over the side of the tanker. They were armed with semiautomatic rifles and laid down a burst of gunfire as they moved quickly across the deck.

"Engaging the pirates," he said into the wireless microphones he and Hamm were both wearing.

"Affirmative."

Laz didn't say anything else. Keeping to the shadows he moved silently over the deck. There was a speedboat moored off the aft and one man remained on the boat. There were at least ten men on the *Maersk Angus*. Laz continued doing recon. He relayed all the information through the wireless microphone back to Savage and the rest of the team. He described the pirate boat and the weapons they were all carrying.

The men all spoke Portuguese, but he recognized them as Somalians. Laz had no real idea if they were part of Samatan's clan. The Somali people were divided by their ancestors. Men could be half-siblings born to the same mothers and grow up to be enemies. It was a complex system that was made up of loyalty proven by blood.

"Men in the hold," Hamm said through his earpiece. "I think they've got our passengers. I'm going silent."

"Affirmative," Laz said.

Two of the men on the deck went up to the bridge. Laz knew he either had to make a move and maybe stay free or allow himself to be captured. Being captured was part of the plan, but it went against the grain as far as Laz was concerned. He didn't like to give up his freedom or to back down.

He tried to stay focused on the end result. They couldn't capture Samatan unless they allowed him to take the ship. But still it didn't feel right to back down.

He eased his way around one of the large shipping containers on the deck and saw two pirates standing back to back. They were definitely Somali, he thought. Tall and gaunt, they held their weapons with an ease that spoke of having held them for a long time.

He pulled his weapon and moved carefully toward the men when he felt the nudge of a gun barrel in the center of his back.

"Put your weapon down and your hands up," the man said. "Or you will die."

Laz started to fight back. He could take all four of these men, but he knew that for the trap to work they had to allow the pirates to take the ship.

He put his weapon on the deck and put his hands up.

The pirates stepped forward, first binding his hands behind his back with duct tape, then shoving him toward the gangway that led belowdecks. He hoped that Hamm would be able to stay free but when he got below to the storage area where the hostages were being kept he saw that wasn't so.

For a minute Hamm looked at him like what the fuck are you doing here?

Laz shrugged and was shoved over to the corner with the rest of the crew and their passengers. The doctors' group looked scared and a bit shocked. For the first time Laz realized he was too close to the bait. This was the first time he was the one on the front line. Normally he was the one who was in the car or on the boat waiting to ride in and rescue everyone.

But since he was the only one on their team with real boating experience—his late father had been a commercial fisherman—Laz had been the natural choice for this position.

But as he looked at Daphne and saw . . . not fear but anger in her eyes, he realized that maybe the ends didn't justify the means.

"No one move and maybe you will live," one of the pirates said in his thickly accented English.

He backed out of the room and closed and bolted the door.

"Is everyone okay?" Laz asked.

"Yes. Other than being scared no one has been hurt."

"Is everyone accounted for?" Laz asked Hamm.

"Everyone on the crew except Fridjtof," Hamm said.

"Our group is complete," Bob said.

One of the women was crying quietly and one of the other men comforted her.

"Just sit tight. We'll figure out what they want shortly. Hamm, I need you."

Laz walked away from the group of hostages and over to a remote corner. "Did you get a message to Savage?"

"Yes. Got it off just as they entered. I also rigged the radio to blind transmit any outgoing or incoming messages to Savage."

"Good. I didn't see Samatan in the group on deck."

"He wasn't with the group belowdecks either. We might have to settle for this lot," Hamm said.

"No way," Laz said. "We're not settling for anything less than the big prize."

"And what prize is that, Captain?" Daphne asked.

He turned to see her. She had stunning eyes, he thought.

They were bright blue and definitely communicated her anger. Earlier he'd thought that the anger was directed at the pirates, but now he saw it was directed at him.

"Taking back our ship," he said to her. "Why don't you go back over with your group while my first mate and I discuss the situation."

She shook her head. "I don't trust you, Captain. I think you are working with the pirates and would sell us out for the cargo of this ship. So I'm going to stay right here until you answer a few questions for me."

Laz shook his head. "This isn't the time to answer questions, Daphne. We need to work on a plan to get us all out of this hold and capture the pirates."

"I can help with that."

"Really? How? Do you have some skills we don't know about?"

She shook her head. "My ex-husband is a Senator and I think I can get him to call for Special Forces to come and rescue us."

Laz shook his head. He knew that Special Forces wouldn't come because the Savage Seven were already here. And this was their job. They were going to capture the pirates and bring down their king.

"I'm afraid you are going to have to rely on me and my crew for right now. Go back to your people."

He turned away from her and waited tensely until she left.

Samatan was known by many different names to many different people. He'd grown up under the dictator in Mogadishu Somalia. He had cut his teeth as a Strongman—an enforcer for local mob bosses—in the north and learned early on that he couldn't rely on anyone but himself to make his way.

The city was now a mass of warring clans, which Samatan

used to his advantage. He knew exactly how to motivate his men, and if he lost one or two on a pirate raid there were always more men to replace them. That was one thing that Somaliland always had—an endless supply of men and boys willing to do whatever they had to in order to survive.

He knew the world saw him and his kind as terrorists, but he didn't care. The civilized nations of the world never realized what life was really like. William Blake said it best: "A dog starved at its master's gate predicts the ruin of the state." Somalia was like that. And each year it seemed to get worse.

No matter how many tankers he captured and ransomed, no matter how much money he brought back to his clan, he couldn't really make the lives of his people better. But he tried. He wanted to see youths growing up with all their limbs and without the scars that he bore.

But tonight that was something he didn't have time to think about. He was patrolling. He seldom went on raids anymore. He saved his presence for times when he was dealing with cargo that couldn't be trusted to one of his lieutenants.

Tonight he was out on the Indian Ocean waiting for his prey. The *Maersk Angus* was a ship they'd taken before, and they had gotten a fair amount of ransom. This time they'd heard rumors that there was a different crew in place—the type of crew that only went out with heavily insured cargo. And that had piqued Samatan's interest.

He had one of his men—a Dane named Fridjtof—onboard. Fridjtof had been an asset to his group for a while. At first he'd relied on gut instinct to find ships to attack, but now he liked having inside information.

He also had several contacts in the ports in the Gulf of Aden, which helped him decide which ships to attack.

He was currently on his own ship. A tanker that housed machine guns, rocket-propelled grenades, speedboats, parts for repairing speedboats, and two helicopters. His ship even looked like the Maersk tankers they often captured. He had spent the last three years perfecting every detail of his operation.

Many nations had their navies patrolling the shipping lanes now to protect the ships so Samatan had had to up his game. He was now using nighttime attacks and men on the inside so that the alarm couldn't be raised.

Instead of taking his hostages to the pirate town of Eyl, Samatan preferred to keep them on his ship. It was easier because his location couldn't be traced to any of the on-land locations. He'd seen his former leader captured that way, and Samatan had no plans on being tried in a Kenyan court for his crimes.

"Sir, we have word that the *Maersk Angus* has been taken," Habeb said, joining him on the bridge. Habeb had been his first mate for the last eighteen months. He was a tall, skinny African who'd grown up in one of the poorer areas of London.

They'd met in the early nineties when Samatan had attended university in Rome. It had been a troubled time for Samatan, whose father had been a vocal opponent of the dictator. Samatan had lost his scholarship money for school and his visa. Habeb had offered him a place to stay and had helped him find papers to stay in Rome and continue his schooling.

"Very good. Was there any trouble?" Samatan asked.

"The Captain had a gun but we were able to capture him and the entire crew. There is also a group of doctors onboard from the U.S."

Samatan hadn't planned on hostages that weren't members of the ships' crew. The crews were easy to manage because they'd been operating in this area long enough that most of the men understood that killing wasn't the objective of the pirates.

"That could be bad. Does Fridjtof know who they are?" Samatan asked.

"I'm not sure. Do you want me to get him on the radio?" Habeb asked.

"Yes. I want as many details on the hostages as he can get," Samatan said.

He had always been careful to keep close contact with his men. He knew that loyalties could quickly change. His men were loyal to him because he paid well and on time but also because he was quick to deal with anyone who betrayed him. And he never showed weakness.

Walking down to the radio room, he knew that he was close to having everything he wanted. The life he'd always craved. It wouldn't be in Somalia. Somalia was a land of broken dreams and death and he'd never bring the family he intended to have there. Instead he'd go to Sardinia, where Mare lived, and marry her. She knew nothing of this life. Of the man he was here. But he'd leave that all behind once he had his fortune.

He could have stopped a year ago but he had made promises to his older brother and his mother. His promises were that he'd try to change the lot of their clan so he was still roaming the seas and taking his fortune from the countries that had turned their backs on Somalia because they didn't want to aid a people whose land had no oil or precious diamonds to offer in exchange.

"Come in *Maersk Angus*," Habeb said once they reached the radio room.

"This is the *Maersk Angus*. P1 speaking."

All of the pirates who'd taken the ship were given a number from 1–5. P1 was the man who would stay on the radio and maintain communication with Habeb.

Samatan had drilled into his men that they could never use their real names or speak in their native tongue. For the most part his crews spoke in Portuguese—a language spoken by many who roamed the seas. Even though Samatan realized that many of the captains whose ships they took realized the pirates were Somali, Samatan liked to think it gave him plausible deniability to pretend to be Portuguese.

"P1 please find M-insider. I have a need to question him," Habeb said.

"Right away, sir."

Samatan and Habeb waited four minutes. Both men were standing looking out at the sea. "It's a nice night."

"Yes, sir, it is. I've always loved a night like this."

"Why?" Samatan asked.

"Feels like we're the only ones in the world and that we own it."

Samatan laughed. "Yes it does."

"M-insider here."

"We need further information on the U.S. hostages," Habeb said.

Samatan preferred to let his second in command speak on the radio. He knew that once they broadcast their voices they had no idea who else was picking up the signal.

"I know only that they are all from the States and got on the ship in Madrid. I can try to find more information but I'm not sure how cooperative they'll be," Fridjtof said.

Habeb glanced at him.

"We need to know what we are dealing with," Samatan said.

Habeb nodded, then spoke into the radio. "Use whatever means are necessary to find out who they are. We need to know what we are dealing with. We've already sent a ransom message to the Maersk shipping company."

"I'll contact you as soon as I have the information," Fridjtof said.

"We will await that information," Habeb said.

"Do you think this is going to be a problem?" Habeb asked Samatan.

Samatan shrugged. "If it is, we will deal with it."

He had learned early on that if he was going to lead this group of men he could never show doubt or fear. Even when he wasn't sure of himself he always projected confidence. In his world it was kill or be killed and a weak man died a young man.

And he had plans to live to be an old man—something that few of his countrymen ever dreamed of. He doubted they even had a chance to dream when every day was a constant struggle of surviving and dreams felt like a frivolous luxury. Samatan had always dreamed of bigger and better things. He'd always dreamed of a life outside the poverty and the violence that was Somalia.

And he'd do whatever he had to in order to ensure he got it.

Chapter Six

The basic difference between an ordinary man and a warrior is that a warrior takes everything as a challenge.
—CARLOS CASTANEDA

Daphne was frightened. Although she'd learned as a mother to mask her own fears, right now she couldn't. Armed men had gathered them all together like cattle and forced them into the main hold of the tanker along with the crew. All around them in the dank and dark hold were large crates. Some she recognized as the supplies her team was bringing with them.

She felt trapped belowdecks, and an insidious panic was starting to grow inside her.

She needed to focus on something. *Laz*. He was something she could do something about.

"Why are you glaring at the Captain?" Franny asked as she came up beside Daphne.

"I just don't understand what happened. I think he should have been better prepared to defend us," Daphne said.

"Look, he's locked up with us," Franny said. Her long black hair was pulled back into a ponytail. She had the same worried look on her face that Daphne was sure she wore too.

"I know that but I don't like . . . I just need someone to blame for this. I guess I'm scared and looking for a fight."

Franny laughed and wrapped her arm around Daphne's

shoulders. "Me too. I almost took Bob's head off because he said that I should put on a sweatshirt so I didn't look too feminine to the pirates."

Daphne tried to smile but she was scared. There was a knot in the pit of her stomach that simply wouldn't go away no matter how hard she tried to focus on being positive.

She'd never been in a life-and-death situation before. She didn't count the times she'd been in the operating room and had a patient code, because in the operating room she was a god and she knew she had the skills to bring a patient back.

But on this ship . . . out here in the real world, she wasn't as sure.

She had no experience in what to do here. And she needed to do something. She needed to be active and not just sitting around waiting for something to happen.

"What did the Captain say?"

"Not much. I still don't really trust that man," Daphne said. "I know that his first priority is our safety and the safety of his ship but . . ."

"I'll go talk to him," Jerry said. "I think maybe he's used to dealing with men."

Jerry walked away and Franny snorted. "That remark had machismo all over it."

Daphne shook her head. "Maybe that's what we need here. Maybe I'm just borrowing trouble by worrying about him, but I need to do something to make us all feel safe."

"Us all? Or yourself?" Franny asked.

"Myself. I hate feeling like a victim."

"Me too. But in this case"—Franny said, gesturing at the room they were locked in—"I don't think there is anything we can do except wait."

"I stink at waiting," Daphne said.

"Well, that's all we can do," Jerry said, returning to their side.

"Why?"

"Because the Captain doesn't want to take a chance on getting us killed."

"So he thinks we're safe," Daphne asked.

Jerry shook his head. "I didn't say that. I think he's not sure of our skills and wants us to just be good little passengers until the pirates make a move so he can see how they are going to treat us."

Daphne couldn't explain it but just hearing that they were to wait and see made her feel like she was going to explode. That was not a plan in her mind. That was like saying an abused woman should sit quietly so she didn't incur the wrath of her abusive husband.

She didn't admit to them that her real anger with Laz stemmed from the fact that he was treating her like everyone else. But then again, why shouldn't he? She was just like everyone else on this tanker—a passenger and his responsibility. She was nothing more important to him then that.

She didn't fool herself that just because they'd had sex anything had changed between them. It hadn't for her. Really, it hadn't.

Laz looked at her for a second and then turned away.

"I can't believe this."

"What?" Bob asked, coming over to join her.

"The Captain wants us to just sit tight and wait this out. See how the pirates treat us."

"Well, it makes sense. These men are unpredictable," Rudy said. "They remind me a lot of the guerrillas I met in South America."

"All criminals are unpredictable," Franny said.

"Not like these kind of men," Rudy said. "These are men who have nothing to lose because they have nothing to go home to."

Daphne understood that mentality. "How do we deal with them?"

"I'm not sure. I think the Captain has the right idea. We should wait this out and get a good gauge of the men who are holding us. Right now they have locked us away, which tells me they don't want to have to kill us," Rudy said.

"I agree," Bob said. "These men aren't really killers unless forced to it."

"So we have no choice but just to wait," Daphne said.

"Definitely. We are going to have to just wait and see what they do next. I think we should all be on our guard," Bob said.

"I have some training in hand-to-hand combat," Rudy said. "And I am damned good with a weapon but we don't have any."

"No, we don't," Bob said. "Maybe we should scavenge around this area and see if we can find anything we could use as a weapon."

"Good idea," Daphne said. "I'll do that."

Jerry laughed. "What's up with you?"

"I just can't sit still. If I do I'll think about all I have to lose and just make a long list of regrets about coming on this trip," Daphne said.

"Me too," Rudy said. "I have enough regrets to live with already. I'll go with Daphne and see what we can find."

"Should we involve the crew?" Jerry asked.

"I'll let them know what we're doing. If they want to be a part of it, then they can participate."

Bob moved off to talk to the others but before any of them could move the door opened and three pirates stood there.

Daphne caught her breath as she looked at the skinny men with mean intent in their eyes. Each of them wore a bandolier with bullets in it and carried two semiautomatic rifles. And though she'd always been a big Second Amendment proponent at home, she'd gladly give up the right to bear arms if it meant she didn't have to face an armed man now.

* * *

Laz didn't like the tension in the room. He knew he'd upset Daphne. He wished he could reassure her and her group, but he couldn't take a chance on letting anyone know what the real agenda was here.

When the door opened and three of the pirates stood watching them, Laz had a bad feeling. The kind of feeling he'd had before Armand had been killed. Armand had been their seventh man and the team still felt his loss. This feeling was the harbinger of something bad.

Two of the men kept their guns trained on the groups of crew and doctors, who stood in separate areas about fifteen feet apart. The other man approached him and Hamm.

"Come with us, Captain."

"Sure."

He looked at Hamm, who nodded at him. Hamm knew he would let Savage and the rest of their team know what was going on, but unfortunately they'd been locked in the hold where radio communications weren't clear. Laz also knew that Hamm would protect the crew and the doctors while he was gone. And since they had gone into this mission with a no-collateral-damage policy that was very important.

The men all spoke Portuguese—something that he'd heard the pirates did to throw off the crews from guessing where they were from. Laz knew, however, that there was no way anyone could mistake the gaunt lost soldiers holding them hostage as Portuguese, mainly because Portugal wasn't the mess that Somalia was.

These pirates looked like they had nothing to lose, and they feared nothing, because death was an everyday reality for them.

Laz's hands were bound behind his back as soon as they were out of the storage area. Laz could fight with his hands behind his back. He hoped that Savage had the team nearby and knew that Mann would be in position as a sniper to protect him. But he couldn't count on that.

He always counted on himself, and then if someone else came to the rescue he was grateful. He'd not only learned early on to look after himself, but also those he cared about. His sister Maureen had been one of the chosen few people that he actually cared about. But that relationship was dead to him now.

"Get up the stairs."

Laz followed directions. Going up on the deck was what he wanted anyway. He needed to see if Samatan was here. Or if they had been the target of another group of pirates.

Besides the three who'd come to get him, there were four other pirates on deck, including Fridjtof.

He didn't like men who lied about their allegiance. Fridjtof took one look at Laz's face and backed away from him, then seemed to remember that he was in charge here. He stepped forward.

"I need the names of the doctors."

"Why?"

"Because I asked for them, Captain. You are no longer in charge here," Fridjtof said.

"And you are?" Laz asked.

He didn't like the idea of giving up the names of the passengers to this man. He knew that they had connections in the U.S. government and knowing their names would only give the pirates more fuel for their ransom demands.

Fridjtof drew back his fist and punched Laz square in the stomach. The impact was forceful and painful but Laz didn't make a sound.

Instead Laz just glanced at the other man; he needed to see how hard he could push before Fridjtof broke. He needed to understand the mettle of the men who held them so he would know what to expect when they took the ship back. And Laz was definitely going to take this ship back.

"Is that all you got?"

Fridjtof backhanded him, hitting him hard on the jaw. He felt his teeth grind together as he caught part of his inner mouth and blood spurted out. Damn it, he hated the taste of blood, especially his own.

"I need their names. You can tell me or I can pull them up here . . . how long do you think they will last? Especially that nosy lady who captured your attention?" Fridjtof asked.

Laz narrowed his eyes, knowing he had to be referring to Daphne. Damn, he knew that sexy woman was going to be trouble the moment he laid eyes on her. Fridjtof was very determined to get the information. Laz wondered if he was trying to prove himself to his superiors.

"I don't think their names are important to this situation," Laz said. "They are a group of humanitarian aid workers going to Somalia. I'd think you could appreciate that and let them go."

"I'll decide what's important," Fridjtof said.

"You don't seem capable of deciding much."

"I can decide if that little doctor talks to me before or after I give her to the crew as a prize."

Laz jerked out of the hands of the men holding him and slammed his shoulder into Fridjtof's stomach. The other man grunted and fell off balance. Laz kicked him to the ground and kicked him in the stomach twice before he was hit hard on the back of the head with the butt of a rifle.

He shook his head to keep the lightheadedness at bay. He was a damned good fighter but four to one wasn't the best odds. Laz tried to hold his own, inflicting as much damage on the men attacking him as he could. But he was outnumbered, and as he continued to take blows to the head he knew he wasn't helping anyone.

He wasn't about to let Daphne or any of the other doctors be "questioned" by these men.

Laz realized that Fridjtof had made up his mind to prove his mettle, and as the other men tried to beat the information out of him, he promised himself that he'd have a very special type of revenge for the man who had betrayed them and threatened Daphne.

Each hit he took just strengthened his resolve. Laz had learned a long time ago how to push pain to the back of his mind. It had been that training and his ability that had cemented for him the fact that he was meant to be a warrior. He'd always suspected it but having the skills of a warrior had made him realize that he was uniquely qualified to be one.

Each blow to his abdomen would have brought another man to his knees, and later Laz knew he'd feel it but right now he stood straight and tall and kept his eyes focused on the man who was hitting him.

It took no skill and little honor to beat on a defenseless man. And it showed Laz exactly what Fridjtof was . . . a coward.

Daphne was worried and scared as the minutes ticked by and Laz didn't return. Their search hadn't netted any weapons. She wished she'd contained her anger toward him and oh, hell. She didn't want anything to happen to him. It didn't matter that he'd told her they'd be safe and then had seemed to go back on his word.

Hadn't she learned that no one could protect her? Hadn't the ending of her marriage reminded her that there were no guarantees in this life? She shook her head and continued pacing the floor.

Bob and Franny were huddled close to each other in the corner. Arms wrapped around each other, taking comfort, she imagined. She wished she'd done that with Laz. Made him stop being in charge and just hugged her before he'd been taken away.

What if he didn't come back? What if the pirates felt like they had to sacrifice someone to make the men they were demanding ransom from take them seriously?

"Pacing helping?" Rudy asked her.

"Not really. I feel . . ."

"Helpless. Believe me I know that emotion well," Rudy said.

She sensed that Rudy needed to talk. That somehow maybe this situation was bringing back to the surface whatever had happened to him in South America.

"Have you been in a situation like this before?"

Rudy shrugged. He was a solidly built man, and in his eyes she saw the same brokenness she'd felt for so long. She reached over and put her hand on his wrist to comfort him and he looked down at it before drawing his arm away.

"I have been held hostage before. And it wasn't the kind of experience I want to repeat. I'm not going to let myself be—"

He broke off and she realized that he didn't want to react the way he had the last time.

"Don't worry, Rudy. None of us are going to take this lying down."

"Sometimes you don't have a choice. Men like these pirates, they have nothing to lose. They don't understand things like our lives and our loves. It makes it very hard for them to be reasoned with."

Daphne nodded, realizing that Rudy and his girlfriend had probably been in a situation like this in South America. "I've never been taken hostage before."

"It's not something you want to get used to," he said. "The men who held us in Peru were with the drug cartel. So it wasn't a ransom thing. But a territorial thing."

"I don't imagine that makes much difference," Daphne said.

"No, it doesn't," Rudy said.

"I read a bit about the pirates in this area before we left and they don't seem to be motivated to kill their captives—just use them for leverage to get money."

"I don't care about that. I'm tired of being used by men with no moral compass. I'm not going to take this sitting down."

Rudy stood up and walked away and all Daphne could do was stare after him. He was a loose cannon—someone without anything grounding him to the moral compass he'd just talked about. Focusing on Rudy would give her something useful to do, but she had no idea how to talk him down from this. How to make Rudy give up his anger. Hell, she hadn't been able to get rid of her own anger until she realized that she didn't want to lose Laz.

It was funny how caring was the bridge that made all the difference. There was no one here that Rudy could care about. Their group was newly formed and they hadn't bonded with each other yet. Who knew when they would?

And the women here . . . well, Rudy wasn't going to fall for Franny, who was clearly involved with Bob, or with her because, well, she wasn't his type. But maybe reminding him of the woman he lost would help.

Daphne walked over to Jerry who was sitting by himself to see if he knew anything about Rudy's past.

"What's up with Rudy?"

"He's agitated and I think he's a bit unstable right now," Daphne said. "He has been in a hostage situation before."

Jerry nodded. "When he lost Maria. This has got to be bringing up some bad memories for him."

"What do you know about that situation?"

"Just that . . . it was gruesome. The banditos that took

Rudy and the rest of the Doctors Across Waters team didn't treat them with respect. The women were violated and the men beaten. I think that Rudy might be feeling like he's back in that situation."

Daphne took a deep breath. Tried to think of something she could do or say to make things better for Rudy. "I can't reassure him."

Jerry nodded. "No one can. We don't know what is going to happen to any of us."

He put his hand on her shoulder and squeezed. "We don't even know if the Captain is going to make it back. I guess if he doesn't it will mean he is either in league with the pirates or dead."

Daphne blanched. She felt like she'd taken a punch to the stomach. She didn't want Laz dead. She wanted to see him again. To flirt with him again. To see if there was more to the attraction between them than casual sex.

But she knew that was out of her control. One of the things her therapist had said after her divorce was that she had to let go. Letting go had been hard then but it was infinitely harder now. She took a deep breath as Jerry got up and walked over to talk to Rudy.

Their team wasn't going to be the same after this. How could anyone be the same after being threatened? She realized that not trusting a man because he broke your heart was infinitely easier to deal with when you were faced with men who might kill you.

In the overall scheme of things Paul's betrayal wasn't that bad. In fact she realized he'd done her a favor. Their marriage had been flat and boring for a long time, and if he hadn't made the move to end it she might have stayed with him for the rest of her life and never experienced anything worthwhile.

Of course the threat of dying wasn't something she really wanted to experience at this moment, but she knew that she wasn't going to continue to define herself by the divorce. It was past time for her to redefine herself by the actions she took. No more letting life happen to her . . .

Daphne looked around the holding area and realized how much her focus had narrowed. Nothing beyond living and getting back to her sons mattered to her right now. She'd been silly to think she had to run off to find adventure and the start of her new life. She was a well-rounded woman who had a good life. As much as she wished she wasn't in this situation right now, she was determined to get out of it and make her life more than it had been.

When she got back home she was going to try something new every season. Take those language classes she'd been talking about for a while now and maybe dabble in a little pottery. She wasn't going to let any opportunities pass her by anymore. She realized that there was no guarantee that they'd come by again.

Why was she just realizing this now? she wondered.

Chapter Seven

A warrior needs to be light and fluid.
—CARLOS CASTANEDA

Daphne and the others waited for the Captain to be returned to them. Hamm had organized all of the hostages into paired teams and given them all a task. Daphne was simply grateful. She'd been paired with Hamm and they were in charge of getting all the water and food supplies they could find.

"Where are you from?" Hamm asked as they both loaded their arms with water bottles.

"D.C. area—Virginia actually. You?"

He was a good-looking man of at least six feet. He had reddish brown hair cut close to his head and silver eyes that reminded Daphne of her youngest son's. He didn't smile easily, but he was relaxed and projected a sense of calm, unlike Laz, who projected tension. Or was that simply her reaction to Laz?

"I . . . um, I heard you and Laz talking earlier on deck and saw some men come aboard. Who were they?"

Hamm pulled away from her. "What else did you see?"

The easygoing man she'd just been talking to disappeared as she saw in Hamm that same tension that Laz carried.

"Nothing. Fridjtof came up the stairs and I had to leave."

Hamm nodded. "Fridjtof is working with the pirates."

"Why did you hire him then?"

"We didn't," Hamm said.

"You still haven't told me anything," she said.

"Get those packages of dried fruit," he said.

She reached for them and then turned to look at the other man. "I'm not going to stop asking questions just because you are trying to avoid them. I think given the situation we are all in, I deserve some answers."

Hamm rubbed the bridge of his nose. "We are working to catch pirates in this area."

"Who is we? And why weren't we informed?" Daphne asked.

"You weren't informed because you don't need to know," Hamm said.

Daphne followed Hamm as he put down their food supplies. "That's ridiculous."

"Why?"

"Because you put us in danger," she said. She didn't like the feeling she had right now. That her entire life was out of control and there was nothing she could do to change that. But Hamm and Laz both had the ability to make things better. Why hadn't they said something before the ship left port?

"No, I didn't. We're the best shot you have of making it out of this alive."

Daphne stepped back as Hamm took a step closer to her. "Now is not the time for second-guessing. Our mission was already set when your people were added to this trip. We couldn't change courses without disrupting everything."

She nodded. "I'm sorry. I was out of line. I hate it when a patient's family demands to know everything that I'm doing in a operating room . . . there are some things they just don't need to know because it would just scare them."

"That's where we were coming from," Hamm said.

She nodded. "I'm so scared."

"You should be. These are dangerous men with nothing to lose, but at the end of the day you have to remember that you aren't the target of this attack. They want money and as long as they can ransom the ship, you and your friends are safe."

Daphne wasn't reassured by his comments. "What if they can't?"

"Then Laz and I will make sure they understand that your group is off limits. Don't worry, Daphne."

"I do worry," Daphne said.

Hamm started to respond but the door opened and a loud thud echoed through the area before the door was slammed again. Hamm cursed under his breath and ran across the room.

Daphne turned to see Laz pushing himself up off the floor and waving off his second in command. Laz stood up and swayed. Daphne and Bob both rushed to his side.

"I'm fine."

"We'll decide that," Bob said.

Daphne could tell that there was mainly external bruising and bleeding. She started toward him, needing to help in any way she could. "Are your ribs cracked? Do you have pain—"

"I'm fine. Hamm, we need to talk. Doctors, stay together. I need to talk to everyone in five minutes."

"I don't think you're in any shape to be giving orders," Daphne said.

"I do," Laz said. He pulled away from them and walked to a corner with Hamm. She was torn between doing her duty as a doctor and just wanting to make sure that Laz was okay.

"Let him go," Bob said.

Laz looked over at her and gave her a small half-smile that was reminiscent of his old grin. She nodded and went with Bob. She wasn't backing down. This wasn't a situation that would serve her well if she hid in a corner.

"I . . . this is something I can help with," she said. "I'm getting the first-aid kit and taking care of him."

Bob smiled at her. "Good. I think he'll feel less threatened if you go over there. We need him in the best possible shape."

"I think so too. This situation is really dangerous."

"Yes, it is," Bob said.

"Have you experienced anything like this before?"

"Never en route. On the ground we've had some tense situations."

Daphne knew that the groups they sent around the world at times encountered hostiles but reading a report and being here . . . well it was a world of difference and she had absolutely no idea how to deal with it.

But she did know how to deal with an injured man, and she wasn't going to take no for an answer. When she and Hamm had searched the storage area earlier, she'd seen inside the crates they'd brought with them. She went over to a large box and opened it up, getting out the things she'd need to make sure that Laz was okay. After talking to Hamm she knew that he and Laz were the only chance they had of making it off this ship safely.

She would do whatever she could to make sure they all made it off. She knew that the others in their group felt that way as well.

"If they take us to Ely, do we have any contacts there?" she asked Bob. Ely was the famous pirate port of call. Usually that's where the ship was held until the ransom was paid.

"No contacts in that city. It's lawless, which is why they take the ships there," Bob said.

"What are we going to do?" Franny asked. "My cell phone isn't picking up any signal at all now. In fact no one can get a signal."

Bob wrapped his arm around her shoulders. "We're not going to panic. We are going to keep level heads and figure this out."

Daphne liked his advice. It made sense to her. Panicking

would only make her worry and be afraid. She needed to stay calm.

"I'm confident the Captain will get us out of here," Daphne said.

"I hope you are right," Rudy said, coming up to join them. The other man still looked tense and out of sorts.

"Me too," Daphne said.

She didn't let her thoughts dwell on any outcome other than them all free and safe. She knew that her negative emotions would just contribute more to those around her. She got the first-aid kit and headed over to Laz.

"They want the names of the doctors. I'm not sure if they know that Daphne is related to a congressman or not. I want to keep them isolated and safe," Laz said.

"Don't worry about it. I'll keep them back. How are you?"

"Fine. Has Savage checked in?"

"Not yet. But we could be having radio problems," Hamm said.

"Doubtful. I'm sure it's this place," Laz said. He was in charge of communications and equipment for their team. He knew his equipment wasn't going to fail. Now if the relay satellite they used for their communications was having problems that was out of his control. But the chances of that happening were slim unless the satellite was over the Southern Atlantic Anomaly.

Laz triggered his wireless mike. "Savage?"

Some static came back over the line but nothing clear.

"Fuck."

Hamm shrugged but didn't say anything else.

"For now it's you and me. We got this."

"Damned straight we do," Hamm said. "Who's in charge?"

"Not sure. Fridjtof was the one questioning me, but I don't think he's the brains of the operation."

"Excuse me, Laz."

"Not now, Daphne. I'm sorry I can't answer any of your questions."

"Not a problem. I'm going to bandage you up. Keep doing whatever you are doing."

Laz glanced at her. He was so afraid for her. For the first time on a mission he had something personal to lose. And he knew it made him weak but he didn't care. He had been fighting battles his entire life with no real ties to anyone and now he had her.

He reached around Hamm and touched her face. Just to reassure himself she was okay. He wanted to kiss her but didn't think that public displays of affection were called for now.

"I'm fine."

"No. You're not."

She wasn't going to take no for an answer. He knew that because she hadn't asked him if she could help. She'd assumed she could.

He was taken aback.

He'd been injured like this more times than he could count and since he was still able to function, taking care of his injuries was at the bottom of his priority list.

"Sit on the box over there," she said.

Laz did what she asked because he was still bemused. No one had ever . . . He shook his head to clear it.

"I'm going to go to the northeast corner of the room. I had a signal from there earlier. I'll try to raise Savage. After the doc patches you up we can regroup," Hamm said.

Laz nodded and Hamm walked away. He turned to look at Daphne and remembered the threats that Fridjtof had made against her and the other woman in the group. He didn't really know any of the doctors who were traveling with Daphne but he'd talked to her. And she wasn't just a nameless, faceless victim that he wanted to protect. She'd become human to him.

"Why are you watching me like that?" she asked.

She had a cotton swab and was putting disinfectant on the larger cuts on his body. The fact that she was doing that told him there wasn't anything seriously wrong with him.

"I like to look at you."

"Why? I'm pretty average looking."

"Maybe that's why," he said.

"Gee, thanks."

He smiled and took her hand in his. Daphne had a look that was all-American. She was his ideal type of woman, though he couldn't explain that to her. There was something about her thick brown hair and deep chocolate eyes that reminded him of home and of why he kept doing this job, which was slowly taking a toll on him. A real toll.

The job had been eating away at him lately, making it harder for him to go back home and blend back into his old life. Even being on the sea didn't bring back his sense of normalcy the way it used to.

"I meant it in that you remind me of everything that is . . . home. You are full-on sassy in a way that I've only ever seen in American girls."

She gave him a half-smile. "Sassy?"

"Yeah. I had a sister, so I know sassy is different from bitchy."

"You are a smooth talker," she said, rolling her eyes.

"I am. What do you say we go for a drink when you get done patching me up?" he said.

Her eyes seemed shadowed as she looked down at him. "I'd like that. But I'm afraid we're going to have to settle for bottles of purified water and a talk with the rest of our fellow hostages."

"Are you scared?" he asked her.

"Yes."

"What part scares you?"

"The men with the guns. I'm . . . I've seen too many gunshot wounds. Operated on too many people who've been hit with a bullet not to really fear them."

Laz reached up and touched her face. "I'm not going to let anything happen to you."

She gave him a haunted look and Laz realized there was more than just fear hiding beneath the surface of this pretty all-American doctor. He wished they had more time together so he could figure out the mysteries that were Daphne. But that would have to wait. And in all reality he'd probably never get to know her.

"Trust me."

"That sounds like an order," she said, tucking a strand of hair behind her ear as she finished bandaging him up.

"It was. I don't have time to coax you into trusting me. This is a life-and-death situation and I'm your best chance of making it out of it alive."

She tipped her head to the side. "I know that. I'm trying, but trust doesn't come easy for me. But if I'm going to trust any man . . . well, it's you, J.P. Lazarus."

She put the last bandage on the worst of his cuts and then stood back to study him. Unlike Daphne, who brought him a sense of comfort and quelled his longing for home, he doubted his looks did anything for her.

He was a rough-and-ready guy who'd been beat up one too many times. He was solid muscle and he knew he could handle himself in any situation, but his kind of living had left marks on him. And despite the trauma Daphne had seen in the operating room, she was too innocent for a man like him.

That didn't mean he wasn't dying to kiss her. To have that

little taste of home that he'd earned getting his ass beat and keeping her name quiet. She'd never know what he'd done to protect her. What he'd continue to do and that was as it should be.

He closed the gap between the two of them and standing toe-to-toe realized her head came to his shoulder. Perfect for dancing or holding her. He wanted to know what she felt like in his arms. But not now.

He cupped her head in both of his hands, tipped her mouth up to his, and kissed her. Just a quick rub of his lips over hers. She exhaled and parted her lips the tiniest bit, and he tasted the sweetness of her mouth.

That was all he wanted. All he needed. He felt like a knight of old who'd received a token from his lady. He pulled back.

"Thank you."

He walked away from her and rejoined Hamm, pretending that Daphne was nothing more than that glimpse of home. But he had never lied worth a damn and especially not to himself. Daphne wasn't a taste of home, she was a glimpse of the home he'd always longed for and he knew that it was right in his grasp if he could only reach out and take it.

He glanced back over his shoulder and saw her watching him and knew that no matter what else happened while they were on this mission, he wasn't going to be able to walk away easily from her.

Daphne stood there watching Laz walk away. She held bandages in her hands and felt like she had lost her mooring. Being a doctor was the one thing that Paul hadn't taken from her when he'd walked away from their marriage.

But Laz . . . he'd shaken her. She'd never met anyone like him before. Never experienced the gamut of emotions she had before she'd met him. It wasn't a power thing, because living in D.C. and being a Senator's wife she'd come into contact with powerful people before. With Laz it was something different. He had a calmness in the face of danger.

The cuts and bruises on his body told her that he'd been beaten. Another person—someone from their group—wouldn't have fared as well as Laz. His body was honed into a machine. She'd felt the strength in his body and from a purely scientific point of view she wanted to explore him.

Yeah, right.

She wanted to explore him because he was hot. And there was something primal about him that called to her on her most basic level.

"You okay?" Franny asked.

"Yes, of course. Why wouldn't I be?"

"Um, you just had your socks kissed off," Franny said with a laugh.

And Daphne had to smile. "You are so right. I'm in over my head here."

"I think you can handle him," Franny said.

Daphne wasn't too sure. When he'd asked her to trust him, she realized that trusting any man was still a struggle. Two years after her divorce and she still hadn't found her way back to just basic trust.

"I'm not so sure. Wow, this day has been . . ."

"Real," Franny said.

Daphne gave the other woman a questioning glance.

"Well, at home we get up, go to work, do our job, and then head home and do it again. I mean there is a little variety but for the most part we live in this insulated bubble. But whenever I'm on one of these trips, it's like seeing the real world. I can't help but feel this is what life is meant to be."

Daphne wasn't sure she wanted this much reality. She'd love the comfort of a chai tea latte from Starbucks and listening to John Mayer on her iPod. Instead she was in a holding cell with people she didn't really know and those who mattered to her were a world away. And she was with a man who was dangerous to her because he was making her feel again.

That was it, she thought. That bubble of her routine at home had insulated her from being hurt by a man and in one day she'd had that bubble popped and now she was here. Living and breathing in the real world with a real man.

It was easy to see why she was attracted to Laz when she thought about her situation in those terms. He represented safety. She didn't fool herself into thinking any of the men on her team could keep her and Franny safe. They were doctors and medics. Men used to saving lives, not taking them. Rudy was the only one who seemed at ease in this situation. Bob of course was doing what any good leader did, trying to keep everyone calm.

"I guess you have a point. But I think this might be more real than I want to experience."

Franny shrugged. "I guess it's different for me because I never found the right man to marry and have kids with, but I've always kept moving on hoping I would someday and instead . . . well, instead I'm here."

Daphne hugged Franny to her side. "It's not any different for you than it is for me. We both left behind another life and another world. I guess we have to adjust to this. I know I do. Otherwise I'm going to curl up in a corner and cry."

"If you do maybe Laz will come comfort you," Franny said.

"Doubtful. That man looks like the type who'd tell me to snap out of it!"

"I see your point."

"Girls, come on over here," Hamm said.

Normally Daphne would take any man to task who called her a girl but tonight that didn't seem important. Instead she gathered with the rest of the hostages. She'd never felt so powerless. She took a deep breath.

She had to stop thinking that this was out of her control. She was still a doctor. Still knew how to save lives. Her boys were safe in the United States and for right now all of her group here was safe.

They'd continue to be until something happened to change the balance of power. She wasn't powerless, she reminded herself. There were ten of them in the hold, and there were a like number of pirates holding them. Something would happen to shift the balance of power.

She had to believe that.

"The pirates are very interested in knowing the names of the Doctors Across Waters group. Rumor has it that one of you is related to a congressman," Laz said. "I've told them you aren't a factor in this hostage situation."

"Thank you," Bob said. "What do you think they will do?"

"Well, for now I think they will let us be. But if the shipping company doesn't step up and meet their demands, they are going to start pulling your group up on deck one by one and demanding that information until they get an answer."

"It won't come to that," Daphne said. "I'll talk to them."

"No, you won't," Laz said. "Hamm and I are highly trained soldiers and our backup is going to make sure that the pirates don't have a chance to question anyone in a hard way."

Laz looked right at her and Daphne knew he was talking to her. She felt an inkling of trust in the pit of her soul. She wanted to believe he would protect her.

In fact, as she watched the intent gaze he kept on her she knew that he would protect her. And that made all the difference in the world. She wasn't as alone as she'd feared she was. She had Laz by her side and trust or not that was more reassurance than she'd expected to find here.

Everything about this summer was more than she expected to find. She had thought of this trip the same way she thought of volunteering at her kids' schools or at the church. It would also give her something to talk about to other people at work functions. She realized that her life had become so routine that she never had a chance to really talk about the things that mattered. And she'd been searching for a way to make herself relevant.

Now she realized how stupid that had been. Laz had made her see that she was enough just as she was. He never made her feel like she should be more of a woman or a different type of person. He simply accepted her as she was and that brought her a measure of peace, which was at odds with the situation she was in right now.

She was in a foreign place and yet she was finding herself more at peace with herself than she had ever been before.

Chapter Eight

A warrior thinks of death when things become unclear.
—Carlos Castaneda

Daphne stayed to herself and her group as everyone settled down for the night. There was little they could do until the pirates came back to get them. And from the crew they'd learned that usually they were left in the hold until the pirates' demands were met. The crew, the doctors, and Hamm and Laz were all held together in the large hold.

The Maersk tankers had been targets before and Laz had reassured everyone that they had a protocol for dealing with the pirates.

Everyone was quiet but she couldn't sleep. She glanced at Franny and saw the other woman wasn't having any trouble. But then with Franny's attitude it was easy to see why. The other woman lived her life and didn't have regrets as far as Daphne could tell.

Daphne always had regrets and doubts and second guesses. There hadn't been one thing in her life she hadn't doubted. She'd like to say motherhood, but that one thing had brought about the most doubts. She rolled over, trying to get comfortable on the floor, but there was no position that was going to help her sleep.

She got to her feet as quietly as possible but then hesitated as there really wasn't anyplace for her to go. She started to sit back down and saw Laz standing a few feet away. He gestured for her to join him and she debated one second before walking over to him. He led the way to a stack of crates piled in a corner. It was the same section she'd retrieved her medical supplies from earlier.

"I never could sleep without being able to feel the air on my face," he said.

"I've never thought about it that way," she said. "Tell me more about the group you are with."

He shrugged. "I'm really not much of a talker."

But she knew that wasn't true. She could tell that the job he had wasn't a social one, but Laz did like to talk. And she suspected that he didn't want to talk about what he did and who he was. That was very different from being reluctant to talk at all.

"Hamm said you had a few more guys on the outside. That you had worked together for a while."

"When did Hamm tell you that?" Laz asked. "I told him to keep an eye on everyone, not gossip."

Daphne punched him playfully in the arm. "He wasn't gossiping. We were chatting while we were collecting supplies. I think I may have been saying you should have told us the dangers involved before we left port."

"That sounds like you." Laz wrapped his arm around her shoulder and pulled her into the side of his body. She wanted to lean against him but remembered bruises he had sustained while he'd been on deck so she didn't. She just lightly rested against him and took comfort from his earthy scent and the warmth of his body.

"Well, I was angry and scared," she said, when she realized she hadn't been talking.

"Was?"

"I guess I still am but a part of me . . . well, I'm trying to figure out how to let that go. If it's out of my control and this entire thing is, I might as well just live in the moment."

"Is that why you came over here?" he asked.

She didn't have an answer for that. She wasn't sleepy and Laz offered her something. She wanted to call it solace but wasn't sure that was the right word to define how she felt.

"Who knows?" she said.

He cocked his head to the side and took her hand in his. His hands were rough and callused. They were the hands of a man who'd worked hard his entire life. By contrast hers were soft and her nails perfectly manicured. She used her hands to heal, he used his to protect. They were markedly different and their hands reflected what she knew deep inside.

"You know. You're not a woman who doesn't do things without knowing why."

"I used to be," she said, not sure why she felt comfortable talking to him except maybe it was because he made her feel safe and she hadn't felt safe in so long. Not since the day that Paul had told her that their marriage was over. Not since she'd realized that the family and the security she'd thought it provided were gone.

He rubbed his thumb over her knuckles. "Don't worry about the group holding us. You'll get out of here and be back to your neat and tidy life soon."

She tugged her hand away. "I'm not worried about that. I don't have a neat and tidy life."

"Sure you do."

"Don't make judgments about me, Laz."

"Fair enough," he said. "I was trying, ah hell, I should have known better, I'm not the kind of guy who knows how to say the right things."

She shook her head. "You do so. You just thought this incident shook me from my moorings, but I came on this trip to try to find myself again."

"You're kind of old to be lost," he said.

"Again with the compliments," she said. But she wasn't offended. Four years ago she'd have thought the same thing. She thought that wandering was what happened when she was young. She'd picked her path and been happy on it.

"Tell me, Daph, why are you lost?" he asked.

"Maybe I was on the wrong path," she said. "My divorce made me feel . . . like I was less than."

He cupped her face in both of his hands and kissed her. It was deep and hot and conveyed so much she was literally shuddering when he pulled back.

"You are not less than," he said. "You are more than any other woman I've ever met. Don't doubt yourself."

She couldn't respond to that. Just swallowed hard and looked at him in the grainy light available.

"Thank you."

"You're welcome," he said.

Silence grew between them and she wanted to know more about him. "Tell me about you. What kind of man sets a trap for pirates?" she asked. She knew what her issues were and there was no path away from them. Not here in this holding cell and not with this man. She just needed a distraction, she thought.

"A crazy one," he said.

She punched him lightly on the arm. "I want to know about the group you are with. Are you SEALs or Special Forces?"

"No," he said, his eyes got very quiet and serious. There was no more evidence of the joking, flirting guy that she'd seen a few seconds ago. "I'm not sure the answer will be comforting to you, Daphne. It might be better if you just know that I'm the kind of guy you can count on in a fight."

"I do know that. I still want to know more."

"Has your curiosity ever gotten you in trouble?" he asked.

"No. I mean there are times when I've uncovered things I

wish I hadn't," she said. She wondered if she would feel better not knowing, but in the end she knew she needed to know more about Laz. He was the distraction she'd chosen to get her through this crisis.

"This might be one of those times," he said.

"I want to know. Whatever it is. I need to know more about your group. We're trusting you to keep us safe."

"You trust me?" he asked.

She did. On this ship she trusted him.

He took a deep breath. "I'm a mercenary."

Mercenary. Well that was something she'd never thought to hear him say. She'd thought SEAL or maybe Special Forces. But not mercenary. Those men were without consciences.

Laz waited to see how she'd react. He'd learned early on in his career with the Savage Seven that saying he was a mercenary elicited myriad responses from women. Some of them were titillated by the thought of being with a soldier for hire. Others found the moral ambiguity of what he did unbearable and sneered at him.

But Daphne now showed no outward reaction. Why did he care anyway?

He couldn't really say except that he really liked her. That was the dumbest thing he could think of right now. He needed to pay attention to the pirates and the situation. They still hadn't been able to raise Savage on the radio, and he and Hamm might have to retake the ship on their own.

They weren't any closer to catching Samatan than they had been before the pirates took the ship. Instead of worrying about that, he was more concerned about what Daphne thought about him.

Goddamn, he was fucked up.

Just because she had those big chocolate brown eyes and the kind of hair that made him long to bury his hands in it didn't mean he should let her distract him. He wanted to be wrapped in her body again. And he knew he'd do anything to see that he got back there.

"How does that work?"

"What do you mean?"

"Who hires you? Do you change sides midway through if you get more money?"

Laz shook his head. "First of all, we never change sides. We fight for the man who hired us, finish that job, and then move on."

"So who hired you this time?" she asked.

"A government," he said. He couldn't tell her too many details because part of the job was to be discreet. The governments who couldn't officially come in pirate territory with their navies hired groups like the Savage Seven to take care of the out-of-control piracy in this part of the world.

"I guess you can't say which one?" Daphne asked. She knew he couldn't. This wasn't the first time she'd learned something disturbing. How many times had Paul learned of some illicit government intervention? When he'd been a young Senator, they'd had a lot of discussions about the ends justifying the means.

"You got that right."

"How many of you guys are there?" she asked.

"Six," he said.

"That's it?" she asked. That sounded like a fairly small team. But then she guessed in a group of men like Laz they'd only want men they knew and could trust.

"Wouldn't seem fair to the bad guys if there were more of us."

She laughed softly like he'd wanted her to. He was cocky but not arrogant. Laz backed up his swagger with true grit. She'd seen it in the dustup on the deck before the pirates' attack and in the way he led the crew, especially down here when he'd talked to the men and their group. He wasn't making false promises, just guaranteeing he'd do his level best to get them out safely.

She needed to believe that. He was someone to watch over her and she took great comfort from that.

"So are you in charge?" she asked.

"Nah. I'm just a solider. Savage is our leader."

Daphne lifted one of her eyebrows at him. "Savage? That's his name?"

"Yeah."

"And you're Lazarus?"

He nodded.

"Do you guys all pick your own names?" she asked.

"Some do. Others just keep their own."

"But you changed yours, didn't you, J.P.?"

He shook his head, loving the sound of his given name on her lips. He hardly ever told anyone. His mom had her reasons for naming him and though he'd legally changed his last name a long time ago, he'd kept the name his mom had given him. A part of him believed that her gift of his name had kept him safe all these years.

"Okay. What's the plan for tomorrow?"

"I'm going to talk to everyone in the morning. I think the best thing will be to get the guards in here so we can overthrow them. We might stage a distraction. I need to get to the radio room to contact our men on the outside."

"Sounds dangerous," she said.

"It won't be. I'm not going to let anything happen to you, Daphne."

He had to figure out how to keep her safe and manage this attraction to her. He liked women. He was known to the others on the team as a bit of a playboy, but this was the first time he'd had a woman on a job that he wanted.

And he did want her. She was curvy and real—a woman

who reminded him of those long-gone dreams he'd harbored as a teenage boy. Dreams where he'd be the army hero and he'd have a girl like Daphne waiting at home for him.

"I believe you will. I can help with the radio room. If you want I saw how to use it when you let me call my family."

"I think it's safer for you to stay here," he said.

"That's all well and good but it will be easier for me to slip away. And I can let my ex-husband know we are hostages."

Laz didn't like that. Didn't like the thought of her turning to any other man for anything. "That's not necessary. I've got this under control."

"It never hurts to have backup," Daphne said.

Laz thought about it objectively. Her connection to the Senator was what the pirates wanted to know about. She was partly a liability. If she was successful and her ex sent the marines or someone else, it could interfere with what Savage had planned.

"Let's save your ex for backup. I need to talk to Savage first. He should be close by and we won't need whoever you can get them to send."

She nibbled on her lower lip as she mulled over what he'd said. He watched her growing more aroused as she just stared at him.

"You like to do things on your own, don't you?"

"Yeah. I don't ask for help unless I really need it."

She smiled then and for the first time it looked like a real smile. "Me too."

He shook his head. "Did you like it when I kissed you?"

She nodded. "Why did you?"

"To reward myself for being so good at my job."

"I'm your reward?" she asked.

Hell yes. He wanted her to be his reward. But he knew that she couldn't be. He had let her get under his skin and that was a stupid thing for him to do, so he simply nodded and sent her back to her pallet.

She couldn't be his reward. Not unless he saved them all in the morning. And suddenly that was damned important to him. He never backed down on a mission and this sure as hell wasn't going to be his first time. No, this time he was going to save the day and win the girl.

He walked over to where Daphne lay and stood over her for a few long minutes. She rolled onto her back and opened her eyes, looking up at him. He wanted to lie down next to her and wrap her in his arms but now wasn't the time. Once they had Samatan and this mission was over, he was going to hold her all night.

Daphne managed a few hours' sleep and woke to a tense room. The pirates hadn't been down and everyone was sitting around waiting. There was nothing to do except wait and that was pricking tempers. Rudy, who had somehow achieved a Zenlike calm the day before, was pacing the room like a caged tiger.

The crew members all roamed the room in an opposite corner from Rudy. Bill and Jerry were talking quietly in the corner and she could tell from the way they kept glancing around the room that they weren't discussing their golf game.

"Oh my, there is too much testosterone in this room," Franny said.

"And no one to direct it toward. I almost feel bad for the pirates who come in this room."

Franny gave her a half-smile. "I don't. You can't lock people up without expecting some sort of retaliation."

"You have a point," Daphne said. But she knew that the men who'd taken this ship didn't fear them. They had grown up in a harsh environment where most people didn't live past their thirties. Some of the accounts she'd read of Somalia had chilled her blood. There was so much lawlessness that its people grew up thinking that they had to make their own justice with guns.

It was one of the reasons why she'd agreed to come on this trip. She'd read stories of kids hit by bullets and having no one to repair their limbs. She'd read horrible things and knew her skills were needed in Somalia. Really needed.

She wouldn't be repairing the shattered knees of athletes, but instead she'd be operating on kids who might not walk if she didn't help them.

"Laz said they are going to try to use a fight as a distraction to get the pirates down here," Daphne said.

"When did he tell you that?"

"Last night. I couldn't sleep."

Franny glanced over at her. "Did talking to him help?"

"It did. I think I just needed to feel normal."

Franny smiled. "I'm glad something worked. I slept but ever since my residency days I've always been able to shut down when I tell my body to sleep."

Daphne knew a lot of nurses and doctors who could do that. She'd never been able to. She needed a good hour between functioning and sleeping. Her mind processed things at the end of the day.

"I wish I could."

"I bet. So a distraction? Like what? Did he say?" Franny asked.

"No, he didn't," she said. But she noticed Hamm assembling the crew members and he waved them over. Jerry and Bob joined her and Franny. Rudy stayed to the back away from everyone else.

"Is he okay?" she asked Bob.

"He said this reminds him of how it felt when Maria was

taken by the rebels. I think he's having some sort of flashback to that time. I offered to get him a sedative from our supplies."

Rudy must have declined it. She would have too. She preferred to deal with things on her own without the aid of medication.

Laz made his way to the front of the group. "Can everyone hear me?"

"Yes."

"Good. I need to get to the radio room to get backup to the ship. If the pirates follow their usual mode of operation they will not come back down here except to deliver some food and water.

"I think if we start a fight in here they will hear it and come in. Then we can overpower them. Hamm will lead the crew in doing this."

"We will help too," Bob said.

"It'd be better if your group kept a low profile," Laz said.

"Too late for that. We know they want to know about Daphne's connection. She'll go with you to the radio room and let the Senator know we are okay and not to pay any ransom," Bob said.

"I don't like that idea," Laz said.

"Too bad," Bob said. "We won't get in your way but we need to be involved in this. Sitting around is making us all crazy and we are a highly intelligent and well-trained group. We will help you."

Laz didn't like the idea, Daphne could tell by the way he narrowed his eyes, but otherwise there was no outward sign that he was affected one way or the other.

"I have training in weapons and hand-to-hand combat," Rudy said.

Laz rubbed his hand through his hair. "Okay. We can use that. I think Hamm and Rudy should be the distraction to get the guards in here. The other woman in your group," Laz said pointing to Franny.

"Franny," she said.

"Good. I want you to scream and yell at them to stop. Be loud and sound hysterical. Can you do that?"

"Yes, I can. Anything else?"

"Stay the hell back. I don't want the pirates to shoot you to shut you up. So pay attention to them. They are dangerous men who will shoot first and ask questions later."

"Then should we be doing this?" Jerry asked.

"Your group can hide behind the medical supplies," Laz said.

"Hell, no," Jerry said. "I was just making sure there wasn't another way."

"Okay. We need you guys to get into it as soon as they deliver food to us. It should be sometime in the next hour or so."

Daphne had never experienced the clock moving slower. In actuality it was only forty minutes later when they heard the scraping of a key in the door and then it started to open. As it did Rudy launched himself across the room at Hamm.

"No you don't, you bastard. We've got women in our group. We should get the food first."

Rudy landed a good punch in Hamm's face and Hamm just slugged back. The two pirates who had opened the door dropped the food on trays on the floor and stepped inside to break up the fight.

They tried pulling the men apart.

Jerry hit Lars hard in the face. "The women aren't bad luck or the reason why pirates attacked the ship."

"Yes they are," Lars said. "We've never been attacked before this."

"Then you were lucky," Rudy said.

"Luck has nothing to do with being at sea," Drew, another crew member, said.

"You just said the women were bad luck," Bob yelled and then the melee broke out. The men were all in a lump of swinging fists.

"Break it up," the pirate yelled.

But the men ignored him. Franny was screaming, which added to the confusion. The pirates stepped into the room and headed toward the knot of men.

"Let's move."

"Will they be okay?" she asked.

"They have to be," Laz said. "Because we can't stay here and help them. We have to do our job."

"I'm not sure—"

"Then stay here. But I have to communicate with my men and I can't do it here. Our friends are giving us a chance to do that."

He looked at her with a very serious intent in his eyes. "Let's don't waste it."

Daphne hesitated, looking back at her friends. She worried that she was jumping from the frying pan into the fire but then Laz tugged on her hand and she looked up into his eyes. There was a promise there, one she knew she was going to have to take a leap of faith and believe.

She did just that by taking a step toward him and then following him out of the hold and into the hallway.

She'd never been so scared in her life and she realized she was counting on Laz to make sure she made it through this. She was counting on a man—on her lover—she thought. And that scared her almost as much as the gun-toting pirates.

Chapter Nine

A warrior seeks to act rather than talk.
—Carlos Castaneda

Daphne continued to follow Laz out of the hold as the fighting ensued. She still wasn't confident that Bob and Jerry could hold their own, but she trusted Rudy to make sure the other doctors were okay. He was their secret weapon with these lawless men.

The sounds came first from the gangway, footsteps, and then the smell of cigarettes. Daphne wasn't sure what was going to happen next. She should have stayed behind. Honestly, why did she always shoot from the hip instead of thinking things through?

"Fall back."

Where? She thought but quietly moved back. All of a sudden she tripped against the wall. The wall opened backward into a room and she realized it was a small supply closet.

Laz followed her inside and closed the door behind them. They were enclosed in complete darkness. The sounds of her breaths echoed in the small supply room. She couldn't hear anything.

She felt fear first, just that overwhelming feeling of aloneness, and she started to shake. She was about to call out to him when she felt his hand on her arm.

"You okay?" he asked in a low, almost soundless voice.

"Yes," she said. But she was lying. She was in over her head and had no idea of how to get out of this situation.

Suddenly she was overwhelmed and felt her throat close up and the spark of tears in her eyes. Damn it, she wasn't going to cry. But no matter how many times she blinked the tears were still there. Feeling overwhelmed, she really had to fight to keep from breaking down.

"You're breathing heavily," Laz said.

"I'm scared and freaking out," she admitted.

He put his arm around her and held her close. She put her arms around his lean waist and her head on his shoulder.

She took another deep breath and this time all that she inhaled was the scent of Laz. Closing her eyes, she let the tears she'd been trying to hold back squeeze out. Laz rubbed her back and she let the confidence and strength that he easily carried soothe her. She wasn't in over her head.

She was smart and savvy and she was going to get out of this situation alive. She knew exactly what she was doing and having Laz by her side only reinforced that.

"Thanks," she said.

She started to pull away but he held her tight. "You're very welcome."

His hand came under her chin and then she felt his fingers wipe away the tears she'd been unable to contain. He sighed then, a deep sound that could be resignation. She had no idea what he was thinking.

"You are the right woman at the wrong time, Daph. Do you know that?"

She shook her head. "I've never been the right woman."

"I find that very hard to believe," he said.

"I . . . I guess that makes me sound like I don't have any self-confidence," she said.

It was oddly easy to talk to him in the dark. His arms were still around her, his scent surrounded the air she breathed, and his heart beat steadily under her ear. She hadn't felt this safe since Paul had dropped his bomb.

She'd forgotten what it was like to be comforted by a man. To just enjoy the physicality of being in a man's arms.

"You have enough confidence for ten women."

Daphne smiled at the way he said it. "I guess I do in certain situations."

"But not this one," Laz said. "I don't mean facing down bloodthirsty pirates, I mean being here in my arms."

She shrugged and would have pulled back to see him but since she couldn't she just stayed where she was. She closed her eyes and pretended that this was nothing but a dream.

"You are right. I don't have a lot of confidence in the basic man-woman level."

He didn't ask her why and she found herself feeling very grateful for that. She wasn't sure she could put into words what Paul had stolen from her when he'd left. She knew that her situation wasn't unique. Marriages broke up every day but those other marriages weren't hers, and she hadn't bounced back from the betrayal and the even deeper sense of rejection she'd felt.

Here in Laz's arms she started to feel the inkling of . . . well, of recovery, she thought. Laz didn't see her as the perfect wife and an excellent mother for his kids. He didn't see her as a good partner in his bid for Congress. In fact, she wasn't too sure how he saw her.

She tipped her head up to where she thought his face was and her lips brushed his stubble-covered jaw. He sighed again.

His jaw moved against her lips as he moved his own head and then she felt his lips against hers. They were soft, softer than she'd have guessed Laz's mouth could be.

He rubbed his lips against hers and then parted them. She felt the warmth of his breath against her lips and then into her mouth. She couldn't help licking his mouth.

He tasted . . . delicious . . . she thought. She slid her arms up his back and rubbed her hand over the back of his scalp. His hair was short and soft. And she couldn't help running her hand over the back of his head as his tongue moved over her lips and then plunged into her mouth.

His arms tightened around her and he drew her closer. She felt the solid wall of his muscled chest against her breasts and the strength of his thighs against her own.

She felt all the things she'd longed to feel in a man's embrace and hadn't in a long time. And she let the rest of the world fall away until the only thing that mattered and existed was being in his arms.

"Damn, Daph, you are one dynamite woman. But we've got to get going if we have any chance of contacting our people while the fighting is going on."

She nodded. She didn't mind. She'd found some strength in being with Laz and she'd take that with her as they moved forward.

Laz was tempted to just stay in that small, dark supply room, making love to Daphne while the world burned around them. But he knew that the consequences that would follow that decision weren't ones he or Daphne were prepared to deal with. She wanted to save her friends and herself and so did he.

And he wanted to capture Samatan. He was tired of ships being preyed on out here.

He and Daphne snuck out the door of the supply room and into the long corridor. The lights flickered, as the *Maersk Angus* wasn't a luxury liner but a working tanker.

"Stay close. Do what I do. If I make a fist, it means stop. If

I point in a direction, I want you to go that way. Stay in the shadows as much as you can."

"Okay," she said.

The radio room was down the long hallway past the main gangway that led to the deck. Laz knew if they had any problems it would be there. The walls were painted the same gray as the floor and ceiling and the hallway seemed long and endless.

He gestured for Daphne to stop and moved forward to make sure they were clear. Daphne stayed close behind him and crouched when he pulled her down. Her breathing was heavy and loud in the small hallway of the ship.

"Breathe quietly," he said in a whisper.

"I'm trying. I'm just nervous."

He nodded and moved down the hallway, Daphne close on his heels. They made it to the radio room but there was a guard outside. Laz didn't hesitate as he came up behind the man. The ROE—Rules of Engagement—for this mission were simple: capture Samatan and have as few casualties as possible.

Moving silently Laz came up behind the guard. Until he heard the way Daphne moved he'd forgotten that he'd been trained to be silent. It had become second nature.

He pinched the carotid artery on the guard's neck, but the man swung backward with the butt of his rifle, hitting Laz in the stomach. He brought his fist up and punched the man in his side, keeping up the pressure on the carotid artery until the guard slumped forward. Laz caught him.

"How can I help?"

"I need to bind his hands," Laz said.

Daphne took off her belt and wrapped it around the guard's hands. A curl fell down over her face, and she realized that if he had met her at any other time he wouldn't have seen the courage he saw in her now. Her hands were shaking but still she did what she was told. She was a good soldier, which was the one thing he respected.

"Stay here."

The blood left her face and she swayed. "Stay here? What if someone else comes?"

He handed her a utility knife. The pirates had taken the one he always carried, but he'd gotten a replacement from the supplies in the hold. "Use this."

"Um . . ."

"You're a surgeon, Daph, I think you know how to handle a knife."

She quirked her head to the side and stared up at him. "I guess I do."

He leaned in, giving her a quick kiss on the cheek before turning back to the radio room. Having Daphne by his side wasn't like having Hamm or the other Savage Seven members but he knew she'd go down swinging. And he couldn't really ask for anything more.

"When I give the signal I'll need you to drag him into the radio room."

"Okay. Do you need me to back you up?"

"I got this. Just be ready when I give you the sign."

She nodded.

He left her to enter the radio room. There was another guard inside and the man turned just as Laz entered. The soldier didn't hesitate to fire his weapon.

Laz tucked low, rolling into the corner for cover. He lifted his own silenced weapon and fired two short bursts, hitting the guard solidly in the chest. He knew it was more humane to just wound and not kill someone but he'd been bit in the ass too many times by that act of kindness.

He walked over and closed the boy-man's eyes before taking his weapon. He went back to the door to find Daphne standing there at the ready. No nerves showed now—just full-on guard duty—and he felt an inkling of admiration for her and the way she handled herself.

"We're clear."

"Good."

She reached down, taking the unconscious guard under his arms and pulling him toward the radio room. Laz nudged her aside and took over. He dumped the guard next to his dead comrade and went to the radio.

"Is he dead?"

"Yes."

"I thought he may have hit you," she said.

"Not this time," he replied.

"Are you okay?"

"Yes, fine. Can you fire a weapon?"

"Yes, but I can't hit anything with it."

He arched one eyebrow at her. "Why not?"

"I think I'm intimidated by the weapon or at least that's what my ex said."

"Can you stand guard? Just fire in the direction of anyone who comes at us."

She swallowed hard and then nodded. He handed her the rifle he'd taken off the second guard. "Just pull this trigger. It's locked and loaded."

She took the gun from him and he turned away from her, working as quickly as he could to switch the radio over to a secure signal to radio the Savage Seven.

"Is anyone monitoring this frequency?"

He heard static and then Mann's voice. "About damned time you checked in."

"We've been taken. No sign of our prize yet."

"We are on our way. Savage made the call about ten minutes ago."

"We need your skills," Laz said.

Mann was a sniper. He worked with the rest of the team and he shared the same skills, but Mann's true calling was as a sniper and he could take a target out with pure accuracy every time.

"What's your ETA?" Laz asked.

"Thirty minutes tops. Seas are a bit busy this morning."

"We may be in the hold."

"We'll check there first. What's wrong with your communications?"

"They won't work in the hold. There must be some kind of lead lining in the bulkhead there." Laz wished he'd had more time to go over the tanker. Missing that outage spot made him downright pissed off at himself. Normally he was better than that.

Was he at the age where it would be better for him to get out of the game altogether? He wasn't trained for anything other than this and maybe operating a fishing boat. Somehow he doubted that he'd be able to spend a significant amount of time alone on the water before he started to have withdrawal symptoms.

He was an adrenaline junkie and always had been. He got off on the danger that came with busting heads and kicking ass. But when he looked over at Daphne a part of him wondered if being with her would be enough to satisfy that crazy part of his soul.

"Laz out."

"Mann out."

Daphne didn't even pretend that she was anything but nervous. She held the gun exactly as Laz had shown her and kept her attention fixed on the hallway. It was dank and gray and smelled of stale air. She heard the crackle of the radio and heard Laz talking, but she kept her attention on the hallway.

She didn't come halfway around the world to die. And she

was tired of feeling like a victim. She was ready to take control.

Dang it. She meant it.

"Behind you. I'll go first—"

"Not yet. I want to contact my ex first. He needs to know what's going on here." As much as she didn't want to have to go to Paul for anything, he was well connected and they did need the U.S. government to get the marines out here. It wasn't that she didn't trust Laz to take care of them; it was only that he and Hamm were two men and the pirates were lawless men who wouldn't stop until they'd gotten the money they came for.

"No. We already discussed this."

"I'm—"

"No. Get ready to move."

"But I really think I should contact him."

"Why? Has your ex ever been there for you? You said earlier that you didn't trust yourself on the man-woman level well so I can only guess that he's the one who put doubt in your mind. I don't trust that kind of bastard."

She had no choice. She wasn't going to stand here arguing with Laz and maybe get them both killed. But she'd wanted—what? Did she really want to run to Paul? He had given up on her. He wasn't her champion anymore.

"Okay, sorry."

"No problem. Do you remember our signals from before?"

"Yes, sir."

"You don't have to call me sir."

"Your attitude says otherwise." He was all business and tough military guy and she had to respect that. There was something about him that commanded authority.

"We can discuss it later," he said with a cocky grin. He took the other weapon. "Can you watch the door another minute while I clear the bodies from this room?"

"Yes. Where are you taking them?"

"To the supply closet."

She nodded. She was nervous. She didn't want Laz to leave her but she knew that she couldn't be a scream queen right now. She had to be brave and confident no matter what. She thought of her two boys and decided they'd be her guiding light here. She'd step up and do things that scared her because she needed to get back home to them.

Laz took the unconscious guard first. She watched the muscles of his biceps bulge as he grabbed the man under the armpits and hauled him out of the room.

Laz was strong and capable—the kind of man she'd often read about in novels but seldom encountered in real life. He walked the walk, she thought. This was a man who lived life on the edge and had carved his own path. Something she realized she wanted for herself.

Daphne heard the radio cackle.

"*P1, está você lá*?"

The words sounded familiar to her, and sounded similar to French, she thought. Maybe Spanish or Portugese—two languages she didn't speak.

"*P1? Está você lá*?"

"Laz?" she called down the hall.

He came running back.

"What?"

"Someone is trying to make radio contact. I didn't recognize the language, maybe Spanish or Portuguese."

"*Olá! Eu estou aqui*," Laz said.

"*P1?*"

"*Sim.*"

The conversation continued behind her while she kept her eyes on the hallway. She felt a little scared but everything about Laz told her he had this situation under control.

"The big shit is about to hit the fan. They have a fucking

mother ship that they are based out of. No wonder we haven't been able to find the bastards."

"What?" Daphne asked. The group that had taken the tanker were well trained and obviously knew what they were doing.

"I need to contact my men again."

"Okay. I'll just stay here."

"Good girl."

He went back to the radio and she heard his conversation and understood it this time since it was in English.

"The pirate leader is on his way to the ship. Apparently Fridjtof's failure to get the names of the hostages has angered him."

"We are on our way as well," Savage said.

There was a burst of gunfire from the hold. Daphne felt a fizzle of fear go down her spine. Her imagination was running overtime and her doctor's instincts were screaming to get down there in case she could save someone's life.

"What was that?" Savage asked.

"Damn it. Someone is firing in the hold," Laz said. "I've got to get back there. Laz out."

"Savage out."

Laz left the dead man slumped on the floor of the radio room. He held his gun at the ready. "Let's go."

He led the way back to the hold at full speed. Daphne followed him unsure of what was happening. Despite the fact that she had a gun in her hands, she felt scared and vulnerable. Laz had proven capable and she trusted him, but this wasn't a normal situation and a part of her couldn't help but feel overwhelmed.

"Laz?"

He shook his head. A second later he came to a halt and she bounced off his back. He reached behind him to steady her. His touch soothed her fears and she realized how much she needed him. Damn it, she wasn't about to depend on another man. No matter how different he was from Paul.

There was another burst of gunfire and then shouting in the hold. Franny's screams could be heard from where they were and this time they weren't hysterical. Her words were clear and they struck fear into Daphne's heart.

"He's dying. We need to stop the bleeding."

Daphne handed the gun she held to Laz. She needed to get in there and do what she was best at. *Saving lives.* She wasn't about to stand out here and wait to see if she could help out.

"What the hell do you think you are doing?" Laz asked.

"Saving that man. I'm trained—"

"It's dangerous."

She shrugged his hand off her arm. "I can't just stand here. I might be the difference between life and death for that man."

"Be quiet," Laz said, but she'd already drawn the attention of the pirate leader who turned on them with his gun.

Laz shook his head as she pushed her way around him. She was a doctor first, and if a life could be saved, then she was going to do her damnedest to save it.

She entered the hold and froze. The gunman turned on her and in his eyes she saw something that made her hesitate. He'd kill her.

She'd never faced anyone who looked at her like he did right now. This wasn't the craziness of a junkie looking for meds in the ER. This was a bold determination to take out any threat.

She put her hands up. "I'm a doctor. Let me help the injured man."

She glanced over and saw that Bob was sprawled on the floor next to one of the pirates. They both were in a pool of blood and she had no idea which man was dying.

"What's the situation?" she asked Jerry.

"Gunshots. I think that Bob was hit in the femoral artery."

Jerry was a surgeon and one of the best. She'd done surgery but not since her residency. She'd spent two years working as a surgeon before she'd decided she wanted something a little calmer and gone back to school to change her specialty to being a pediatrician.

"Tell me what to do," Jerry said. "I can help you."

"We need to stop the blood. And then we are going to have to operate on them."

Daphne was very aware that the pirate wasn't about to just let them do whatever they wanted to but with this much blood, the seriousness of the situation had to be brought home to him. They needed action. They couldn't stand around acting like hostages.

In this moment there was no hostage and pirate—just injured men and doctors. And she and Jerry would do their best to save the injured men.

She saw that in Jerry's eyes. She knew that the pirate might have other ideas but she could only follow her instincts.

Chapter Ten

Courage, above all things, is the first quality of a warrior.
—KARL VON CLAUSEWITZ

Daphne didn't care that Laz had ordered her not to go. She was locked onto the situation and her instincts made her take control. Jerry was on the floor next to Bob. *Oh, no, not Bob.* He looked bad. His skin was pale and the pool of blood on the floor made her realize how serious Bob's injury was.

It looked like Jerry was applying pressure to the inner right thigh. Oh damn it. Bob's wound was a femoral artery. He could die. Probably would unless Jerry was able to start operating on him.

And they weren't prepared to operate. There was no operating room or sterile environment here.

The stench of blood was in the air, and her first thought was they needed to get the bleeding stopped and then protect the open wounds from infection.

They were at sea so the risk of infection was higher. All the bacteria in the air and the constant threat of mold spores had her worried.

Bob was their calm-headed leader. He was their rock. Jerry was on the ground next to Bob doing CPR while Franny held her hand over a wound that was still bleeding.

Fridjtof was the other injured man. He was holding his own

stomach and she feared that if his wound was in the abdomen, either the aorta or inferior vena cava could be affected and he'd bleed to death. The lighting in the hold wasn't that great and it was impossible to see where he was hit. Seemed it might be near his upper chest rather than his abdomen, but until she got closer she wouldn't know where she was needed.

"Jerry, do you need me?"

"No, I need supplies."

Daphne took a closer look at the situation. One of the pirates was holding his gun pointed at Franny. She was halfway to their crates.

"These men are going to die unless you put your weapons away and help us save them," Daphne said.

"Shut up, woman."

"No," Daphne said.

Laz stepped into the room, using his body as a barrier between her and the leader of the pirates. Daphne paused to realize that Laz had stepped up every time she needed him. No man had done that for her before.

"Captain, this was very stupid of you," the man said.

"Who are you?"

"You may call me Jamac."

"Well, Jamac, we need to see to the wounded."

"Not yet. Our leader is on his way and he will want to take care of the troublemakers."

"They will be dead before he gets here unless we can operate on them. I will not let these men bleed out," Daphne said. "Rudy, get the supplies from our crates. Get the GSW kit and the QuikClot to stop the bleeding on Fridjtof."

"Franny, what does Jerry need?"

"Pressure pack and an operating room. Bob's been hit in the femoral artery."

"Damn it. Let her pass and get what she needs. Are there

beds in the infirmary?" she asked Laz since he was most familiar with the tanker.

"No. The mess hall would be the best place to operate."

"Okay, we'll do that. I need four men to carry the bodies down there when we are ready to move," Daphne said.

Years of working in the ER had inured her to gunshot wounds but this was different. She knew the men involved and had spoken with both of these men recently.

"We aren't going anywhere," Jamac said.

She turned on him and all of the timidity Laz had seen in her earlier was gone. She marched over to the armed and dangerous Jamac and got right in his face. "As long as I can save his life I'm in charge. We're not going to do anything stupid and you can stand at the door over there and keep an eye on us while we move the injured, but I am going to help this man Fridjtof—your comrade—and Jerry is going to take care of Bob."

Jamac seemed thrown by her brazen behavior. Laz wondered what a man who'd grown up in the broken land of Somalia would make of an American woman. At this moment Daphne was so much more than a doctor, she was an in-your-face American who wouldn't be deterred from her path.

Jamac fired a shot at Daphne's feet. "You are not in charge here. I am."

Laz took two steps toward Jamac and then leapt in the air with a flying side kick, hitting Jamac solidly in the chest. He followed him the ground, placing his foot on the other man's throat. "Listen to the lady."

Jamac struggled to breathe under the pressure of Laz's foot. Laz glanced at the other pirates. "Anyone else want to argue?"

The other four pirates shook their heads.

"The lady is in charge. Do what she says or your comrade will die."

"Give up your weapon and become my hostage and my men will help."

"Agreed," Laz said.

"You and you," Daphne said pointing to two of the men. One of them was Josef from the ship's crew and the other was a pirate. The men looked at Jamac and then shrugged. They lifted Fridjtof and took him to one of the large crates.

"Now go and get Bob and put him over there. Jerry, do you have that under control?"

"Yes. I . . . it's going to be touch and go but I've got this."

"Okay. Everyone else get out of the way and let us do what we need to."

Laz didn't like the situation at all but it was working better than he anticipated. The mixed crews of the *Maersk Angus* and their pirate captives worked side by side with the doctors as they operated on the two injured men. Jamac had assigned an armed guard to each "operating table" in the mess hall.

Laz had managed to keep himself free but had given up his weapons in order to get Jamac to cooperate. The situation was tense and no one was feeling that more than the two doctors.

Daphne and Jerry worked quickly and efficiently, barking out orders to both the nurses—Rudy and Franny—assisting them and the crew. Daphne was unwavering in her demands and if someone didn't move quickly enough she let them know.

Laz sat on the floor where Jamac had ordered him to sit when they'd entered the mess hall. His hands weren't bound and though he was weaponless he was hardly without the means to take over the situation if he needed to. Right now it was more important that the doctors take care of the injured men.

Both men were uneasy around each other. Thirty minutes into the operation Jamac offered him a cigarette.

Laz shook his head. "How did you get involved in this?"

"It's my job," Jamac said. "You?"

"This is my job as well," Laz said.

"Well, captaining a boat. But you know how to handle yourself . . . like a weapon."

Laz had been trained all of his adult life to give up little information and he didn't forget that in this moment. He knew if he could befriend Jamac the other man would lower his guard and that was his goal.

"I like UFC. You got that over here?"

"UFC?"

"Ultimate Fighting Champs. It's a combo of street fighting and different martial arts disciplines."

"You fight much?"

"Every chance I get," Laz said. This part of the story was true. Every new persona Laz took on was based in the reality of who he really was.

"What for?"

"Money and fun."

Jamac laughed. "I do this for the same reasons."

"Is the pay good?"

Jamac nodded. "Better than I can get on the land. And since I'm in charge of these men I get an extra bonus."

"Truly? So you're the leader of this group?"

"This unit. We work for another man."

"Ah, I understand. I'm a captain but my boss is the man who books the tanker."

Jamac took a drag on his cigarette.

"How much ransom did you ask for?" Laz asked after a few minutes passed.

"Three million American dollars."

"Do you think you will get it?"

Jamac smiled at him. It was odd to see such wisdom in a man so young. But Jamac had lived a lifetime in his young years and it was all written on his face. "Yes. They always pay."

Because of that the pirates would continue to operate in this region. The first time that a crew fought back, the pirates would start to rethink this easy way to make money.

But fighting back would mean death to many of the crewmen on the tankers and ships that used this shipping lane. The Somali pirates who operated in these waters—hell, all Somalis—were used to death. Few of them looked forward to a long life. Instead they would fight and die young.

"What made you choose this life?" Laz asked. In his experience the more questions he asked the more information men gave up. He'd learned over the years that all men liked to talk about themselves and pirates were no different. They all wanted someone to listen to their story. And right now while he waited for Savage and the rest of the team to get here, there was little else to do. They were at a stalemate. Laz with his weapon and Jamac with his.

"My brother-in-law got me into it," he said. "I was thirteen the first time I did it."

"Scared?" Laz asked. That was one thing that always disturbed him about young soldiers. They had been thrust into their lives as boys. Many of them didn't make it past that initial foray into manhood. But somehow Jamac had and he had thrived.

He nodded. "But it was . . . how you say? Exciting?"

"Exciting, I bet."

Jamac smiled and Laz felt a bit of sympathy toward this man. He didn't want to kill him or any of the other pirates. They were all so young—though dangerous and a threat that he would stop. Still their youth made him feel each of his years like an anchor around his neck.

These boys should be flirting with girls and going to college, not taking boats and pirating in the middle of the Indian Ocean.

"Is your brother-in-law still doing this?"

"Yes, he works on the mother ship with the boss."

"Where is the mother ship?" Laz asked.

"I think that is enough questions for now," Jamac said. "I'm going to have to kill you."

"You think so?"

"Yes. You aren't one of the captains who will calmly let us take your boat."

"No, I'm not."

"You are a worthy adversary," Jamac said. "As soon as the doctor is done fixing my man, this stalemate will be over."

"I know."

"What led you to the sea?"

Laz thought about it for a moment. The sea had always been there. An escape from the dirt and poverty of his life in South Florida. An escape from the old man's drinking and his younger sisters' tears.

"On the sea you make your own destiny."

Jamac nodded. "I like you, Captain."

Laz just nodded back. They fell into a companionable silence as they watched the surgery that was taking place in the mess hall. Laz had his earpiece in and realized from the open buzzing on the line that his radio was working again.

"I hope this stalemate ends soon," he said.

"It will," Savage said in his earpiece.

"I think it will," Jamac said. "They look to be finishing up."

Laz glanced over at Daphne and saw that she was exhausted, but something in her eyes told him she didn't have good news about her patient.

Daphne had never sweated so much through an operation. And her tension had everything to do with the fact that with the inferior vena cava wound and this crude operating room there was no way she was going to save Fridjtof's life.

Failure wasn't something she liked and she refused to let

this man's life slip away from her. True, he wasn't a good man but that didn't mean he should die like this.

"Get me another liter of plasma, Rudy."

"You're wasting it. He's not going to pull through."

"I'll decide what's a waste. I've almost got it," she said.

But she wasn't sure.

Rudy reached over and put his hand on her shoulder. "In this situation . . . there's no way we're going to be able to stop the bleeding enough for you to get this repaired."

"I know," she said. "I guess we'll have to call it."

"I'll do it. You go wash up."

Daphne turned away and felt a wave of exhaustion and fear wash over her. It had been easy to be brave when she was filled with the desire to help the injured men but now that was over. She realized that her gamble could have gone wrong. She walked to the sink built into the wall of the galley. Jerry was still working over Bob, and after she washed up she'd go over and see if he needed her help.

The scent of cigarette smoke reached her, and she looked over at the door and saw that Jamac was stubbing out his cigarette. He and Laz were standing there blocking anyone from entering or leaving the room.

She shook her head and washed her hands, realizing she was crying as she massaged the soap into her hands. She shook her head. She never cried when she lost a patient.

She felt a hand on her shoulder but refused to look up. There was nothing she could say, and she didn't want anyone to see her this vulnerable. And she was vulnerable right now.

"You okay?" Rudy asked.

She felt like a first-year resident crying like this. "Fine." She turned the water off and shook her hands dry. "I need a towel."

Rudy snagged one from farther down the counter and

handed it to her. She wiped her hands with the paper towel and then tossed it into the trash.

"Thanks. I'm going to see if Jerry needs my assistance."

"I checked with him and he said he's fine."

"We need to talk about final arrangements for Fridjtof's body."

"Want me to handle it?" Rudy asked.

"No. I'll do it. What happened? How did those men get shot?"

"The fight got a little intense and the pirates started shooting. Hamm took out one of the pirates with some martial arts move and relieved him of his weapon. He told Fridjtof to drop his but the other man fired and Hamm returned fire hitting him in the upper chest area."

Daphne was shaken by what she heard. "What about Bob?"

"Everything went a little crazy for a minute or two. The pirates all started firing and Bob was hit in the melee. Jamac came in and then you guys did."

"That sounds . . ."

"Scary, Daphne. It was scary and I've seen some things that a man shouldn't have to and it scared me."

She reached over and patted Rudy's arm. He was a tough guy and to hear him say he was scared . . . "Do you ever wish you'd stayed in South America?"

"Not at all. I was dying there."

She nodded. "I . . . it doesn't really compare but when my husband and I divorced I felt the same way."

"It does compare. The death of a relationship is hard whether your lover dies or just decides to leave."

She nodded. For all his tough and gruff ways Rudy had comforted her with his words more than her friends who'd just said that Paul was an ass.

"Thanks."

"No problem."

"We're going to have to preserve the body until we can get it out of here. Are any of the freezers big enough?"

"I'll check."

Daphne walked over to where Laz and Jamac were standing. "I'm afraid Fridtjof didn't make it. The wound to his inferior vena cava was fatal."

Jamac nodded and then looked over her shoulder, to where Jerry was still working over Bob.

"What of your comrade?"

"I don't know. His injury was severe. I'm not sure if Jerry can repair it. Why?"

"Why can your friend be saved but not mine?" Jamac asked.

"If we had a better operating table I would have saved him. The wound hit a major vein. There was no way to stop the bleeding and repair it."

"Maybe Dr. Jerry is just better than you are."

Daphne looked at Jamac and fought the urge to punch the man. She was shocked at how violent her thoughts were but she was on the knife's edge. She was tired and scared and had just lost a patient. A man that she had known though she didn't like him. It was hard.

"I can't talk to a man who is this ignorant. We need to figure out where to store the body until we get to port."

"Leave him. My men will take care of it."

"Fine," Daphne said and walked away. Rudy waited near Fridjtof's body.

"What do they want us to do?"

"Nothing. They will see to it. Jamac thinks that Fridjtof may have died because I'm a woman."

Rudy shook his head. "That's ridiculous. Jerry couldn't have saved him."

Daphne nodded and walked away. The mess hall was

smaller than the hold and there were too many people in here now that she wasn't operating. She needed some privacy and everywhere she looked there were men with guns and flashlights. The smell of blood was overwhelming and she thought she could sense death in the air.

Laz felt the tension in Jamac as Daphne walked away, and though a part of him wanted to comfort her, he knew that this situation was about to go from sugar to shit. Damn. He didn't need this now.

He turned away from Jamac as the other man spoke in Portuguese to one of his men.

"Savage?" Laz said under his breath.

"Ten minutes. I heard that one of the pirates died. Keep the woman close to you. I wouldn't be surprised if they decided to punish her for the death."

"Will do."

Laz glanced over at Hamm to see if he'd heard the exchange and he noticed the other man was moving toward Daphne. In fifteen minutes a lot could change. Having Savage and the team en route was a nice fallback but it didn't help the situation now. And Daphne was in danger.

He stepped away from the door and was walking toward Daphne when Jamac stopped him. "You stay here, Captain."

"Bring the woman to me," Jamac said. Hamm was close to her but not close enough. One of the pirates who'd held the flashlight for Daphne now grabbed her. She struggled, trying to pull away, but couldn't escape his strong grip.

Laz walked over to them intent on stopping Daphne from being taken but felt the barrel of a gun in the small of his back.

"Don't interfere."

He glanced over at Jamac but before he could act Jerry spoke up.

"I need her help. Send her over here."

"Too late for that. The doctor needs to come with me. Take her up on deck, Michel."

Michel forced Daphne across the galley. Laz couldn't move. He had no doubt that Jamac would shoot him if he moved. He needed to wait until the other man was distracted. There had been enough bloodshed today. And he wasn't going to let Daphne be part of it.

Hamm stood a little more alertly than before. It was a bit frustrating that the other man hadn't moved to protect Daphne before Michel had gotten to her. But Laz didn't waste time on regrets.

"He will die," Jerry said, referring to Bob.

"I don't care," Jamac said. "If you continue to argue you can stop what you are doing and join us on deck as well."

Daphne looked over at him. "No, you take care of Bob. I'll be fine."

Laz wondered if it was simply wishful thinking that had motivated her comments. She had to know that Jamac was probably going to try to kill her.

"Savage?"

"We copied everything. Mann has the situation under control."

"I'm going up to the deck."

"Don't do anything stupid."

"Hey, it's me."

"That's what I'm afraid of," Savage said.

As soon as Michel and Jamac left the galley, Hamm made his move to overpower one of the pirates. Laz joined in the fray, not wanting to leave this situation until he was sure that Hamm had the upper hand.

He was afraid for Daphne and fear was something new to him. He'd spent a lifetime pretending that nothing and no one mattered to him and now he was going to have to admit to himself that she did.

A woman was the thing that would make him experience fear. It fit with what he'd always believed he'd find when he found that one woman. The woman who would make the sacrifices he'd made worthwhile, he thought.

He had someone he wanted to go home to.

Chapter Eleven

Courageous, untroubled, mocking and violent—that is what Wisdom wants us to be. Wisdom is a woman, and loves only a warrior.
—FRIEDRICH NIETZSCHE

Daphne had never been as scared as she was at this moment. She had no idea what would happen once she was on deck. Jerry had tried to help her and she'd seen Laz give Hamm a signal of some kind but she wasn't sure that meant he'd try to rescue her. And as out of control as things were on the tanker right now, she wasn't even sure she was even a priority to him.

She shook her head as Jamac's hands tightened on her arm and he shoved her up the gangway in front of him. She knew that she was important to Laz. She didn't kid herself that he was going to let her die up here without at least trying to rescue her.

She had to be ready. She had to help him in whatever way she could. But honestly she was drained, and as a wave of humid air hit her face she felt like fighting was the last thing she wanted to do. She knew that her boys were safe with their father in his home in the States.

Laz would survive without her and she was ready to just give up until they dragged her across the deck of the tanker and she heard the sound of the approaching chopper.

She lifted her head toward the sound of the twin jet engines. It made very distinctive sounds as it approached the tanker. A large waft of air circulated on the deck as it touched down. She stepped backward as the door opened and a man stepped out of a Eurocopter. This had to be the pirate king. The man that Laz and his team were trying to trap.

"Is that your boss?" Daphne asked.

"Yes, missy, and he is the one who wanted to see the murderer who killed Fridjtof."

She shuddered as Jamac started to laugh. She wasn't a murderer and she knew she was dealing with men who might see it differently. Fear choked her and made her knees weak but she knew she couldn't show that fear to Jamac.

"I didn't kill your comrade. I tried to save him."

"Save your breath."

She did. Jamac's body language changed as the chopper landed. He was no longer the man in charge but someone waiting for his boss. Daphne had seen this many times in D.C. There was always a bigger dog, she thought. There was no arguing with a madman and perhaps Jamac's boss would be more open to listening.

He stepped out of the chopper and stood on the deck for a moment. He had midnight dark skin and his head was completely bare of hair. He was tall—at least her height—and he had a long scar that ran along the right side of his face. Wire-rimmed aviator sunglasses concealed his eyes.

He held himself with authority and wore the success he had carved out for himself like a cloak. As he moved she saw the way the pirates on the deck bowed and were ready to do whatever he asked.

This was no mismatched group of untrained desperate men who were hoping to eke out some money. These were men who were highly trained. The fact that Laz had set a trap for them worried her.

Did he know how well trained these pirates were?

Would he still attempt to rescue her from a man such as this one?

"Bonjour, Madame," he said to her.

"Bonjour," she replied.

He turned to Jamac and spoke to the man in a dialect she now recognized as Portuguese, but the words were gibberish to her. Her own fear was growing by the minute.

Would they let her explain that the severity of the injury made it nearly impossible for anyone to have saved Fridjtof.

"I tried to save Fridjtof," she said. Waiting wasn't her style and standing while they discussed her fate wasn't an option for her.

"Madame?"

"I just wanted to let you know I did everything I could to save him. I'm a pediatrician, not a surgeon, and the wound was . . . well, it was fatal. I can't think of a surgeon who could have saved him even in the best rated trauma facilities."

"Are you under the impression that you will be punished for letting one of my men die?" he asked her.

"Yes."

He shook his head. "No one will die because of that man's stupidity. Guns shouldn't be in the hands of our hostages, which Fridjtof learned the hard way. Jamac, have you made sure that everyone is unarmed?"

Jamac said something she couldn't understand and a terse conversation between the two men left her alone a minute later with the pirate king.

He removed his sunglasses and she found herself staring into midnight black eyes. She thought he didn't look like a madman.

But then she'd heard that Ted Bundy had nice eyes and he'd been a serial killer.

"I am Abdu Samatan and I would never harm a woman for another man's mistake," he said to her. Taking her hand in his, he kissed the back of it.

"Daphne Bennett," she said. "Doctor Daphne Bennett. I'm with Doctors Across Waters. We really have no political affiliation at all. We are a humanitarian group who provides much-needed medical care to people in countries without the means to provide it to their people. Somalia is one such country."

"It is a pleasure to meet you, Daphne. I think you will find that you and I aren't that different."

She shook her head. "I would never use someone else to achieve my goals."

"Yet I have no choice. The reason why you are needed in Somalia is the same reason my men have taken this ship. There is no government looking out for the people of my homeland. No one to provide for them except me and men like me. We are the only source of income for our villages."

She took a deep breath as she did not feel safe as Abdu spoke to her. He saw himself as a modern-day Robin Hood; she looked at him and just saw a dangerous man who would do whatever he had to in order to survive.

Where was Laz? Had he been recaptured by Jamac as the other man went back belowdecks? She had depended on him to save her and now she was on her own. She had been in tense situations before. Hell, she lived inside the beltway in D.C. She knew tension but this was entirely different and she had no idea what to do.

"Come with me, Dr. Bennett. I want to show you something," Abdu said. He had a gun in one hand and her elbow in the other. She tugged on her arm but he tightened his grip until she felt he might break her arm. He was that strong.

"Don't make me have to hurt you," he said. "I don't like hurting women."

Tears stung her eyes, though whether from pain or fear she

had no idea. She'd ceased to think and instead had become a creature who simply reacted to what was going on around her.

Daphne had no choice but to follow Abdu. There were four other men on deck clad in head wraps and long flowing robes which she recognized as common garb for Muslim men. They all were armed with semiautomatic rifles and had on sunglasses to combat the hot late afternoon sun in the Gulf of Aden.

The smell of the sea and a breeze comforted her for a second. The smell of sea air and the rocking of the boat was familiar, but Abdu's grip on her arm was foreign and reminded her of how fragile she really was.

Two of the men she recognized from when the tanker had been taken; the other two men were new faces and these new men were harder and leaner. She didn't know if the men who'd originally taken the ship were a B-team or what. But these new men weren't going to be easy to overthrow. To be honest the other team hadn't been either.

It was funny because the sun was shining down on her head warming her skin. She'd always loved the daytime and been absurdly afraid of the dark. Even as an adult she'd slept with a night-light on. And now she realized that being afraid of something she couldn't see had been silly.

Real fear was seeing the devil in a charming man's clothes and realizing that you had no way to fight him. That no matter what you did or said that devil was still going to be looking you in the eyes when he stole the soul from your body.

While Daphne was up on the deck, Laz was on the heels of Jamac as they headed down the gangway. One of the pirates who'd held a flashlight while Daphne had been operating tried to stop him, but Laz was done laying low. He decked the other man and quickly relieved him of his weapon. He pulled the man toward the large storage cabinet in the galley.

"Savage?"

"Here. We are in position. Wait a minute. Damn it, Laz, get on deck. There's a Eurocopter heading toward the tanker."

"Not friendly?"

"Not that I know of. Mann is lined up to take the shot, but there are five men on deck with the lady doctor. We want Samatan alive. I think he's the one who has the lady," Savage said.

"Is she in danger?"

"Probably," Savage said.

Savage had never pulled his punches and didn't now. "I'll go get her," Laz said.

"Confirm that. Hamm? I need you to secure the galley. Once Samatan receives word that we aren't going to pay the ransom he might start harming the hostages."

Hamm left the operating table where he'd been helping out. "I'll secure the galley. These men will be our hostages now."

"How will you do that?" Laz asked.

"Rudy is a good fighter," Hamm said. He signaled to the man who had helped Daphne work on Fridjtof. Rudy walked over to join them and Laz saw the pirates who'd helped Daphne stand a little straighter.

"What do you need?" Rudy asked.

Hamm smiled at the other man. "More fighting. The galley is ours."

Rudy nodded.

Hamm led the way to the two pirates and Laz heard the sound of fighting behind him. Then he heard the clatter of flashlights as the other two pirates helping at the operating table dropped them to come to their compatriots' aid.

Laz intercepted the men. He used the lethal combination of street fighting and martial arts he'd learned from years of doing this job. Fighting two men at once wasn't what he preferred but he knew time was of the essence. He had to act quickly so he could go and take back Daphne.

He landed a solid punch in one man's gut and then used a sweeping sidekick to take down another. He used a blunt-force punch to the throat to incapacitate the man he'd just dropped. He turned to the other man and ended his fight with a one-two jab to the solar plexus and then the jaw. These men were trained to fight with guns but they weren't as skilled in hand-to-hand combat.

"When you're done we need someone to hold the flash-lights," Jerry said.

"In a minute," Laz responded.

Savage asked, "What's going on there?"

"The galley is ours." Hamm got a spool of duct tape from one of the cabinets and they bound the hands of all the men they'd just taken down. Then they tied them separately to the legs of the bolted-down tables in the galley.

"We've got this," Hamm said. "You go help Dr. Bennett."

"On my way. I am going to free Daphne—"

"Negative, Laz. We've got the girl covered. You go to the bridge. They sent a man up there. Go to the bridge and make sure the tanker is under your control. Mann will take the shot needed to protect the Doctor."

Laz had never really argued with Savage on a mission. He'd been trained to take orders and he automatically started to do it now. But this was Daphne. He wanted to say she was just another civilian that he was sworn to protect. But he knew she was so much more than that. And if goddamned Kirk Mann let her die, he'd kill the man who'd been his best friend for longer than Laz wanted to remember.

"Laz?"

"I'm going. But, Savage, you tell Mann to make sure that he gets his man. I . . ."

"He will. That doctor isn't going to die on the deck of the *Maersk Angus*."

Laz sprinted down the long dank hallway toward the gangway and heard the clatter of footsteps.

"Pirate on his way to your position," Savage said.

"Just one?" Laz asked.

"Affirmative."

"Do you need backup?" Hamm asked.

"Negative. Going silent," Laz said.

He stood in the shadows cast by the sun coming down the gangway. He saw the battered shoes first, then the tip of the semiautomatic gun. Laz attacked with a single-mindedness that he'd always been able to summon on a mission.

Everything else faded away as he took down his enemy. He disarmed Jamac and had him in a chokehold in a matter of seconds. In another time he and Jamac might have been warriors together; in this life they were enemies. Jamac was now his prisoner.

"Hamm, I'm bringing another prisoner to you."

"Affirmative."

"You're needed on the bridge, Captain," Savage said.

"I'm going there as soon as I deliver my prisoner."

"Move quick."

"Will do," Laz said. He delivered Jamac to Hamm and ran for the stairs, then slowed his pace. He couldn't just step out onto deck without risking giving his position away.

"Where is Daphne?" he asked.

"She is with Abdu Samatan," Savage said.

Laz felt a surge of satisfaction that they'd lured their man into this trap, but it was laced with concern for Daphne. He knew that Samatan wouldn't kill her outright unless she got obstinate. And knowing Daphne like he did, she would. He wondered how she could have ever survived being a Senator's wife. She didn't have a PC filter between her brain and her mouth and just said whatever was on her mind.

He admired that, really, he did. He only hoped it didn't get her hurt or killed.

"Easy, Laz. They are headed to the bridge."

"So am I. Why hasn't Mann taken the shot?" Laz asked.

"The girl is in the way. And our client wants Samatan alive."

"Makes our job that much—"

"Harder?" Savage asked.

"I was going to say more fun," Laz said.

Savage laughed and Laz switched his mind from talking to his boss to the mission. He flattened himself against the wall at the base of the bridge. He scanned the deck for pirates and saw one man stationed by the chopper.

"Should I take out the chopper?"

"Negative. Just get the bridge back."

"Will do."

Laz tuned out everything else and concentrated on getting to the bridge. He climbed the stairs.

"Freeze or the woman dies," Samatan said.

"Who are you?"

"I'm Captain Lazaraus and this is my ship."

"I'd beg to differ, Captain."

"Where is Jamac?"

"He is now my prisoner," Laz said.

"There will be no shift in power. Habeb, go and find Jamac," Samatan ordered.

A slim man who was no taller than Daphne stepped behind Laz and went down the stairs. Laz knew that Savage was monitoring him and hoped he had enough time to warn Hamm that he was going to have company.

Samatan held Daphne with one hand on her arm; in the

other hand he held a SIG Sauer semiautomatic handgun pressed to her temple. Daphne was pale and sweat had beaded on her lip. She didn't look tough or stubborn now. She looked scared and Laz vowed he'd never see that look on her face again.

Samatan was taller than Laz had expected and muscular. He had the body of a man who was well fed and well trained. He was not like the lean, almost gaunt pirates that had taken the ship.

It took Laz less than a second to analyze the situation. He put his hands up and stepped across the threshold.

"If you make one false move the woman dies and then you will."

Laz nodded in agreement. He wasn't going to do anything to jeopardize Daphne's life and right now he had orders to take back the bridge.

"Do what Samatan orders. We will be there shortly to free you," Savage said in the earpiece.

"What do you need me to do?" Laz asked.

"I need you to talk to your masters. To tell them that we want three million U.S. dollars or we will start killing passengers," Samatan said.

"Three million is too much for this tanker. We're not carrying cargo worth that much," Laz said.

"I don't need your advice. It's not just the cargo that has monetary worth, Captain. Rumor has it that you have an important passenger onboard. The wife of a U.S. Senator."

Laz shook his head. He was confident they didn't know the identity of the person related to Senator Paul Maxwell. Not that he was going to gamble with Daphne's life but right now he needed to level the playing field. Samatan clearly thought he held all the cards.

It was up to Laz to make sure he realized that he didn't.

"All of our passengers are important. Why don't we take the ship to Eyl and we can negotiate from there?" Laz suggested.

Laz knew that Mann couldn't make a shot on the bridge. There was reinforced glass on the main windows and tinting. It would be nearly impossible for the sniper to hit anyone. He might be able to entice Samatan off the bridge and into an area where Mann could hit him. But Laz thought that there was a reason Abdu Samatan hadn't been captured yet and he suspected it was because the pirate king was savvy.

"I don't deal in port towns, Captain. So you will get on the radio and relay that information to your bosses."

"Okay, but I still think—"

"Don't."

Laz looked at the other man.

"Don't what?"

"Don't think. That's not a job for a man such as yourself, Captain. You do what I say and no one will get hurt."

"Hamm hasn't checked in," Savage said in Laz's ear.

What did that mean? Had Samatan somehow taken over the tanker again? Habeb didn't look all that lethal but Laz had learned the hard way that a man didn't have to be a bodybuilder to be a threat.

"My only goal is to ensure the safety of my crew, passengers, and cargo."

"Then radio your bosses," Samatan said. "The sooner they pay the ransom, the sooner you will be on your way."

Laz reached for the radio. Tankers International was listed on the shipping papers as the owner of the cargo *Maersk Angus* was carrying but for this trip a client of the Savage Seven was footing the bill. That client was a consortium of interested governments and shipping companies.

"Contact us. Wenz will answer and relay the info to the proper authorities," Savage said.

Laz made his way over to the radio. Did Samatan realize that the one on the bridge wasn't as sophisticated as the radio room? Laz didn't care. He'd make the call and then take care of Samatan. No matter how big and strong the pirate king was, Laz was determined to take him down. Samatan was only human after all, and all men could be killed.

Daphne was beyond nervous. She could no longer process or function. A man was holding a gun on her, she'd just had another man threaten to kill her, and she was facing the man who was her onetime lover and wondering if he was simply going to out her as the politician's ex-wife and let this man kill her.

It'd be easier, she thought. Then Laz could capture Samatan and she'd be out of the picture.

But when she met Laz's gaze, he winked at her. She felt a sudden lightening of her soul. She wasn't alone in this land of death even though that was how it had felt to her. She had Laz here with her and he wasn't about to let her die.

She needed to get her head around helping Laz take this guy down. Part of it was that she was tired. She'd been running on empty since . . . well since she'd arrived on the tanker. Being part of a captured team, running the risk of being caught but going to the radio room, performing surgery when she hadn't since she'd been a resident had completely drained her.

She was breathing heavily. She realized she was going to hyperventilate if she didn't calm down but her body was on a runaway train. It needed rest and an escape from the nerves that were dogging her.

"You okay?" Laz asked.

She nodded, but felt herself swaying.

"Don't worry about the woman," Abdu said. "Just make contact with your bosses."

Laz moved around Abdu to do that and Daphne watched as the pirate king kept his eye on Laz. But the gun to her head never faltered. Even as she swayed a bit on her feet, the muzzle of that handgun remained in constant contact with her skin.

She started shaking.

"Would it be easier if I knocked you out?"

She turned to stare into those midnight black eyes of Abdu and realized he wasn't a cruel man. Just a man fixated on his goal.

"Maybe," she admitted.

He laughed then and it was a rich deep sound as unexpected as the bitterness of 99 percent pure chocolate. This man looked hard and cruel, but with that laughter Daphne realized he was more than the devil on this ship. He was a man and with that came all the complications of being human.

"Why don't you let her sit down?" Laz said. "I will still do your bidding."

"Just do what is asked of you, Captain. What is between the lady and I isn't any of your concern."

Abdu didn't loosen his grip on her arm or take his concentration from Laz. He was capable. Even though she'd been thinking of him as just the pirate king she realized that he was like a real king and to him this was a battle that had to be won.

She was just a pawn that was in his way. "Why do you do this?"

"Do what?" Abdu asked.

"Risk your life by taking ships. Wouldn't it be easier to be a doctor or a lawyer? Someone who makes a good living in a safer way."

The gun against her forehead moved slightly as he turned them both to follow Laz's moves. "There is no opportunity to do those things and still make a living in Somalia. My people are lost and leaderless and all that is left us is whatever we are brave enough to reach out and take for ourselves.

"Now, Captain, my patience is running thin, make that call."

Laz picked up the microphone for the radio and fiddled with the dial. She watched his long fingers as they moved over the control panel and she realized how very much she'd enjoyed being his lover. It was an odd thought when her life was in danger, but she realized one of the things that brought her peace was having him here with her.

"This is the *Maersk Angus*. I need to be patched through to Tankers International."

"This is Port Authority and we will relay your message. Go ahead."

"We have been taken by a group of pirates. And ransom is being demanded."

"How much?" the voice came back.

"Three million U.S. dollars."

"Is there a deadline for it to be delivered?"

"Tomorrow," Abdu said. "Five P.M."

Laz relayed this information. They waited three long minutes before there was a response. "Tankers International refuses to pay that large amount of ransom. Instead they offer five hundred thousand U.S. dollars and no prosecution."

Abdu's hand tightened on her arm as anger coursed through his body. He was so tight she feared he might explode and she'd be left tethered to a madman.

"Tell them not to insult me again. We will not negotiate with them. They will pay the ransom or we will start killing the passengers and crew of this ship one by one."

Laz started to speak but Abdu stopped him.

"The deadline is now noon tomorrow. The first person will be killed at 12:05."

Laz relayed this information and the radio went silent. Daphne wasn't sure what would happen next.

* * *

Samatan wasn't sure what to do with his captives. Until he heard back from Habeb he needed to keep them locked up. There was a small room used for storage at the base of the bridge and he decided to keep them there.

He didn't take his eyes from the Captain for a minute. There was an aura of danger around the man, and Samatan had learned early on in his life that he couldn't trust any man when that man was pushed into a corner.

The sound of gunfire drew the attention of all of them. He saw a long low speedboat off the aft bow.

"Do not let them board," he yelled to Tomas and Bin, who were on deck. He saw his men move to do his bidding.

The Captain leaned forward and watched the other boat intently.

"Do not worry, Captain. I will keep your ship better than you did."

The other man lunged toward him and Samatan pressed the barrel of the gun harder to the woman's face. "Do you want her death on your hands?"

The Captain cursed and shook his head.

He shoved the woman to the floor and then reached over her head to rip the radio from the control panel. The Captain leapt toward him as Samatan fired, hitting Laz in the fleshy part of the thigh. The Captain kept coming and Samatan lifted his hand back and hit the Captain in the face. Blood spurted from Laz's nose and lip as he staggered backward.

"Stay put," Samatan said as he left the bridge. He stopped to lock the door with the key Habeb had found earlier.

"Stop them," he yelled to his men.

Tomas aimed a burst of semiautomatic fire at the speedboat, hitting the driver. The man slumped forward and the boat careened toward them. The throttle was still down. The other pirates continued to fire.

Samatan took his time finding his target and then fired

three shots, hitting each of the men who'd been attacking them. There was only one man remaining alive on the boat and he stopped it and put his hands up.

"Board the boat and take supplies for us," he ordered Tomas.

"Bin, go below and make sure that Habeb has the situation under control."

Alone on the deck he looked around the tanker. This mission was to be his last in charge of the pirate group. He'd been doing this for better than ten years now and he was ready to retire and start a life for himself in Madrid. He knew this was a young man's game and he had been dancing to the piper for too long.

Tomas tossed the weapons from the boat onboard the deck of the tanker. "What should I do with this man?"

The man who had driven the speedboat looked up at him with pleading eyes. But he was unmoved.

"Kill him. No one steals from me," Samatan said.

Tomas turned and shot the man at point-blank range. Then let his body drop on the floor of the speedboat with the others.

"The boat?"

"Burn it. I want to send a signal to any other poachers who might think they can take what is mine."

Tomas nodded and went to work. Samatan watched as his man found the spare fuel can and poured liquid gas all over the floor of the speedboat. Tomas worked quickly and efficiently. He never questioned any of Samatan's orders and he'd been with his crew for almost two years now. Samatan liked Tomas because he did what he was told.

Tomas climbed back onboard the tanker and then tossed a match down onto the floor of the speedboat. Flames spread quickly over the floor of the boat as it drifted away from the tanker.

Soon a big black cloud of smoke could be seen, sending the

signal to anyone else on the seas that Samatan wasn't a man to be fooled around with and this tanker had been claimed, and soon would be ransomed.

Samatan had debated briefly taking the hostages to Eyl where he could keep them in a real brig. But doing so would make him like all the other pirates on the seas, and he had never been like everyone else. He'd keep them on the tanker, and if it came time to kill the hostages, he'd do it here at sea.

Unlike the other pirates who preyed in this area, he wasn't in awe of the money he made. He always knew there was more. He did hire men from the village where he'd once been Strongman and he tried to give back to his people whenever he could, but at the end of the day he was in this line of work to make a living for himself.

He did this because it was one of the most lucrative careers a Somali man could have. And if that Somali man was as educated as Samatan he'd grown to crave a life and a lifestyle that couldn't be obtained by working as Strongman.

Besides, Samatan wanted to live a long life. He wanted to have sons who would grow up and not in a death-filled village as he had, but in a nice village where they'd learn to play football or soccer as the Americans called it. They'd go to school without the fear of being shot on their morning walk. And someday they'd grow up to give him grandchildren.

That was it, he thought as Tomas came to stand next to him on the deck. His dreams were simple. They were the same as any other man's. He knew that the woman he'd left on the bridge thought him evil and he didn't care what her opinion of him was. His life had been hard. Not because he'd chosen it but because he'd been born on the wrong continent.

The wrong continent for a man with dreams. Big dreams and the drive to make them come true. In another land he'd be a captain of industry or famous for his acumen. In this world he was famous or infamous for his brutality and his success rate. The *Maersk Angus* would be just another tanker he successfully took and ransomed. And the U.S. Senator's relation would give him a nice bonus on this operation.

Bonuses were always nice, he thought.

"Sir?"

"Yes, Bin?"

"Habeb has all the hostages in the mess hall. Two of the men were armed. But he took them down and freed Jamac and the others."

"Good. Tell Habeb to separate the crew from the passengers. I think leaving them together has made them brave."

"Yes, sir."

Bin left and Samatan realized he had to see to the two hostages he'd left on the bridge. They needed to be moved.

"Follow me," he said to Tomas.

Together they returned to the bridge where the woman was standing over the man he'd shot. "Stand up."

The woman helped the Captain to his feet. "Lean on me."

"Captain, you will lead the way back down to the deck. Don't try anything or the lady will die."

The Captain followed his orders, hobbling down the stairs on his injured leg. At the bottom of the stairs he would have turned to the deck that was sunny and open, but Samatan directed him toward the maze of containers that lined the deck. They were huge and used for transporting goods between countries.

Samatan didn't care what they were used for now, he just needed a place to store this man and woman. He thought about killing them but until he ransomed the tanker and found the relative of the U.S. Senator he didn't want to kill any of the hostages.

The information he'd been given said that one of the women was related to the senator. His boss was very eager to have that woman and Samatan was smart enough to know that though they'd ask for money for the woman his boss really wanted to use her for political purposes.

Samatan didn't know exactly what his boss wanted and he didn't care. His only concern was doing what he'd been asked to do and getting his money.

He scanned the deck looking for someplace to put these two. A container seemed like a good place but he didn't want them to die in the heat of the day. And he knew the metal containers would reach deadly heat.

"Open the room to the left, Captain."

Samatan was careful to watch the Captain as he did his bidding. He knew such a man must be looking for some weakness. Some chance to jump him and change the balance of power. He knew that because he'd do the same thing if a man were holding a gun on him.

But Samatan knew he was strong enough to keep this man and this woman his hostages. He didn't doubt himself for a second because to do so would invalidate who he was.

Chapter Twelve

The warrior's approach is to say "yes" to life: "yea" to it all.
—JOSEPH CAMPBELL

Laz hesitated; he didn't want to trap them in a locked room. His leg ached like holy hell and he was angry that he'd missed his chance at Samatan.

They were amidst the tall towering containers and the room was one they used to store the anchor chain and other supplies for the deck. The room was small and windowless. A dark little room, which during the heat of the day could turn into a crypt. He hoped that Daphne didn't realize that.

Samatan shoved Daphne inside and she fell to her hands and knees as he did. Laz lurched and caught himself before he fell on top of her. He moaned as his injured thigh took the brunt of his weight. Daphne had bandaged the bullet graze and packed his nose with gauze to stop the bleeding.

The door was closed and they were locked in the darkness.

Laz lay next to her on the cold hard floor of the tanker. He wrapped his arms around her and his breath brushed her face.

Daphne was terrified of the dark. She always had been and falling on the floor with Laz had shaken her. She clung to him like he was a life jacket and she'd been plunged into the sea. Instead they were in the musky room and she had no idea how they were going to get out of here. Had no idea if they could be saved or if they'd die of heat exhaustion in the supply room of this pirate-held tanker.

She shook, though she tried to hide it, as her emotions overwhelmed her. Laz was on top of her and she was pressed to the floor. Tears burned the back of her eyes. She wondered if the reaction was from having the gun pressed to her head for so long or if everything that had happened was just too overwhelming.

She'd survived the crumbling of her perfect life back home but this far surpassed that kind of stress. She had lost a patient, been attacked by pirates, and had a gun held to her head. She was sobbing now and wanted to stop but in her mind the thoughts circled like vultures sensing a meal.

"Shh," Laz said. He whispered it against the back of her neck. His hands moved awkwardly over her as he rolled to the floor next to her. She felt him pull her on top of him.

Suddenly she was lying on his body and he was holding her. His arms were big and strong and she felt safe, but that safety was a fleeting feeling. She heard the sound of the guns, making her fear that more pirates were arriving. More people to point guns at her and threaten her.

"This isn't what I signed up for," she said in a voice that sounded pitiful.

"No, it wasn't. But you're not alone. I won't let anything happen to you."

"You're locked in here with me," she said.

"That's right, I am. It's better than you being alone, isn't it?" Laz asked.

His hands continued to move over her and she was slowly becoming aware of the fact that he smelled good. There was something familiar to his scent and feel and it brought her more comfort than she'd expected. In the dark there was only Laz.

Though she'd promised herself she'd never rely on one

man again, there was something solid about Laz that she couldn't help but lean on.

She turned her head into the curve of his neck and he whispered her name softly. Just hearing her name on his lips made her think of that brief time they'd spent making love together.

She remembered how he'd felt when he'd entered her body, how his hands had felt caressing her. She wanted more. She wanted him again.

Now.

An affirmation of life in case she didn't make off the tanker. If these were to be her last hours, she didn't want fear to be her dominant thought.

"Make love to me," she said, sitting up on his lap. He still lay on the floor of the dark room and death shadowed her with the fear beating in her heart but with Laz she felt alive. Really alive like she hadn't since she'd been young. Back when life had been lived in black-and-white terms and not in the nebulous gray area she'd settled into.

"Are you sure?" he asked. "I know you are scared, but that will pass."

She felt around for his face and found it. The stubble of his beard rubbed against her fingertips as she caressed her way over his jaw to his lips. They were full and hard—he had a man's mouth but the skin was surprisingly soft. She leaned down and rubbed her lips back and forth over his.

Daphne felt the exhalation of his breath and felt that they were both alive and she needed him more than she could rightly say in this moment.

"I'm more sure of this than I have been in anything else in the last twenty-four hours."

He slipped his hands under her shirt and pushed it up over her head. The next instant she felt him lift the cups of her bra and his palms rubbed over her nipples.

She found his shirt and pulled it up over his head. She was careful of his thigh even though she'd put a topical ointment on it and bandaged it well so it shouldn't give him any problems.

"We almost died," she said.

"Don't think about it," he replied, sitting up. He bent over and she felt the warmth of his breath against her breast before his tongue touched her nipple.

"We're alive and we have each other," he said. His voice was low and husky as he spoke right into her ear. She shivered and braced her weight on her knees as she moved over him.

As she rubbed her center over his erection, using his shoulders for balance, Laz groaned her name. She found his mouth with hers and felt his hands moving between them. He undid her pants and then she felt his fingers slipping beneath the fabric of her panties and touching her. His finger circled her clit and then he rubbed it lightly in a circular motion.

Suddenly everything dropped away except him and how he made her feel. She closed her eyes as she rocked against him. He whispered hot sexy words into her ear, urging her to come for him.

She felt her body clench and tighten as her orgasm washed over her. Laz continued caressing her between her legs and she reached between them to find his cock and free it from his pants.

"I want you now," she said.

He shifted between her legs and then she felt the tip of his hot cock at the entrance of her body. He thrust up into her, using his grip on her buttocks to force her down on him. She took his entire length and he held her still for a long moment. She leaned down against his shoulder and felt him inside her, wrapped around him by the clench of her pussy.

She felt completely surrounded by him, and as he urged her to move she did. Slowly at first but then quicker as she heard his breaths quicken and felt his hands tighten on her.

He was grunting as she felt another orgasm teasing her. So close to pulling her over the edge.

"I'm going to come again," she said.

"Me too," he said in a deep low voice that pushed her over the edge.

He held her and she just rested against him. "Thank you, J.P."

"Thank you, Daph," he said.

They pulled apart to clean up in the dark. She laughed as he took off his T-shirt and let her use that to clean between her legs. He was rougher than any man she'd ever met but he was also kinder, and she knew deep inside that her reactions to him were motivated by more than her fear to the situation.

"Laz?"

"Yes."

"You have a plan to get us out of here, right?"

"I hope so. I need to check in with Hamm. I lost radio contact with him when we entered the bridge."

"What can I do?" she asked.

"Sit tight and be quiet," he said. "My team are en route, but aren't as quick as we'd hoped."

She lay there next to him with her head resting on his shoulder and her body aching from the fall. She knew she hadn't bruised her body badly but she was tired.

She tried to concentrate on what Laz was saying but all she could do was listen to the timbre of his voice and let it soothe her.

She realized this was a mixed blessing. If they'd both been free, she'd never have been able to feel his arms around her but captured as they were it was okay to just lay here and draw strength from him.

And that was exactly what she did. She wrapped her free arm around his lean waist and felt his hand tighten on her arm.

She tried not to relive the last twenty-four hours but realized her life had changed more than she knew how to handle.

She'd asked for adventure and gotten it in spades. Though this wasn't what she envisioned she realized that for once she was truly alive.

Laz was distracted but tried not to be. He concentrated on what Savage was saying when all he really wanted to do was blow the hell out of this room and take Samatan down by whatever means were necessary.

He knew that his anger sprung from the fact that the other man had held a gun to Daphne's head and that he had locked her in this room.

He needed action or he was going to make love to her again. Now was not the time. Right now it was more important to figure out what the hell had happened to Hamm and how to get them out of this locked room.

"I've got to try to contact my boss, okay?" he said to her.

"Savage?" Laz asked.

"Laz, are you and Daphne okay?"

"We're fine. What happened to Hamm?"

"He was taken with the other crew members to another room. The rest of the doctors' group is in the galley under armed guard."

"Are they safe?" Laz asked, relying the information to Daphne that Savage had just given him about their respective groups.

"Is Bob alive?" she asked.

"Tell her I don't know," Savage said.

"Savage doesn't have that information," Laz said.

"Right now I need you to assess your situation and let me know when you can be back on deck. Do you have a weapon?"

"Not anymore," Laz said.

"I know. You're doing great. Just tell me when you will be back in the game."

"I'm not out of it," Laz said.

"Out of what?" Daphne asked.

"The game. I need to figure out how we are going to get out of here."

"Do you have a flashlight?" she asked.

"I have a penlight in my boot."

He sat up and felt her move with him. Her touch on his face was gentle and then he felt the brush of her lips against his. "Thank you for being in here with me."

"You're welcome. I wish I could have kept us from this."

"How could you?" she asked.

He shrugged and reached down to take the penlight from his boot. He found her hand and pressed it to her palm. "See what you can find in this room."

"What will you be doing?"

"Trying to open the door from the inside."

"Wenz is tracking your GPS, Laz," Savage said. "Once we get a fix on you, Mann is going to try to shoot the lock."

Laz shook his head. "That's an impossible shot."

"Mann thinks he can take it."

"Have him get Samatan. That man is serious about killing hostages. We don't want that to happen," Laz said.

"I'm not about to let it," Savage said. "I need you and the woman off the deck. Once you are out you are go to the chopper and disable it."

"Will do," Laz said.

Savage's way of thinking was always on the next task. It kept Laz from dealing too much with the impossibility of his current predicament.

"I found this crowbar we can use to get out of here. And there is a breeze coming up from the anchor chain."

"Show me," Laz said.

"What is it?" Savage asked.

"She's found the anchor opening. We might be able to shimmy down it."

"Great thought, Laz," Savage said.

Laz moved toward Daphne and the light. There was a small thin ray of sunlight coming in from the outside.

"Can Savage hear me too?" Daphne asked.

"Yes," Laz said.

"In your own time," Savage said. "We are monitoring the communication wave but so far have only heard bits of conversation in Dutch. Is that your crew?"

"Yes, that would be the crew." Laz didn't like having two conversations at the same time. He'd done that more times than he wanted to admit when he'd been undercover but right now he wanted out of the room, which would give him the clarity he needed.

"Should I just be quiet?" Daphne asked.

Laz took her shoulder and squeezed it. "Yes."

"Okay," she said. She stood next to him as he sized up the room. Savage was quiet as well, probably working a different angle at his location.

"What's your twenty?"

"We are close but holding. I'm waiting to make sure that speedboat that he set on fire doesn't blow up," Savage said. "There is something on the radar that Wenz is tracking. Might be another ship."

"Copy that. Did you have a chat with Tankers International? Are they going to pay the ransom?"

"They are counting on us to get you out of there," Savage said. "So that's a negative. But they did relay the information to the United States. It seems that the taking of the tanker was leaked to the media. And Senator Paul Maxwell wants to know what the hell is going on."

"Fuck. That's just what we need."

"I know. The navy is sending one frigate. I told them we have it under control but we're not the U.S. military."

"Nice. How much longer?"

"No more than ten minutes."

"J.P.?" Daphne asked.

"J.P.?" Savage said in his ear.

Laz reached up and muted the earbud so Savage couldn't hear their conversation.

"Yes?"

"I hope this works and we can get out of here," she said.

He walked to her. "Me too since Hamm is locked up and possibly unconscious and Savage and the team aren't going to be able to get here for a while. Though he does have a plan."

"What's that?" she asked.

"Having our sniper try to shoot the lock off the door," Laz said.

"That's almost impossible. My boys watched a special on shooting off locks and depending on the steel it can be very difficult."

"And on the shot," Laz said.

"How old are your boys?"

"Fifteen and sixteen. They are barely eleven months apart. They hate it when I lump them together."

"But you do it anyway," Laz said.

"I do," she said. "They are united in my mind. I treat them like individuals."

Laz took the crowbar back to the front of the room. "Talk to me while I work."

"What about?"

"Your life back home. I've been doing this for so long I've forgotten what it's like to have a normal life," he said.

"Surely your friends have 'normal' lives," she said.

"Nope," he said. His circle of friends had narrowed to men he could trust and that meant the Savage Seven. There wasn't anyone else that he'd let into his inner circle. He had learned the hard way that trusting men became dead men. And he intended to live a good long time.

But first he had to get them the hell out of this room.

* * *

Daphne realized how much she liked Laz over the next thirty minutes as he worked to find the best way to free them from the room. It was very hot inside and she struggled to breathe sometimes, but he kept calm and cool.

Occasionally he'd talk to Savage on the earbud but for the most part he just worked at finding a way out of the anchor storage room and talked to her.

He asked a lot of questions about her everyday life. "When did you decide that you wanted to be a doctor?"

"Third year of college. I didn't go to medical school. But I'd been studying philosophy and one day the question was about legacies and what we live behind and I started thinking about that."

"Why?"

"Because if I continued to study philosophy I'd be an observer of life and mostly of abstract things instead of a real participant. I wanted to really be out there making a difference, not discussing the differences that other people made."

Daphne realized how young she sounded when she made that statement. It had been a young woman's desire to make a difference and she'd thought she had to be in a profession to do it. She always knew she wanted to be more than a wife and mother.

"What are you thinking?"

"That I can be incredibly naive sometimes."

"Still?" he asked.

"Yes, I think so. What about you?"

He shrugged and then turned back to his work. She had kept the penlight pointed wherever he directed her to. His features were stark in the filtered light and he seemed very capable. She didn't imagine Laz ever had worried over what he would do and the impact of it. He was the kind of guy who went after his goals and damn the consequences.

"I enlisted at eighteen. I had a pretty good idea of what my legacy would be. And if I died for my country then I'd be okay with that. Making a difference . . . well, I've always had that on my mind."

The sound of metal on metal scraping made her shiver, but she knew they were that much closer to being free and freedom was just a step toward taking back the tanker and getting back on track. Back on the path she'd started down for this summer.

"I can see you had. Was your family in the military?" she asked, needing to know everything she could about him. Here on the tanker he was becoming her reality.

He didn't answer as he repositioned himself and tried one more time to wedge himself down the opening.

"Nah, they were fishermen."

"Truly? Is that why you're a sea captain?" she asked. Then realized that he was a mercenary, not a sea captain.

"Yes. My knowledge of boats and the seas came in handy for this mission. Savage knows how to put the right guy in the right job."

"Why a mercenary, Laz? Is it for the money?" she asked because that question had been in the back of her mind for a while now.

Another shift of his long lean body and he almost lowered himself through the opening. "No. I do it because—you won't get this because you're from D.C.—but sometimes the government has to make decisions that aren't in the best interests of the people and I was tired of watching my CO have to be pulled back because someone in Washington thought stopping before the goal was reached was okay."

She laughed. "Man, you sound just like Paul. The frustration comes from having to find a solution that everyone can get behind and he always says that means no one is happy."

Laz made a grunting nose.

"Sorry. I guess you don't like politicians."

"I don't care about them one way or another," Laz said. "I just don't like thinking about your ex."

Daphne wasn't sure what that meant. "Why?"

Laz turned to her, supporting his weight on his arms, and then he vaulted back out of the hole around the anchor chain. He pushed the penlight aside so it didn't illuminate his face. Then he came in close and kissed her hard and deep. She shivered as his tongue brushed over hers and then plunged deep into her mouth.

He pulled back. "I don't want any other man on your mind except me."

She put her hands on his jaw. It was impossible to tell him that after being married for seventeen years she inevitably thought of things that Paul liked and said. She couldn't help that, but she no longer thought of Paul as someone who mattered to her.

"That . . ."

"What? Is it too much? Am I too possessive for a man you've known for so short a time?" he asked. He ran his callused thumb over her cheekbone.

It was hard to imagine that this man could compare in any way to Paul. "I'm not thinking of Paul. You just . . . listen, I lived with him most of my adult life and it's not that I'm pining over him. It's just that he was a constant in my life."

"Why did your marriage end?" he asked.

"That's not really any of your business," she said. No way was she going to tell Laz, who radiated an earthy sexuality, that her marriage had ended because Paul had been tired of her. Both sexually and personally.

"Damn it, Daph, it is my business. I'm not the kind of man

who has a girl in every port. Hell—I was that kind of man," he said. "But you changed all that."

She shook her head. "Me? The girl next door? I don't think so, J.P."

"You did. I can't explain it any plainer than the fact that when I look into your eyes I know that we are meant for more than this time together on the tanker," he said.

And those words scared her. Plain and simple. She didn't want any man to say something like that to her because she'd be tempted to believe him, and if she did and he betrayed her, she'd die. She'd just wither up and die and never be able to trust any man again.

"Laz . . ."

"No, don't bother to say anything. I know I sound like I'm just saying whatever I have to," he said, "but this time it means more."

She shook her head. *This time.* He'd used words like that with other women. "My husband cheated on me, Laz. For two and a half years he had short-term affairs until he met a woman he finally felt like he could leave me for."

Laz cursed under his breath.

"So when I say it's not you, it's me, believe it. I'm not sure I'm ready to trust any man when he says he's going to be with me forever. I'm not even sure I believe in forever any more." Her voice cracked and she felt the sting of tears in the back of her eyes. She hated that the thought of not having a man by her side still made her cry but she'd grown up expecting to be married for her entire adult life and divorce had rocked her world.

Almost as much as having a gun held to her head.

Paul had killed dreams that had always been something she'd used to define herself. Abdu Samatan had stolen her sense of personal security and made her accept that she really was mortal. And J.P. Lazarus held the promise of security against both of those things yet she was too afraid to reach out and take it.

Laz went back to working on getting them out of the room. At first he'd enjoyed being in here alone with Daphne but now he needed to get out. He needed to do what he did best—action. He plain sucked at talking even when he was buried deep in her body and he knew she wasn't thinking about her ex or her old life. Just look how well it had gone when he'd told her how he felt.

Damn it. It pissed the hell out of him that her ex had hurt her that way. It didn't matter that if Paul hadn't been such an ass then Daphne would never have come on this trip and he'd never have met her. He wanted to be the only man she thought of and the man who always kept her safe.

But how could he protect her from her past?

He sure as hell hadn't been able to protect himself from it. He still had nightmares of the first man he'd killed up close and the comrades he'd lost on battlefields all over the world haunted him most nights.

But that was different. He didn't have mixed feelings about the way those men had died . . . well maybe Armand. Armand had been killed because a dirty double-crosser had betrayed him. Of course the rest of the Savage Seven had sent that bastard straight to hell.

He reached up and turned the mute off his earbud. He'd wanted privacy to talk to Daphne but that had backfired. He'd do better to remember that he was a warrior. And warriors didn't make good mates. Hadn't his first wife told him that?

"Savage, you copy?"

"Savage here."

"Did you get in touch with Hamm?"

"Sort of. One of the men mentioned that he was concussed.

I've tried to raise him but can't," Savage said. "Samatan and another man are on the bridge. They've radioed for someone to prepare for hostages. I think that means they are going to try to move everyone off the ship."

"That might be better. You can intercept."

"Indeed we will. And Mann is ready to take out the pirates one by one if he has to."

Laz laughed. "I bet it's like sitting on a caged tiger trying to keep him calm until he can take his shots."

"Copy that," Savage said.

Daphne stood quietly behind him. He knew she was listening to his side of the conversation and a few minutes ago he would have stopped to explain things to her, but she'd angered him when she'd said she couldn't trust him. So he didn't.

"Any word on the doctors in my group?" she asked.

"Tell her no. Still nothing. We don't know where they are being held. At first we thought they might be in the galley but we haven't been able to confirm," Savage said.

"They haven't talked to them since the groups were split. We'll be out soon and can see what's going on," Laz said. "Savage thinks they might be planning to move the hostages."

"Where? If they take us to Eyl, our group has someone there who might be able to help," Daphne said.

"Who?" Laz asked, surprised.

"I don't know. Bob said there was a contact there who would help us if we got taken to that port."

"Nice. Isn't Bob the one who's had the surgery?"

"Yes," Daphne said. "But Franny will know who it is as well. We can ask her."

"Did you copy that, Savage?"

"I did. Confirm that Franny will know the name."

"Confirmed. Do you want me to stay out until they take the hostages?"

"Negative. I want you to get free and get to Hamm. Then see if you can arm the groups and have them ready to overthrow Samatan on my command."

"Copy that. There's an emergency boat on the port side that I will take the women to once I have the group assembled. Which direction should they go in?"

"Northeast. I'll send you the exact coordinates on the GPS unit we stashed on the boats," Savage said.

"Confirm."

"Confirm all you want," Daphne said. "I'm not leaving on my own."

"It's the only way. Besides you know that you're the prisoner he really wants to get his hands on. Think about that, Daph. Do you want to be ransomed to your sons and Paul?"

Laz would use whatever means necessary to get her off this tanker and to safety.

"I guess not."

"Good. Now we need out of here."

Laz continued to work on trying to get them out of the room but it was a time-consuming job. Finally he figured out the best way to slide his body through the opening. He put his foot through first and then his thigh. It was tight around his lean hips and his shoulders scraped as he pulled himself through. He had to awkwardly bend over to get his head out. But in a manner of minutes he was below the well room and in the bowels of the tanker.

He checked the area to make sure they were still clear before he reached up into the opening. "Come on, Daph."

She wriggled herself through the space he'd made and soon was standing next to him. Her face was pale and sweat beaded her upper lip and had left marks on her T-shirt between her breasts. The heat, which he'd been largely ignoring, had affected her.

"How do you feel?" he asked. He hadn't thought to stash

water around the tanker, never suspecting that they'd be imprisoned in one of the rooms.

"I'm fine. I just want to get back to my group and check on Bob."

"We'll do that. But first we have to get to Hamm," he said. "The pirates can't know we're free."

She sighed. "What do you need me to do?"

"Stand guard while I figure the best way out of here," Laz said. He walked across the deck to one of the life rafts, reaching below the tarp that covered it. He drew out a semiautomatic handgun. Hamm had stashed weapons onboard just in case.

He handed the weapon to her. She shuddered but took it. He wanted to kiss her again but made up his mind that he wasn't doing that anymore. She didn't want a man like him, even if she hadn't said that in so many words. He knew they were worlds apart and he was in an uphill battle if he wanted more from her than this brief tanker affair.

Hell, he knew that. He never had been a forever man, he thought, while he looked around for the direction they should head.

He glanced sideways at Daphne as she stood like a trained sentinel watching the two avenues that could possibly bring an enemy to them. She was everything he'd ever wanted in a woman and some things he'd never considered good qualities until this moment. It was hard as hell for him to remember that he was a warrior and not just a lover.

He moved next to her and took the gun out of her hands. She let it go easily, but her hand lingered on his. She took his wrist and looked up at him with those big brown eyes of hers.

"Thank you."

"Just doing my job, ma'am," he said.

She shook her head. "It's more than that and I wish I was in a better frame of mind where men are concerned, Jean-Pierre, because I'd never let you go."

Laz had never been touched by something someone had said to him before. Well maybe his old man's words when he told him he wasn't any son of his but that was a different feeling altogether. Daphne had just made him feel like he was the right sort of man for her. That feeling was more powerful than he would have believed it could be.

Chapter Thirteen

To achieve the mood of a warrior is not a simple matter. It is revolution.
—CARLOS CASTANEDA

Daphne followed Laz through the maze of the underbelly of the ship. He led them up a rope ladder that was composed of several joined together at the end of the tanker. He went first and she spent a few tense moments waiting for him until he signaled her to come up on deck. The sun had began to set over the Gulf of Aden.

"This has been the longest day of my life," Daphne said.

Laz didn't respond as he led her toward the end of the row of containers. He was looking for somewhere safe to stow her. *His words not hers*. She wasn't sure that she was going to be able to hide out while he went and faced bad guys. Not that she was particularly skilled at fighting armed assailants but hiding out felt cowardly, and she was tired of letting the pirates control her emotions.

"Some days life is like that," Laz said at last. "I need to go find Hamm and check on him—"

"Don't go alone. I know I'm not much help but I don't want to be left up here by myself," she said.

"Daphne, you'll be safer here."

"How do you know? Samatan could find me again and . . . I just know I'll be better off with you," she said.

"You don't even trust me," he said.

"I do trust you, Laz. Way more than my mind thinks I should. So far you are the only man ever to not let me down."

"Ever? What about your dad?"

She bit her lower lip. She shouldn't have started this conversation. "He died when I was ten. I never really knew him."

Laz tipped his head back and looked up at the night sky. All around them the stars were starting to be visible as the sun sank over the horizon. Daphne remembered the first night she'd come up on deck and talked to him. "I thought you were a pirate that first night we spoke up here."

"You did? Why?"

She licked her lips trying to think of the right words to say.

"Don't do that," he said. "Don't try to find words that will sound nice. Just say the real reason."

She bit her lip and then took a deep breath. "There was something about you that made me think you were hiding something from me."

"You didn't trust me," he said.

"But I wanted to," she said. "You're a rascal of a guy, Laz. You can be charming one minute and deadly the next. You are like no man I've ever met before and even though I know you'd grow bored with me in the real world I want to see if it would work between us."

Laz shook his head. "Woman, you are making me crazy. I just said the same to you and you got your back up. This isn't me leaving you alone at your place and not calling back. This is a life-and-death situation."

"I know," she said, interrupting him because she just couldn't let him continue. "I know I sound like I'm half crazy and maybe I am. But I can't be up here alone. I will freak out."

Laz gave her that lazy half-smile of his. "Okay, fine. You can come with me but when it's time for you to leave . . . you will go and not argue."

"Sure," she said.

"I need you to be quiet and understand we can't help someone if they are injured. I'm going to free Hamm and that's it. Savage believes the rest of the hostages will be transferred tomorrow and they will be rescued then."

"But Samatan said he'd shoot us if he didn't get his money."

"And he will be planning to," Laz said. "Just not here. They like to do it public."

She shivered. "I don't understand the people here. Why wouldn't the Somalian people stop him?"

"He is a leader here. The people in Eyl and other towns up and down the coast get their money from the pirates. That's why they are treated like kings here."

"I wonder sometimes why I ever left D.C."

"Me too. You don't exactly seem like an adventurous person."

"I'm not. I did it because I was lost. I know you won't understand it but I had to figure out how to find something of who I used to be. Some part that hadn't been stolen. I thought doing this would be the best way."

Laz took her hand in his and drew her into the shadow behind one of the containers. "It was a good thought. Doctoring the people in this part of the world will touch that philosophy major who decided she wanted to leave a legacy."

She smiled to herself as he led the way through the containers to a gangway that she hadn't known was on the tanker. It was on the far end away from all of the common areas and crew quarters.

"I think you are right."

"I usually am," Laz said.

He paused for a second. "Shut it, Savage."

"Is your boss disagreeing?" she asked. She'd noticed that Laz had a very good relationship with Savage. Just from the one-sided conversations she'd observed that their relationship seemed to be based on respect.

"He has his own opinions on the topic. We are heading down now so communications might be spotty."

Daphne didn't say anything.

"I'll be using hand signals again," Laz told Daphne.

"I still remember them. I'll be as quiet as I can."

"You'll be fine. If anyone comes at us just stay low and out of my way. We've reached the point where we can't allow any pirate to survive."

"Do you think the ones we captured were freed?" she asked.

"I know it," Laz said. "Samatan isn't a man to underestimate. He sent his number-two man down there to let them out."

"I don't want to see how he reacted to Jamac being captured. He was already mad at him," Daphne said.

"Samatan can't have incompetent people working for him," Laz said. "Otherwise his entire operation will fail and he'll end up like those pirates whose boat capsized and are washed up on shore dead."

Daphne somehow thought that Samatan would never make a mistake like that. Even with Laz and Hamm onboard the *Maersk Angus*, he had managed to take it over and keep them hopping.

She knew with his backup Laz would get the tanker back and keep his clients from paying ransom. Yet a part of her wasn't too sure that he could do it before anyone else got hurt. "I'm sorry Fridjtof had to die."

"I'm sorry that any man has to," Laz said, "but that's simply the way of the world and men who work for two masters don't live long."

She let those words echo in her mind as they walked down the long dark corridor. It turned and snaked around the belly of the ship. She wasn't sure she'd ever be able to find her way back, but that didn't matter. Right now all she had to do was follow Laz and let him keep her safe. And she trusted that he would. No matter what else she knew about him, she knew he wasn't going to let her die or be used to extort money.

"I'm surprised that you didn't shoot your way out of the situation with Samatan," Daphne said as they snaked their way through the belly of the tanker.

This part of the ship was all large tubes and low-hanging ceilings. Laz carefully led the way knowing that Daphne's nerves had to be getting to her at this point. His were.

He was ready for action but he lived by the motto that brain was better than brawn. And in most cases that was true.

"I don't think I could have protected you if I had," Laz said. "And I don't want anything to happen to you."

"Thank you," she said. "For everything. I know I probably would have made your life a lot easier if I'd just sat quietly and let you do your thing. But that's not my way."

Laz glanced back at her. "You didn't do anything wrong. There is nothing that you did that contributed to anything going on right now. Don't feel like you should have done something else."

She shrugged. "I should have—"

"Shoulda, woulda, coulda . . . it's useless thinking that way unless you can time travel and change the past. And hell if you can then you need to tell me right now."

She smiled at him and Laz felt lighter. He liked this woman more than most. He suspected it might have something to do with the fact that he'd spent more time alone with her than he normally did with women. Well, when they weren't in bed.

"No, I can't time travel. I just . . . I don't want to make those some mistakes again. If I'm screwing things up then I want to know so I can stop doing that."

Laz nodded. "Just do what I say when I say it and we'll be okay."

"I'll try," she said dryly. "You know many times I've been in charge in the office and ordered my staff around because I know what needs to be done, but it never occurred to me how many time they must have bitten their tongues. It's very difficult to just blindly follow someone."

Laz wanted to laugh at the way she said that. But he didn't. Instead he shrugged and kept walking toward the end of this hallway. Once they exited this room they'd have to be quiet. They'd have to make sure no one heard them as they moved toward Hamm's location.

"Savage?"

"Go ahead."

"Has anyone moved?"

"No. There are two men on the bridge and we can see on the radar that two smaller crafts are approaching the tanker. I think you have less than forty minutes before there are more reinforcements on board."

"Confirm that."

"What did Savage say?" Daphne asked.

"That we need to move quickly. I think you'd be safe here. Do you want to wait while I go free Hamm?"

She shook her head. "Unless you think I'm going to be a detriment, I'd rather stay with you."

"You're fine," he said.

She put her hand on his shoulder. "I'm not fine, Laz. I'm trying to be but this is so much more than I ever expected to experience in my life."

He patted her awkwardly on the shoulder. "It's okay. You're doing great. And if you decide you want to just sit this out someplace quiet, that's fine too. We just need to keep moving so if you can't do that . . . well say so."

She nodded. "Will you do something for me?"

"Sure thing. What is it?"

She took a step closer to him. "Will you hold me for just a second?"

Laz opened his arms and she stepped into them. She put her head down on his shoulder and he felt the warm exhalation of her breaths against his neck. He rubbed his hands down her back and she settled even more fully against him. Her breasts pressed against him, reminding him how long it had been since he'd held her. Really held her.

And it reawakened the craving inside him for more of Daphne. She was more than he expected, and when he held her he felt like he was more than a warrior. More than a man put on this earth to do his job and then move on to the next one.

Laz felt like he might have a future that didn't involve fighting. He lowered his head on top of hers, resting his cheek against the silky smoothness of her hair, and just breathed in the essence of Daphne. Let everything that was her just wrap itself around him.

She tipped her head up and he leaned down and kissed her. He kissed her like it might be the last time because the next few hours would be intense and he needed to go into battle with the taste of her on his lips. Damn. If he had the time he'd take her one more time.

Cement the bond between with his flesh. Make her remember that he was the one man she really needed. But first he had to get them out of danger. And he would. The promise of holding her in his arms was just an added incentive.

"Come on. The sooner we capture Samatan the sooner we can be alone."

She nodded. "Be careful, Laz. You're not impervious to harm."

"Hell, I know that, I have the bruises to prove it."

"How are you feeling? How's your leg?"

"It's fine."

"Really?"

He nodded. "I've had worse and still gone on to do my job."

He kissed her one last time and then forced himself to step back from her. "Let's move out."

She fell into step behind him. He carefully opened the fire door, which kept the engine room sealed off from the rest of the ship. He opened it cautiously hearing Daphne's breaths in his ear.

"Hold position," Savage said in his ear. "There is something going on up on deck."

"What?"

"Some kind of gathering. There are eight men up there. Wait a second. It looks like he is addressing them all."

"Can Mann take a shot and get him?" Laz asked.

"No. It's rocky on our boat and we are just as likely to hit any of the other men. You are clear to move."

Laz led the way quickly down the hallway. "Am I close to Hamm?"

"Two more feet," Savage came back.

Laz saw the doorway to the crew quarters on his left. He stopped in the hallway. This was the worst type of scenario. He didn't like going in blind with no chance of backup and that was exactly what he was going to have to do.

He had no idea what was hiding on the other side of the door. They knew Hamm was in there because everyone on their team had an embedded GPS tracker. But beyond that he had no idea who else was with him and if he was going to be facing an armed adversary.

"You stay put, Daph. If you see anything or hear anyone duck into that room over there and out of the way."

"I will. Be careful," she said.

Laz entered the room low with his weapon drawn. Hamm was sitting in a corner with the rest of the crew members around him. Hamm had a cut above his eye and the crew members looked ready to leap at Laz and defend Hamm.

Savage had let J.P. know that his teammate had a concussion earlier.

"Captain? We feared you were dead."

"I am alive. And I am here to rescue you all. How's Hamm?"

"He is dizzy. He fought hard but there was no way to keep the skinny little man at bay."

Samatan's second in command was a fighter. But that didn't surprise Laz. What did surprise him was that Hamm had been injured. The cut over his eye didn't look that bad.

"I'm bleeding from the back of my head," Hamm said.

"I've got Daphne with me," Laz said. He backed out of the room and signaled her to join him.

She came into the room and he saw her hesitate when she saw all the men. Then she caught sight of Hamm and he saw a change come over her. The doctor with her full-on confidence was back. She walked past Laz to Hamm and started asking questions and checking his pulse.

"You got this?" he asked.

"Yes," she said.

"I need two men to come with me," he said. He had two volunteers quickly.

"What do you need from us, Captain?" asked Bjorn.

"We are going to retrieve some weapons I have hidden on the ship," Laz said.

"The rest of you men need to guard the door. Don't let the pirates see Daphne since they believe we are locked up in another part of the ship."

"Yes, sir."

Laz looked at Daphne. "Will you be okay?"

"I'm fine. Hamm will be too. He is a slightly concussed but I think he'll be fine."

"Good to hear," Laz said.

"Amen," Savage said in his ear. "Ask her if Hamm should be evacuated with the women."

"I'm not going to ask that," Laz said. "Hamm will kill me if I suggest such a thing."

Savage laughed.

"Come on, men," he said.

They followed him out the door and into the hallway. Weapons had been stowed in the crew quarters in the expectation of pirates taking the ship.

"Why do you have weapons stashed, Captain?" Bjorn asked as he followed him into the main crew quarters.

"To catch pirates, Bjorn," Laz said.

"Well we've certainly got them. Not sure it's what you had in mind," Bjorn said.

Laz shook his head and led the way to the crew lockers at the end of the narrow bunk area. There was enough room in this area for twelve hammocks. While some tankers had cots or navy-style bunks bolted to the floor, this one used hammocks for the men.

"How familiar are you both with weapons?"

"I grew up on a farm and can handle a single-shot rifle," Drew said.

Laz nodded. "Bjorn?"

"I was in the army so I can handle just about anything."

"Good. Just what I wanted to hear."

Laz went to the last locker and used the key on his key ring to open it. He started pulling out semiautomatic rifles and RPG launchers. He handed ammunition to Bjorn and Drew, and both men took as much as they could hold. Laz felt much better once he was loaded down with weapons.

Being a sea captain had been okay but as he slowly put on the tools of his chosen trade he felt more like himself. He was a warrior and without his weapons he felt like a fraud.

He paused for a moment to wonder what Daphne would say if she saw him now. But that didn't matter. He hadn't hidden who he was from her. She knew that he was a warrior. And he knew she'd be happy when he got her off this tanker and back to safety.

"I don't want a lot of dead bodies so think before you just fire. But don't be a hero. If your life is threatened and you have the shot, take it," Laz said.

"Yes, Captain." Both men both examined their weapons and loaded them. Laz did the same thing with his.

"Savage?"

"Here."

"I have the weapons and we are heading back to Hamm. Then we will free the doctors and bring them to our group," Laz said.

"Who is Savage?" Bjorn asked.

"Someone on the outside who is helping us," Laz said.

"Do they have a twenty on the doctors?" Savage asked.

Laz knew that the while finding Hamm had been easy because of his GPS tag the doctors didn't have a tracking device. Searching the rooms on this level was going to be risky and might lead to them being recaptured.

"Do you know where they are holding the doctors?" Laz asked Bjorn.

"No, sir. The one doctor couldn't be moved, so the woman insisted they keep him in the galley. I don't know if that is what happened because we were shuffled out of there."

"Thank you. That gives us a place to start the search. Let's get back to our men and then we'll find the doctors."

Laz led the way back down the hall. They reentered the room where Hamm and the other crew members were. Daphne was sitting next to Hamm on the floor, and his teammate and friend looked much better now.

"Is he okay?" Laz asked Daphne.

"I'm fine. She gave me some pills and some water," Hamm answered.

"Where did you get pills?" Laz asked.

"This is the room you assigned to Franny and I," Daphne said.

Laz nodded. He handed Hamm his weapon and ammunition. He gave the other men weapons as well. Daphne blanched when she saw the RPG launcher.

"What are you going to do with that?" she asked.

"Shoot down Samatan's chopper if he tries to escape," Laz said.

She shook her head, but she didn't say anything else.

"Do you want a gun?" he asked her.

"No."

Laz shook his head. He asked Hamm, "Do you feel up to coming with me to get the doctors?"

"I'll go," Daphne said. "Hamm needs to sit still for another twenty minutes before he starts moving around."

"I'll take one of the other men," Laz said.

"J.P., what if Bob's condition is bad? I need to be there to help out. If Bjorn or Drew or any of these other men have medical training then I'll stay behind but otherwise I think I should go."

"She makes a good point," Savage said.

"Fine. But I don't like taking someone unarmed with me. This situation is dangerous and people could be hurt," Laz said. But he knew full well if it had been Jerry or Rudy or, hell, even Franny, for that matter, he wouldn't be arguing with them. He wanted Daphne to stay behind because he wanted her safe.

He didn't doubt that he could protect her, because he knew he'd give his life to save hers. It was just that he wanted to keep her in cotton. Make sure she was protected from all the dangers that were on the tanker.

And he also knew he couldn't say that to her. So instead he shook his head and led the way to the door, very aware that she was behind him the entire time.

He knew she had to be tired and scared but she just kept doing everything he asked of her. His admiration for her grew with each minute they spent together.

There weren't that many people he admired in the world. He wasn't a true cynic but in his line of work he tended to see the worst in people.

Situations like this one where they were being held against their will and she was being asked to do things out of her comfort level—well, he wouldn't have been surprised if she'd simply said no. But each time he turned to her, she said yes no matter what it was he asked from her. No matter how many times he asked her to reach deep inside of herself and find the will to do something she had never done before, she did it.

And he flat-out couldn't think of another civilian he wanted with him in a situation like this. It had nothing to do with the fact that he thought he might be falling for her.

Chapter Fourteen

In fighting and in everyday life you should be determined though calm.
—Miyamoto Musashi

Daphne didn't like all the weapons that Laz had on, but then she admitted that what she really didn't like was the fact that Laz was a warrior. But that was ridiculous. From the beginning he'd been honest with her about the kind of man he was.

Well, not honest, she thought. At first he'd wanted her to believe he was a captain of a tanker and she'd thought he was a pirate and now she knew the truth. He was a mercenary.

Seeing him armed to the teeth made that very real, forcing her to accept the man she'd had sex with was very different from every other man she'd ever met.

She'd known that but she hadn't realized how different. She hadn't fully expected him to look the way he did now.

There was that aura of danger she'd first sensed in him but more than that was a driving focus on his mission. And she had no real idea what he would do to get them off the tanker. To retake the tanker from a man like Samatan. But after what she had witnessed on the bridge when the pirate king had shot and killed those other pirates and then set their boat on fire . . . well, maybe Laz did need all those weapons.

Samatan wasn't a run-of-the-mill hostage taker and Laz wasn't your average hostage, she thought.

"You're awfully quiet back there," he said in a low voice.

"I thought it would be best to just stay silent," she said. Part of her had no idea what to say to this man. She knew that Jean-Pierre Lazarus was in there somewhere—probably buried somewhere beneath the steely eyed, weapon-toting man.

And she was worried about her friends. She dreaded finding them and feared that Bob might be dead.

"Say what's on your mind," he said at last.

"I'm tired and scared," she said. "I'm not sure there's anything else on my mind but that."

"Fair enough," he said. "The galley is going to be our first stop. I want you to stay close to the wall and I'll go in low. If it's clear I'll signal you to join me."

"Okay."

Laz moved ahead of her and she felt kind of petty since she'd worried about the weapons he had on. Now that they were facing the unknown, she was so glad he had those guns and that he knew how to use them. In fact she was counting on him to keep her safe.

"I'm sorry," she said.

"What? For what?" he asked.

"For . . . I don't know, doubting you, I guess. I know you are doing this to protect everyone. I should have just said thanks."

He shook his head. "There's no right or wrong way to react, Daphne. This is out of your comfort zone and so am I . . . I guess I'm surprised it took you that long to look at me like you did."

"How did I look at you?" she asked.

"Like I was a monster," he said. "Now stay put. I'll be right back."

He pulled his weapon and used the tip of his toe to open

the door to the galley. It was locked, which made her believe—hope anyway—that her friends were in that room.

"Come and get my key," he said.

She nodded and moved to his side. He handed her the key ring and she fitted the key in the lock and opened the door so Laz could keep focused on whatever lay beyond.

The smell of blood and disinfectant greeted her as Laz eased over the threshold. He crouched low and swept his weapon from side to side just as she'd seen cops do on TV shows.

She almost started laughing. This was so surreal she almost felt like she'd had too much to drink.

"You okay?"

"Yes," she said. "Are they here?"

"No, they aren't. Your friends aren't in here."

"It smells like blood," she said.

"From the surgeries," Laz said.

"Is . . . is Bob in here?"

Laz glanced over at the table where he'd been operated on. It was empty. That didn't mean her friend was alive. It simply meant that he hadn't been left here.

"No, he's gone too."

"Good."

"He might be dead," Laz said, wanting to warn her.

"I know. I . . . I just can keep hoping he's recovering. Why did they lock this room?"

"Probably because it's the galley and the food is in here. They aren't going to feed us and Samatan will keep his men hungry so they stay loyal to him."

"He is such a barbarian," she said.

"Yes, he is. But he was raised to be one. Let's go check the other rooms," Laz said.

"Wait a minute," she said. She didn't like the idea of being without a weapon and carrying a gun was out of the question but being in here reminded her that scalpels were sharp and had been used as weapons in ERs when necessary. So she went to the sink where she'd washed up after her surgery and took the one she'd used.

"Good idea," Laz said.

She nodded because she wasn't sure she could use it on a person who wasn't prepped for surgery, but she knew that she didn't like feeling as defenseless as she had when Samatan had held that gun to her head.

Laz led the way back out into the hall. He made her wait while he swept the hall with his gun. Then signaled for her to follow him. Absurdly she was struck with the memory of playing *Charlie's Angels* with her two best friends in middle school.

They'd spent lots of hours with their hands held together like guns, posing and chasing after phantom baddies. Now here she was trying to rescue her friends and fighting off a real-life pirate attack.

Pirates! When she thought too much about it this entire situation, it made her feel like she had stepped into the twilight zone. But this was real. The aches and pains in her body and the nerves that were making her think these things proved it.

Laz came to a stop in front of another door. He tested the handle and it was locked.

"Ready to do it again?" he asked.

She nodded. She fit the key into the lock and looked at him before she opened the door. He went in like he had in the galley and this time someone grabbed his arms as he made his sweep. Laz tucked his head and rolled, breaking free of the grip and raising his gun at his assailant.

Daphne stayed poised in the doorway with the scalpel held tightly in her right hand.

"Hell, you scared me," Rudy said.

"That kind of action could have gotten you killed," Laz said.

Daphne stepped inside the room and closed the door behind her. Rudy stood over Laz and Jerry and Franny were behind him. Franny's eyes were red and Jerry looked like he'd aged ten years.

"How's Bob?" she asked.

Franny shook her head. "We don't know. They took him to the infirmary."

The doctors' group looked like they were exhausted and strung out. It was clear that Franny wanted to be with Bob. Laz didn't think she'd be much use to them in any situation. He didn't relish the thought of taking her to find Bob but he had no other ideas about what to do with the woman.

"We need to move. I have weapons with the crew members and we will all arm up and then move to take the ship back from the pirates."

"I need to see to Bob. I'm not going to be any good in a fight and I . . . I just need to be with him," Franny said.

Laz shook his head. "Leaving this room makes us more vulnerable to discovery."

"I'm not asking you for permission, Captain," Franny said.

He glanced over at Daphne to see if she could help him with this. He wasn't going to risk them all being locked up or maybe even killed because of one stubborn woman.

Daphne walked past him to Franny. The men stayed by him.

"Savage?"

"Here."

"What's your twenty?"

"We are almost at your location. When you are together we will tell you where to rendezvous with us."

"Affirmative," Laz said.

"Who are you talking to?" Jerry asked.

"My boss. I'm working with a group to capture the pirates."

"That's reassuring," Rudy said. "Do you have more weapons?"

"Yes. I have enough for you both as well. We really need to get moving. Daphne?"

"You can go," Franny said.

"If we leave you here, I will lock the door. I can't risk the pirates knowing that we are not locked up," Laz said.

Franny twisted her fingers together. "I love him. I can't stand not knowing how he's doing. What if he dies? I don't want him to be alone."

Laz could understand that. But his hands were tied. One man's life versus everyone else on the ship. Well, the math just didn't add up.

Daphne seemed to know that as well.

"Let's go back to the rest of the crew," Laz said. "Once everyone is together we'll try to go to Bob—"

"He's in the infirmary," Franny repeated.

"You've got fifteen minutes," Savage said.

"This is the most FUBAR situation."

Savage agreed. "If she's going to be a problem, you're going to have to deal with it. I leave it up to you."

"Thanks, Savage." Laz realized how much he appreciated the calmness that Daphne had exhibited the entire time. She hadn't gotten hysterical one time even when Samatan had held a gun to her head.

"Okay. Time is wasting. If the hallway is clear we will try for the infirmary. But I can't leave you there, Franny. And we are risking—"

"Everyone else's life," Jerry said. "I think we should leave Bob in the infirmary. Let's go back to your men, Captain. Bob would want us to."

Franny started to cry and Daphne put her arm around the other woman. "You're right, Jerry. He wouldn't want anyone to be put at risk because of him."

"So you'll come with us?" Laz asked her.

Reluctantly Franny nodded. Laz took a deep breath. He wasn't too sure the other woman wasn't going to flip out at the first sign of trouble. But for now they could move.

"We will go out single file," Laz said. "Rudy, you seem the most knowledgeable about fighting, I want you at the rear."

Laz took his spare weapon and handed it to the big man. He checked the weapon and then tucked it into the small of his back.

"Daphne will be behind me and then Franny, Jerry, and Rudy. When I hold my hand up like this, I mean for you to stop. If I point at you and wave you ahead, that means go. I need you to be as quiet as possible. That means no talking and try not to breathe heavy or step loudly."

"How far are we going?" Jerry asked.

"Just to the other end of this hallway."

"What if we're discovered?" Franny asked.

"If we are then I will cover you all while you come back in this room. Bar the door and don't let anyone in. Rudy will be able to defend this single doorway with his gun. Here's an extra clip," Laz said, tossing it to the other man.

"Any other questions?" Laz asked.

"Who are you?" Franny asked. "You're not just a sea captain, are you?"

"He's a man who is trained to rescue people like us," Daphne said.

"Ready?"

"Yes," they all said.

Laz led the way out of the room carefully. His thigh felt tight and he thought he might have torn the bullet burn when Rudy had grabbed his arms and he'd had to roll. But he didn't allow that to distract him. He kept focused or tried to because where his mind kept going was to Daphne.

She'd defended him, she'd championed him to her friend, and that had made him feel . . . well, a way that warriors weren't supposed to feel. He wondered if Kirk or Savage ever felt this way. They'd both found women and married them.

Laz had never felt anything like this before. He wasn't a soft guy. And . . . a shadow moved over the opening where the gangway was. He held his hand up and the procession behind him stopped. He eased forward, weapon drawn, ready for whatever or whoever came down the stairs, but the shadow just turned and made another circuit.

Samatan had one of his men on sentry duty guarding the stairwell. Laz tucked the knowledge away for now. He signaled the others to follow him as he went the rest of the way down the hall. He opened the door where he'd left the crew and entered it a moment later.

Once they were all inside and the door was closed, Laz breathed a sigh of relief. Hamm was looking much better and he helped arm the doctors.

"Savage?"

"Here."

"There's a sentry at the stairwell," Laz said.

"Affirmative. We are docking at the back of the tanker," Savage said.

"We can meet you on deck."

"Let me get a good look at it first. Is everyone armed?"

"Affirmative," Laz said. "I need to leave the women in a secure location."

"And you're thinking the infirmary?" Savage asked.

"It seems like a small thing to do for her," Laz said. He had been the one to hold Armand's hand as his friend had died. He knew what it was like to fear dying alone, and if he could do something to prevent that he would.

"Go ahead. Take them to the infirmary," Savage said. "Hamm, can you lead the other men until Laz gets back?"

"Affirmative, boss."

Daphne sat with Franny in the corner while the men armed up for the coming fight. They were talking quietly between themselves and she imagined this feeling of pride and fear was something that women had felt since the beginning of time. Whenever men went off to war, the women were left behind.

No matter how much she appreciated the men going off to save them, a part of her was afraid—afraid that they would lose and then she and Franny would be at Samatan's mercy. She was doubly afraid of breaking down the way Franny had about Bob.

There was no longer any doubt in her mind that she was falling for Laz. He was not like other men and that was part of why she wanted him. He listened to her when she talked and he always respected her point of view even if he didn't agree with it.

She was still touched that he'd considered taking Franny to Bob. Though she felt sad for her friend even she had thought that was a selfish thing for the other woman to ask for.

"Are you okay?" Daphne asked Franny, pulling her eyes from Laz where he was talking with Hamm. Would he say good-bye to her before he left to lead the men? What would she and Franny do if they were discovered in this room?

She had the scalpel . . .

"No, I'm not okay. I'm an emotional mess and I'm so worried about Bob I can't . . ." Franny took a big sobbing breath and then put her face in her hands.

Daphne hugged the other woman close. "It's okay. Bob is tough. One of the toughest men I know. He's not going to die. You know how stubborn he is. And he gave his word to get us all safely to Mogadishu."

Franny tried to smile. "He is stubborn. He'll want to make sure we all get there safely."

"He's not going to die on you, Franny. He would want to say good-bye first."

She nodded. "I know. He already said good-bye before the surgery started. That's why I'm so afraid. We didn't get to bring him out . . . the anesthetic hadn't worn off when we were separated. Oh, Daphne, what am I going to do?"

Daphne had no idea. It was hard. This entire situation wasn't something any of them had planned for and just surviving from one minute to the next was taking everything that they had.

"This is a life we didn't choose but we have to survive and we will," Daphne said.

"We didn't choose this but we did know that we were going to a dangerous part of the world. Do you wish we'd turned back when the plane was disabled?" Franny asked.

Daphne looked across the room and found Laz watching her as he readied his weapons. Did she wish she'd gone back to the States?

No, she thought. She didn't want that at all. Coming here and meeting Laz felt like the adventure she'd been longing for. She didn't want the danger that she'd found but she did want the man—the warrior—that she'd found. And she would never regret coming here.

"No. I don't. I was lost," she said.

"And you're not anymore?" Franny asked.

"I'm not sure. I don't feel lost. Maybe it is simply that I don't have time to feel sorry for myself here. That I don't have time to go over every detail of the life I left behind and see if there was something I should have done differently."

Franny squeezed her hand. "I think that is it. I wouldn't have stayed behind. This is the only time I can be with Bob. And no matter what, it is worth it."

Daphne realized that she and Franny weren't that different.

It wasn't that the lives they lived at home were lies exactly but out here they had the chance to be themselves. For Franny that meant being with the man she loved.

Daphne was coming to see that for her it meant being accepted for who she was. And that had come from Laz.

"Should we get a weapon?" Franny asked.

"I can't fire a gun. I know I wouldn't be able to shoot someone no matter how big the threat," Daphne said. "But I do have a scalpel."

Franny laughed softly. "That will be very helpful."

"Well, it is sharp and I know how to use it."

"Yes, you do," Franny said. "I'm sorry you lost Fridjtof."

Daphne nodded. "Me too. I tried my best but we didn't have the right facilities. Rudy was a great help. That man knows his stuff."

She didn't really want to talk about the man she'd lost. She hadn't had a chance to process Fridjtof's death yet and she knew she'd keep going over the surgery she'd performed in her mind to try to figure if she had made a mistake. "I should have kept up my surgery skills. But I haven't done even the most rudimentary thing since my residency."

"No one does."

"Ladies, I've spoke to my team leader and if you want to I will take you to the infirmary to wait while we go to take back the ship," Laz said.

"Really?" Franny asked. "Oh, thank you. Yes, I want to do that."

Daphne just nodded at him. Laz smiled at her and she knew in that moment she loved him. He was so much more than just a gun for hire. She had no idea if there was a future for the two of them but none of that mattered. Her life was richer because she'd met Laz.

"Thank you," she said softly. Franny had gone to retrieve her medical bag.

"You're very welcome. I figured if you had to sit somewhere . . ."

"Don't make it sound like it was nothing. I know that it's going to be dangerous to take us to him and it means the world to me that you are offering to do it."

He arched one eyebrow at her. "I do my best."

"Yes, you do. You make sure you are safe, J.P.," she said. "Don't forget you promised me that we'd have some alone time once this threat was past."

"I'm always careful but I will be even more so because of you," Laz said. He reached out and touched her, tracing his finger over her face. First he traced her eyebrows and then down the blade of her nose and then he reached her lips.

She sucked the tip of his finger into her mouth and saw his eyes narrow. He cursed under his breath and leaned in and kissed her. It was a quick brushing of their lips. With so many people around there wasn't time for anything else, but she cherished it.

He was her man, she thought. Her warrior. And when he came back from battle they would celebrate. That kiss was a promise of another embrace to come after he had stopped Samatan.

She wanted to give something of herself to him, something that he could take with him while he was fighting. She touched the medallion of Mary she wore. She had never taken it off since it had been given to her at her confirmation.

She reached behind her neck and unfastened it.

"Wear this. It will keep you safe until you come back to me," she said.

"I don't believe—"

"I do," she said. "And I want you to have something of mine with you."

He nodded at her and then put the necklace on. It was tight

against his neck and he tucked it under his T-shirt, but they both knew it was there.

She leaned in and lifted the medallion up and kissed his chest where it lay. Then she hugged him so tightly that he knew she was trying to ensure he'd come back to her.

He'd never had a woman waiting for him before and it changed something deep inside of him. He was going to make it back to her because he realized he wasn't ready to let her go. He didn't know that he'd ever be able to let her go.

He led them carefully to the infirmary, listening for pirates and on edge. He didn't want to leave Daphne alone with a sick man and another woman.

He had no idea what her reaction would be if he told her that so he kept that knowledge to himself.

Chapter Fifteen

If a warrior is to succeed at anything, the success must come gently, with a great deal of effort but with no stress.
—Carlos Castaneda

As Laz led the way to the infirmary, Savage, Wenz, and Van were moving together toward Hamm's location. Laz kept track via his earpiece. Mann had been ordered to hide. Laz knew that the sniper would choose the top of one of the containers for his location. The Savage team all had night-vision goggles, including himself and Hamm, which they'd retrieved with their weapons but the doctors and the crew members were all reliant on the deck lighting, which was poor in the darkness now that the sun had set.

Daphne and Franny followed close behind Laz as he led the way to the infirmary. He felt like he'd made a million trips up and down this hallway tonight.

He reached up and touched the medallion that Daphne had given to him. He wasn't religious. He'd been in enough near-death situations to know when it came to the end of his life he wasn't going to call out for the Lord. But having the medallion that Daphne had worn around her neck . . . well, it meant a lot to him.

"Thank you for doing this," Franny said quietly. She had taken up a position behind him.

"No problem," he said. He hadn't done it for Franny; he'd

done it for Daphne and he suspected that everyone knew that. And he didn't care.

There had been a time in his life when it had been important that he be the lone wolf but lately . . . hell since he'd realized he was getting older and this was a young man's game, he'd been looking.

Not actively but just keeping his eyes open for a woman who might be different. A woman who would make all the hard work and sacrifices he'd made over the years worth it. And he'd never suspected that the woman to do that would be a pediatrician from D.C.

He had no idea if there was a future for the two of them but she made him dream again. That was enough. He wasn't ready to quit the Savage Seven and he knew that she wasn't ready for a new man, not after the crap her ex had put her through.

Why did men do that?

His own sister had had husband problems but Laz had fixed those for her. He hated to see women treated poorly. He knew there were women in the world who were just as faithless as Daphne's ex, but he figured most men knew how to deal with it. Women didn't. Or rather women like Daphne didn't.

Laz heard a sound in the dark area near the stairs. Someone had doused the lights. *Fuck.*

He gave the signal to stop and sensed the women stopping behind him.

He made a clicking sound, which was a signal the team used when they were running silent. "Savage here."

Savage could talk so soft and low it was like a lover whispering in your ear. "Lights out at the stairwell."

"Hold."

Laz pulled his military-type fighting knife from the chest web he wore. Guns were noisy when fired and he hadn't put his silencer on his weapon before moving out. A mistake he'd rectify at the first chance.

"Clear," Wenz said.

Laz gave the signal to move out and walked a lot faster than he had before. "Is your presence known?"

"Unsure," Savage said. "Act as if it is."

"Will do."

The infirmary was the last door at the end of the hallway. The lighting was flickering and weak, But Laz knew that wasn't anything different than it had been. He hadn't taken the time to make sure they were prepared for Bob to be dead. He hoped that Bob was okay but given the circumstances of his surgery it was iffy at best.

He got to the door and signaled for the women to stop and stay back.

The infirmary was dark and with his night vision goggles Laz swept his gaze around the room. He saw nothing out of the ordinary. There was a mound on the bed shaped like a body. He wasn't sure if the person was breathing or not. He went back to the door and signaled the women to enter the room.

They did and he closed the door behind them all.

"Where's the light switch?" Franny asked.

"No lights. We can't risk someone seeing it when they look over the edge of the ship. Everything must stay as it is," Laz said.

"I have a penlight, Franny," Daphne said, handing it to her friend.

Franny flicked it on and then hesitated. Laz sighed and walked around the women. "Keep the light pointed down. I'll check the bed. Stay where you are."

He walked over to the bed and glanced down. Bob was lying there. Laz saw his chest rise and fall and put his hand on the man's wrist to find his pulse. "He's alive. His heartbeat is thready, though."

"Thank God!" Franny said, racing to his side. She pushed him aside to stand next to Bob. She started talking to him in a low voice and the words she said were so heartfelt and private that Laz felt uncomfortable hearing them.

He left those two alone and went back to Daphne. "I'm going to lock the two of you in this room. If you hear anyone at the door—hide."

"Hide?"

"Yes. If things go poorly for the pirates I'm willing to bet that Samatan has ordered his men to kill the hostages. And Bob will be easy to kill. Take care of your friend but keep yourself safe too."

"I will."

Laz cupped her face and kissed her, giving her the kind of kiss he'd wanted to earlier. Here in the dark with no one around to see it he took his time. He felt sunshine in his soul when their lips met and he kissed her long and hard.

"Laz?"

"Hmm?"

"Lazarus. You're needed on deck," Savage said.

"On my way, boss."

Daphne held his hand as he walked to the door. He wanted to give her some more advice but didn't know what to say. He'd known how to fight for his entire life. He had no idea what he'd do if he didn't.

"Just stay safe."

She nodded and he turned and left. He didn't hesitate or look back because he had a job to do. And as much as he wanted her to be his future she couldn't be unless he focused on this mission now. If he didn't stay sharp they wouldn't make it out alive.

He locked the door behind him, pulled out his silencer

from the web on his chest, and put it on his weapon. He was ready to fight.

More than ready. Nothing would stop him from taking back this ship. With his team he was unstoppable.

Laz moved silently through the hallway back to the gangway where Wenz had taken care of the pirate guard earlier. He made his way up the stairs slowly, keeping his weapon drawn and his senses sharp.

He panned from left to right and then was on the deck of the tanker. "Twenty?"

"Aft stern," Savage said.

Laz made his way through the maze of containers on the deck of the *Maersk Angus* to the aft stern of the boat. He stayed light on his feet and was very careful to watch for pirates. From his position he saw that there were two men on the bridge and the Eurochopper was still on the deck.

A minute later he was at the rendezvous location. Savage greeted him with a handshake and a chest bump.

"'Bout time you got here. I thought I was going to have to start the party without you."

"No way. Wenz, Van," Laz said nodding to his teammates.

"What's the plan?" Laz asked.

"Hamm is on his way with the main fighting force. Laz, I want you and Wenz to take back the bridge. I need someone up there who knows what they are doing. You might not realize this but Samatan has held you all in Somali waters and we need to get the tanker to international waters so we can arrest him."

"Will do. Liberate the bridge and move the tanker. Anything else?" Laz asked.

"Nah, smart ass, that's all."

Laz stepped back to talk to Wenz. "Have you reconnoitered the bridge?

"I saw the figures of two men when I was on my way here.

We can't count on backup from Mann. The glass is bullet-proof."

"We don't need Mann's help," Wenz said. "We've faced tougher situations."

"We have. I think that Samatan will probably be up there and he's mine."

"Why?"

"Because he is," Laz said, not about to talk about the way the pirate king had held a gun to Daphne's head.

"We don't do revenge," Wenz said.

"It's not revenge. Damn it, man, this guy shot me in the thigh and took over my ship. I think I've earned the right to take him out."

"Why didn't you just say that?" Wenz asked.

"Damn, you're a pain in the ass."

"You'd be the same way. A man with revenge on his mind is a dangerous fool," Wenz said.

That was true. Laz made it a point to stay out of emotional situations. He didn't like to react with anything but his instincts, which he'd honed to a razor's edge over the years. Then he thought about the necklace that Daphne had given him. Was he being a fool? Because fools were usually the first to die in a battle. Hadn't he seen many young saps go down? Hell. He wasn't going to be one of those. He took a minute to clear his thoughts—to renew in his own mind his mission objectives.

And then he did what he always did before he went into a fight. It was his ritual. He took two steps away from Wenz so he was alone at the railing of the ship. He looked out and remembered the face of his good friend and fallen comrade Armand. He took a deep breath and remembered the way they used to psych each other up for battle.

The egging on the running tally they had for hits and misses. Armand had died with more hits than Laz but Laz had kept the tally going in his head. "I'm going to catch up to you this time, *mon ami.*"

Laz closed his eyes, imagining the sound of Armand's laughter. His friend would have seen that as a challenge. And Laz did too. He was fighting the good fight for fallen men like Armand and he'd never forget that.

The team was assembled and Savage had spoken to each group individually. Laz felt confident that they'd get the tanker back. He had known from the beginning that they would eventually.

"Do you think we'll get Samatan?" Savage said as the men moved out.

"I'd have Mann keep a close eye on the chopper. He's going to make a break for it as soon as he gets wind that something is going on," Laz said.

"I'm on it," Mann said.

"Good. Nice to have you close by," Laz said.

"Aw, didya miss me?" Mann asked.

"Like I miss a blister on my foot."

"All teams check in," Savage said. "Mission is now green and we are go. Everyone must check in with command as they move. Your assignments are as follows: Laz–one, Wenz–two, Hamm–three, Van–four. Mann is command and I'm team leader. The rest of you must follow your unit commander, understood?"

They nodded. Then they tested their earpieces and Savage gave the order to move out.

Wenz took a position beside Laz as they retreated around the containers toward the bridge. The containers provided big shadows, which covered their movements, and the moon was waning tonight so it wasn't as bright as it could be.

Laz had the lead and they were as one as they communicated. They moved forward one at a time. "One in position."

"Two moving."

"Two in position."

"One moving."

"Hold one," Mann said. "Someone is at the end of that container. Command lining up shot."

"Command you are go to take out target," Savage said.

A second later Laz heard the thud of a body hitting the deck.

"One you are clear."

"One moving." Laz moved to position and bent to check the body of the pirate. The man was dead and Laz closed his eyes and dragged him out of the main pathway. "Path clear. One in position."

"Two moving."

Laz waited for Wenz and thought of how many times he'd done this same maneuver in the dark. It was as comforting as the way a pair of faded jeans or worn tennis shoes felt. He knew the men on his team as well as he knew himself, and they were like extensions of each other.

"Two in position. Stairs are clear."

"One moving," Laz said, keeping low and moving to the stairs. "One on stairs."

He tried to keep his body as low as he could but climbing was difficult. This was the time when they had to be careful not to be seen.

"Two moving behind."

Laz got to the top and went to the right of the doorway. Wenz came up behind him.

"Hold one and two."

"Holding," Laz said.

"Teams in position?"

"Three ready."

"Four ready."

"Team leader causing a diversion," Savage said. He detonated a flash bomb, which made a loud noise, and then there was a ton of smoke. The door to the bridge opened. Laz tripped the first man out the door and Wenz followed him down the stairs.

Laz rolled into the opening and came to his feet facing a pirate but not Samatan.

Samatan sent another message to Tankers International via his negotiator. Samatan worked for a larger group and all monies they received from piracy were wired into Swiss accounts before the men were paid.

At first that policy had been difficult for some of the Somalis on his team to understand, but after the bodies of pirates who had a crate of money dumped on their boat had washed ashore, his crews had agreed to the Swiss accounts.

Samatan was the leader of this bunch of pirates but he had a boss he answered to. And his boss wanted that U.S. Senator's connection. Now he had to get the two women together and take them to his ship. The one that was anchored away from the *Maersk Angus*.

"Habeb?"

"Yes, sir?"

"Please retrieve the woman from belowdecks. I will get the other from the container."

"Yes, sir. Where shall I bring her?"

"To the infirmary," Samatan said. "I think torturing their sick friend will give me the answers I need."

"At once," Habeb said.

But just as Habeb started to leave, there was a huge explosion of bright light and smoke started to cover the deck. Samatan grabbed his gun as did Habeb.

"We are under attack."

"Find the men responsible and kill them," Samatan ordered.

"What about the women?" Habeb asked.

"I will see to them. Shoot to kill. This ransom is ours and we won't give it up easily."

"Yes, sir."

Samatan moved across the deck quickly. He had a speedboat stashed on the port side of the ship. If it became necessary for him to leave he'd go. But he wasn't leaving without the women. One of them was the key to a lot of money.

He went down the stairs two at a time and headed for the room where Habeb had stashed the woman and the tanker captain. When he opened the door he found it empty.

He cursed.

Somehow the hostages were trying to take back the tanker. He went to the infirmary next. He'd kill their sick friend as payback. No one would be alive after tonight except the one woman he needed. And then she would die when this was over.

Samatan got to the infirmary and forced the door open. It was quiet in the room but he hit the light switch as soon as he entered. The man on the table was breathing fitfully as Samatan walked over to him.

He put his gun to the man's temple and fired. The body jerked and there was a scream.

A woman launched herself at him from behind the table. She had her hands extended and clawed at his face. The scratches hurt as he backhanded the woman and knocked her to the floor. She started to get back up but he kicked her hard in the gut.

She curled into a ball moaning. The other woman—the one he'd held his gun on earlier—lifted her hands up and stood on the other side of the bed.

"I surrender. Don't shoot me," she said.

Samatan was so angry he almost shot her. They'd taken away his bargaining chip. "Get your friend up and come with me. If you do anything other than what I say I will shoot you."

She nodded and went over to the fallen woman, who seemed to be completely out of it. Samatan's face stung as the air stirred around him.

It would be easier to take just one woman but he didn't want to take the wrong one and not get paid. He saw a roll of medical adhesive tape on the counter. "Tie her hands together."

"That's not necessary. We'll come with you," she said.

"Do what I say or I'll put you both in a body bag and carry you out that way."

She shuddered and reached for the tape. She bound the other woman's hands. "I'm Daphne by the way and this is Franny."

"This isn't a social gathering," Samatan said.

"Just wanted you to know who we were so it'd be harder to kill us."

"It's not hard to kill someone whose name you know," he told her. "Hurry up."

"I'm done," she said.

"Bring the tape to me."

She did.

"Hold your hands out, wrists together."

She did and he bound her wrists tightly, double-checking the other woman before binding their arms together so they were effectively chained to each other's side. Samatan had learned over the years that it was harder to run when you were tethered to another person.

Franny was still crying and he could tell from the way she walked gingerly that his kick to her gut pained her.

He knew how vulnerable females were there. Back when he'd been Strongman, sometimes he'd had to beat women to make their men behave. And they'd used a bag of oranges to smack them in the gut. That way there was no outward marks of the beating.

"Move. If we encounter anyone along the way or you attempt to raise the alarm I will kill you."

The women stayed huddled together as he forced them through the door and then down the hall. "Go to the end. There's a rope ladder that leads up to the deck."

"We're not going to be able to climb the rope ladder tied together," Daphne said.

"Stop talking and do what I say."

They would do it. Fear was a great motivator and he assumed they both wanted to live. One thing he'd seen again and again was people doing all kinds of things to stay alive. It was funny how badly most humans wanted to live.

They got to the ladder. "Climb."

They were awkward but Daphne did most of the work and pulled her friend up and onto the deck. Samatan stayed right behind them, nudging them both with the gun when they hesitated.

Once they were on the deck he dragged them to their feet and to the port side of the tanker.

Habeb was waiting for him. When he saw the women he came forward. "The crew has retaken the ship."

"Not for long. Let's get these two back to the mother ship and then we will come back."

"Yes, sir. We lost Jamac."

Samatan nodded. "You can tell me later. Let's get out of here."

"Overboard, ladies," Samatan ordered.

Franny shook her head. "I can't swim."

"There's a boat down there," Daphne said. "I've got you. Lean on me."

"I want to die," Franny said.

"Keep whining and you might get your wish," Samatan said.

Daphne gave him a look of pure venom but helped the

other woman over the railing and down to the speedboat. Samatan followed the women and Habeb stood and waited for orders.

"Take the chopper so they think we are airborne."

"Yes, sir."

Samatan was angry and more than a little pissed off at his men who were responsible for the loss of this tanker. He'd have to deal with those men. Anyone who made it off the *Maersk Angus* alive was going to be very aware of his wrath.

"We need life jackets," Daphne said.

"Too damned bad," he said. "Sit down and shut up or I will drag the both of you through the water as we go."

"No you won't," she said. "We'd drown and die and you'd only have a corpse to ransom."

As angry as he was he didn't care. "Don't tempt me by talking. I might decide the ransom isn't worth the aggravation of keeping the two of you alive."

The other woman started sobbing in earnest and Daphne shook her head. Samatan cast off the boat and worked it up to full speed as soon as they were away from the tanker. This was the first job he'd taken that had gone this way. He wasn't used to losing and he realized he didn't like it.

He would take steps to ensure that it never happened again.

Chapter Sixteen

A warrior must only take care that his spirit is not broken.
—Carlos Castaneda

Laz was bloodied and more than a little exhilarated as he and Wenz took over the bridge. He monitored the fighting on the earpiece. Wenz stood guard at the door as Laz readied the ship to get under way. He had missed this, he realized. Sitting still had been a nightmare. Now he was back on the bridge and things were about to wrap up on this mission.

Soon they'd arrest Samatan.

"Movement around the chopper," Mann said.

"How many?" Savage asked.

"One target. I have him in my sight," Mann said.

"Hold. Is it Samatan?" Savage asked.

"Unable to confirm."

"One? Can you go?"

"Affirmative. Two is in charge of the bridge."

Wenz took over his position. Everyone on the team had read the specs on the tanker before they'd come on this mission so Wenz could pilot it if need be.

Laz vaulted down the stairs two at time. He wasn't going to take a chance on letting Samatan escape now that they were so close to taking him down. That pirate king had been a menace in the Indian Ocean and the Gulf of Aden for a long time.

Many, including their client, believed he worked for someone else because of the sophisticated operation he had. For instance the Eurochopper was something that most governments bought for their militaries to use. The U.S. government used them in the Coast Guard.

Laz pulled his weapon as he got to the bottom of the stairs. There was no one on the deck and he sprinted toward the chopper as he realized the man was going to enter it.

"Freeze!"

The man hesitated and then fired at Laz. Laz tucked his body and rolled across the deck toward the pirate. He came to his feet and returned fire.

Laz aimed for the pirate's kneecap and saw the man stagger and fall into the side of the chopper. Laz was on him before he could make another move.

The pirate raised his own gun and fired at Laz. Laz moved quickly, feeling the burn against his cheek as he turned his head just in time to miss being hitting by the bullet.

"Damn it," he cursed. He brought his heel down on the pirate's shooting hand and bent over to take the gun from his grip.

The pirate punched him on the side and reached up to grab him between the legs. Laz danced out of range and brought the butt of his weapon down on the side of the man's head.

The pirate slumped on the deck. "This one. Target down. Not Samatan. Repeat not Samatan."

"Copy that. Do you need backup?"

"Hell no."

"Medical?" Savage asked.

"Negative," Laz said knowing that he'd have Daphne patch him up later. Her hands were way softer than Wenz's, and she was always caressing him when she bandaged his cuts.

"I think we're all clear. Everyone gather on the main deck

by the chopper. Flex cuff all the pirates. Four, prepare to process them."

"Affirmative, leader."

Van would take pictures of everyone they captured and record their name and nationality. Then that information would go into an international criminal database. If for some reason they couldn't make the piracy charges stick, then their clients would search for other outstanding warrants.

Savage walked out into the open leading two pirates whose name Laz didn't know.

"Did we get Samatan?" Laz asked. "He wasn't on the bridge."

"Or at the chopper. Did he leave while you were locked up?" Savage asked.

"I don't know. This man was attempting to get on the chopper. Maybe he can tell us."

"Revive him," Savage ordered.

Rudy brought over a bucket of water and splashed it on the man's head.

"Who are you?" Laz asked him.

"Go to hell," the man replied.

"Is Samatan still on this ship?"

The man kept his mouth shut and looked up at him with disdain. Laz didn't give him the satisfaction of getting upset. Van would question him and get answers whether this guy wanted to give them or not.

"You're going to be in jail for a long time. It might go easier on you if you cooperate now."

"I know nothing," the man said.

"Leave him," Savage said. "Van, take him first. We need to know who he is and why he was attempting to leave on the chopper. And where the hell is Samatan?

Van lifted the man by his arm and dragged him across the deck.

"I think that man needs medical attention," Jerry said. "I'd be happy to patch him up and anyone else who needs our assistance."

"Thank you," Savage said. "Your help tonight was invaluable."

"You're welcome," Jerry said. "I was glad to help. If you don't need me anymore, I'll head down to the infirmary and get it ready to treat the injured."

"Sounds good. Rudy, thanks man."

"No problem. Like I said, I saw some action in Peru."

"Nasty place," Savage said.

Laz waited for orders. "Want me back on the bridge?"

"Yes. Then you can head to the infirmary and check on your girl."

"She's not a girl."

"No?"

"No, she's a lady," Laz said.

"Is she yours?"

Laz walked away from that. He had no idea how to answer that loaded question. He wanted her to be his. How was that? He was a man who called nothing but a shack in Florida and an old fishing boat his own and now he wanted to lay claim to a woman who was worlds better than he was.

Slowly he climbed the stairs to the bridge. Wenz waited until he was in position before he backed away. "That went well."

"Except for Samatan not being in the captured group," Laz said.

"Van will find out where he is," Wenz said.

"I hope he gets the information soon. I want this wrapped up."

"Got plans?"

Did he? He and Daphne had said when this was over they'd

do something together but who knew if they'd have the chance. She might change her mind once the danger was past.

"No plans. Just want the mission wrapped up," Laz said.

"Me too."

"Team leader, confirm we are ready to move?"

"In a minute," Savage said.

Laz looked down on deck and saw that Van had returned to Savage. At the same time Jerry came running up to Savage and Laz had a sinking feeling in the pit of his stomach.

"Team leader? Is Daphne still on this tanker?"

"Negative, one. She and the other woman were taken hostage by Samatan. Whereabouts unknown."

"Wenz, you have the bridge," Laz said.

He ran down the stairs again and got on deck in no time at all.

"Habeb is Samatan's second in command. Samatan is heading to the mother ship, which is great for us. We've been wanting to capture his hive," Van said.

Jerry was standing next to Savage. His face was white and Laz put his hand on the doctor's shoulder. "You okay?"

"No," he said. "Bob's dead."

"I'm sorry he didn't make it," Laz said.

Jerry shook his head. "You don't understand. He was shot in the head. He's dead."

Laz felt his blood run cold. Samatan was going to kill one of the women. And if he knew Daphne she'd do everything to make sure that neither she nor Franny were injured—an action that would make the pirate king mad.

"Where is this mother ship?" Laz asked.

"I haven't gotten the exact location yet," Van said. "But I will. Right now, Habeb revealed that Samatan is in a Sea King speedboat heading toward international waters."

"I'm going after them," Laz said.

* * *

Daphne held Franny as they continued to speed through the night. She was numbed by what she'd seen this man do: just walk up to a vulnerable person and shot them like he had. She knew that Samatan had no soul. If he had he wouldn't have been able to do that. She was still shaking and felt almost physically sick.

Her hands hurt where she was bound to Franny. Franny was in even worse shape so Daphne was trying to hold it together, but it was really hard and she felt like she might start sobbing at any second.

For the first time since pirates took over the *Maersk Angus* she actually felt like she might not make it back home. She prayed with all of her conviction that God would watch over her and Franny and help them to survive whatever Samatan had in store for them.

The moon offered little light this dark night but there seemed to be a million stars in the sky. As she looked up at them, Daphne wondered if this memory would always be the one that rushed to her mind when she saw a starry sky.

Samatan slowed the boat and put it in idle.

"There is no need to bring both of you with me. I only need the one who is related to Senator Paul Maxwell."

Franny's hand started to shake in hers and Daphne held onto her hand more tightly. "We are both related to him."

Samatan raised one eyebrow at her. "I don't believe so. I've only been authorized to collect the ransom on one woman."

"Well, you're going to have to take both of us," Daphne said.

She had no idea if Franny could swim or not or if Samatan would simply kill Franny outright if he knew she wasn't related to Paul. Technically, she thought, neither of them were related to him.

"What are you going to do with us?"

"One of you will be starring in a video begging for your life. The other will be going over the side of this boat."

"We're in the middle of the ocean."

"We aren't that far from the tanker. I'm sure they will have discovered that you are missing and started looking for you."

Daphne suspected that he wanted to get rid of one of them to slow any rescue attempt down.

"I'm running out of patience," he said. "I'm going to start hitting you until you give me the information I want."

Franny whimpered.

"I am the one," Daphne said. "But she can't swim and I will jump overboard myself unless you provide her with a raft or floatation device."

"You are in no position to make demands," Samatan said. "How do I know you are who you say?"

"You don't. But I will tell you—but only if you free Franny."

He nodded.

"I am Paul Maxwell's ex-wife. We were married for seventeen years and have two sons. I live in a suburb of D.C. as does Paul."

"Very well. I believe you. I have no raft for your friend," he said.

"Then a life jacket. You aren't killing another of my friends in front of me."

Daphne wasn't sure he understood how serious she was. She'd rather take her chances in the ocean with Franny than wait until Paul declined to pay ransom for her and have Samatan shoot her in the head like he had Bob.

He took a knife from his pocket and walked toward them. "Stop. You said she could go."

"Be quiet, woman. I'm cutting her free. There is a life jacket under the bench. She may get it out."

Samatan cut them free and Franny just looked at Daphne. "You can do this, Franny. The life jacket will support you."

"I'm scared," Franny whispered.

Daphne gave the other woman a hug and then lifted the bench as best she could with her bound hands. "Get the life jacket."

Franny just stood there. Out of the corner of her eye she saw Samatan move closer. He was going to throw her overboard without anything if Franny didn't hurry.

"Franny! Get the life jacket," Daphne yelled.

Franny blinked at her, then bent over and pulled out the life jacket.

"Cut her hands free," Daphne said.

"No."

Daphne reached for Franny's wrists, brought them to her mouth and bit through the medical adhesive tape that was holding them together. She hurriedly stuffed Franny into the life jacket.

"Someone will come for you. The Captain will," Daphne said. She pressed the penlight into Franny's hand. "Be safe."

Franny started to speak but Samatan pushed her over the edge of the boat. Daphne turned to make sure that Franny had bobbed to the surface. She thought she saw her friend's head but had no time to be certain as Samatan put the boat back into gear and started moving again.

Daphne fell back against the floorboard and sat there. She knew she should probably try to overcome Samatan and rescue herself but she couldn't do it. She was tired. Physically she ached from everything she'd been through today and emotionally she was drained. She'd lost a patient and then she'd lost a friend.

She was alone with a madman and she had no idea how she was going to get back home to see her boys. At this moment coming on an adventure seemed like the stupidest decision she'd ever made.

She'd give up everything just to see her boys one more time

and hug them close. If she didn't make it back to them, she hoped they'd always remember how much she loved them.

"I thought you only ransomed tankers," she said, screaming to be heard over the roar of the boat.

"Normally, we do," he said, turning to face her. His accent wasn't that thick and his English had a lyrical sound to it.

"Where are you taking me?" she asked.

"To my ship," he said.

He turned to face the bow of the ship and then continued flying over the water through the night. The breeze was cold after she'd been so hot all day. She shivered a little and wondered if she had fatigue. Who cared? That was the least of her worries.

She wondered if Laz would come after her. But then she stopped herself. Of course he was going to come after her. Laz was the kind of guy who'd always rush to her side when she needed help. That was just a part of his nature that wasn't going to change because there was danger or even if it was inconvenient for him. If she needed him he would be by her side.

That thought comforted her and she started to get some of her spirit back. She wasn't going to let Samatan harm or kill her. She'd just found herself and she wasn't about to end up lost again.

Laz didn't wait to hear what else Savage had to say. As soon as Van had a location for the mother ship, as Habeb referred to the floating headquarters of Samatan's piracy operation, he got in one of the speedboats and went after Daphne.

"Laz, wait for backup," Savage said in his earpiece.

"You can follow me. I'm not waiting. You saw what he did to Bob. That man was injured and Daphne—hell, that woman will argue with him and fight with him. I have to get to her, Savage."

There was silence in his earpiece and Laz just kept going full throttle. He had a spotlight on the boat and he turned it on. It would have been better if he'd brought someone with him because they could have acted as a lookout or spotter. But he hadn't been able to wait another minute. He had to get to Daphne.

He saw something bobbing off the starboard side of his speedboat. He circled around and came back to it.

It was a person.

He killed the engine and let the boat drift closer.

"Help me."

The voice was feminine but not Daphne's. "Franny?"

"Yes. Oh my God. He killed Bob. Daphne's still with him."

"It's okay. We're going to get him. Can you swim over to the boat?" he asked.

"I can't swim at all," she said.

Every second he wasted here with her was another second it would take him to get to Daphne but he wasn't about to leave Franny in the ocean. The other woman had seen Samatan kill Bob and a part of Laz wanted nothing more than to comfort this poor lady.

He found the life ring that was tethered to the rope and tossed it to her. "Can you grab this and I'll pull you to me?"

She tried but she was simply too tired. He could tell because her movements were lazy and uncoordinated. "Savage?"

"Here."

"I'm going in the water to rescue Franny. Be aware that there are two of us as you approach."

"Confirm that."

The earpieces their team used were waterproof up to fifteen feet. Laz didn't bother taking off his shoes or shirt, which would only slow him down. And he'd been a SEAL. The water was his second home.

He dove over the side of his boat and swam to Franny with strong strokes. She was crying a little and he thought she might be suffering from exhaustion and shock.

"Hello, Franny."

"Captain. I'm sorry I couldn't reach for the ring."

"It's okay," he said. Her face was pale and she had some bruising under her eyes. He towed her back to the boat.

"Hold on here," he said, guiding her hands up to the side of the craft.

"Can you do that?"

"Yes," she said.

But her hand slipped off and he had to guide it up again. He had the feeing he could do this all night and not get her into the boat. Finally he swam them around to the back and lifted her onto the step in the back of the boat.

"Sit here. Don't fall in."

She nodded and he moved around the motor to a place where he could pull himself up and out of the water. His body didn't even feel the strain despite everything that had happened to him today.

He knew he was in the battle zone. That place where he could do anything to his body and keep moving. Tomorrow he'd feel but tonight he was on autopilot.

He went to the back of the boat and helped Franny into the craft. She was mumbling softly to herself and Laz was truly worried about her.

"This is One. I'm back on the craft."

"We're nearly to your twenty," Savage said.

"Someone is going to have to take the hostage back to the tanker. She needs medical assistance."

"Wenz is with us. He will do that while Mann and I accompany you in pursuit."

"Affirmative."

Savage didn't say anything else. Laz knew when this was all

over his team leader would have words with him and make sure he didn't disobey orders again. But right now Savage would stay focused on the mission.

"Why aren't you going after Daphne?" Franny asked.

Laz looked at her. "We have to make sure you are safe first."

"I'll be fine. I can stay on this boat and just . . ."

"Just what?" Laz asked her. "A few minutes isn't going to affect Daphne. I'm not going to let Samatan hurt her."

Franny shook her head. "He killed Bob at point-blank range. Bob wasn't even threatening him."

Laz sat down next to the other woman as she started crying. He wrapped his arm around her and held her for a minute trying to give her comfort. "I'm sorry."

She didn't even hear him. That brief moment of lucidity was gone and she was back to the moaning and mumbling she was doing before.

The sound of an engine reached him first and he knew another craft was approaching. He stood and drew his weapon in case it wasn't his team.

"Hello the craft," Savage's voice boomed across the water.

"Come on in," Laz said.

The other boat slowed down. Wenz stood toward the back of the boat with his medic kit in one hand. Laz tossed a rope to Mann and the two men drew the speedboats side by side.

Wenz came onboard to treat Franny and Laz crossed to the other craft. "I think she's in shock and might have some injuries."

"Don't worry. I'll take care of her," Wenz said. He was already kneeling next to Franny and checking her pulse. Franny was still mumbling but stopped when Wenz touched her.

"Do you need me to follow once the woman is safe?" Wenz asked.

Savage shook his head. "The three of us got this. If we

need backup we will radio and you and Hamm can come in the chopper."

"Will do, team leader."

Wenz and Mann tossed the ropes that held the boats tethered together back to each other and Savage put the boat back in motion.

No one said anything to him and that was fine with him. He didn't want to discuss anything with either of the men. He was already going over the moment he killed Samatan. In his mind he saw Daphne whole and healthy and back in his arms.

But in his heart he knew fear for another person and that made him cringe because he knew that men who had something to lose oftentimes lost.

He closed his eyes and carefully compartmentalized everything he felt for Daphne. He shoved it to the back of his heart and his mind. All those emotions weren't helpful to a man who was born to win. A man who stop at nothing to rescue a civilian. He had to stop thinking of her as the woman who held his heart, but that was harder than he'd expected it to be.

If she died he'd continue to mourn her until his deathbed. He remembered the lyrics of that old George Jones song, "He Stopped Loving Her Today." It would take his own death for him to stop loving Daphne.

A mission like this one made him realize—hell, the only thing that had changed his thinking was Daphne. She was sweet, sexy, sassy, and just perfect for him.

It hadn't mattered that she was right woman at the wrong time. Hell, she still was, but he guessed that there was never a right time for a woman like her to come into his life.

And he knew if he hadn't happened now on this ship and on this mission he'd never have found her. He would have gone his entire life alone.

He hadn't found a woman because Mann and Savage had. He'd found *the woman*—the one woman that God had made for him. He wasn't about to let a pirate like Samatan take her from him.

He looked up at the night sky and saw the stars he and Daphne had stood under just two nights ago and promised himself that they'd have a lifetime of nights to spend together.

But first he had to take care of the man threatening that dream he held in his heart.

Chapter Seventeen

A rule of thumb for a warrior is that he makes his decisions so carefully that nothing that may happen as result of them can surprise him, much less drain his power.
—Carlos Castaneda

Daphne had never been more tired or scared in her life. Samatan continued to pilot the boat into the dark horizon after he'd dumped Franny over the side. She was all alone, and though she'd stopped thinking that she would die at this man's hands, she had no thoughts of what she could do to save herself. She did briefly think of diving over the side of the craft and trying to swim away from him.

But she knew that Samatan would double back and pick her up. And when he did he'd be mad and perhaps hit her. Not that being hit was bad in the scheme of things. It was way better than being dead.

But she decided to wait and see what happened once they got to his ship. She'd try to make a break for it then.

She saw the lights first, like those of a small city. "What is that?"

Was he taking her to the port town of Eyl? Had he fooled them all by making them believe he was different than the other pirates who operated in this area?

"That is my ship," he said. He picked up the radio and said something in rapid-fire Portuguese. She really wished she had an ear for languages but she didn't. So she was stuck in the dark.

Less than five minutes later they had pulled aside a large freighter that was bigger than the *Maersk Angus*. She thought this freighter was very similar to an aircraft carrier and realized that she was seeing a city.

This was a city at sea. They moored to the larger craft in no time flat and Samatan grabbed her arm and lifted her up to the largest man she'd ever seen. He was just shy of seven feet tall. He was all steely roped muscle and had a face that was both scary and fierce. He reached under her armpits to pull her up on deck and then held her arm tightly while Samatan joined them.

"Take her to my conference room. If she gives you any trouble, knock her out. We can revive her when we need her."

"Yes, sir," the other man said in thickly accented English.

She had the feeling that Samatan had switched to her language just so she could understand the threat. "Thanks."

"For what?"

"Speaking my language. That makes me feel so much better."

"Sarcasm is an American trait and not one I appreciate. You don't have to be unharmed to be ransomed, my dear. You would do well to remember that."

"Take her, Djimon. Don't leave her alone until I return to you," Samatan said and turned to walk away from them.

Djimon led the way across the deck and down the gangway stairs to a room. It was elegantly appointed with thick pile carpeting and a walnut table. On the walls were paneling and there were two portholes in the far wall offering a view of the dark night. They weren't that large, like the small ones on the cruise she and her family had taken to the Bahamas several years ago.

At the far end of the conference was the equipment for video conferencing. There was a rather expensive looking video camera on a tripod. It was connected to a laptop and a man was sitting at the end of the table.

He was small and wiry and wore a pair of horn-rimmed glasses. He didn't look up as they entered.

"Put her at the end of the table," the man said.

"Yes, sir," Djimon replied.

He led her to one of the large captain's chairs and sat her down in it. He wrapped his two large hands around her shoulders and chest to restrain her in the chair.

"I'm not going to try to escape," she said.

"We know," the man at the end of the table said. "This is to remind you that we are in charge."

Djimon bent down and tied her feet to the legs of the chair. She hated the feeling of being bound even though she knew she probably wouldn't have tried to make a run for it. Having them do this to her—well, it took away that comfort. She now knew she was stuck in here and helpless against whatever they chose to do to her.

She hadn't felt like a victim until this moment. She closed her eyes, focusing on her prayers, and realized that Laz's face was in her mind. She wished she had some kind of superpower telepathy thing. She wanted to tell him how much meeting him had changed her life and made her realize that she hadn't been lost at all when Paul left.

The weakness—the problems—had been with Paul. Laz had shown her that she was enough just by being herself. He hadn't needed her to go to the gym at five every morning or be on the PTA and continue to increase her pediatric practice. Laz hadn't needed anything from her except who she was, and that itself was a gift.

She thought of her boys Josh and Lucas and how very much

she loved him. She wanted to tell them so again now. She felt tears in her eyes and blinked rapidly to stem them. She wasn't going to start crying now. She couldn't.

If she did, she'd never stop and then she'd be a mess. It didn't take a genius to realize that they were going to videotape her with some message and upload it to someone.

She wondered if they were going to e-mail it to Paul. His family had old money but Paul wouldn't pay any ransom for her. They had a policy of not paying that went back generations to when his great-uncle had been kidnapped. The family had used the FBI to try to rescue the great-uncle, but in the end he had been killed before they could.

She had a knot in the pit of her stomach that said this might be the end of the line for her.

Eventually though she suspected they'd have to untie her . . . which made her think. "I have to go to the bathroom."

The men ignored her.

"Hey! Did you hear me?"

Djimon looked over at her. "You may not leave this room. If you must relieve yourself you may do so where you sit."

Horrified, she shook her head. She wasn't about to pee on herself. They weren't going to untie her. Not for anything. She was going to die tied to this chair.

She only hoped they weren't going to videotape that. She didn't want her sons to see it. She wondered if she'd be able to talk. Some of the hostage videos she'd seen didn't have audio. She wanted to tell her boys that she loved them, and that she was so proud of the men they were becoming.

Oh, God, please let her be able to do that. If she was going to die she needed to know that she'd at least have a chance to comfort her sons one last time.

Samatan had a shower and changed his clothes. He didn't like to appear to his boss looking anything other than his best.

One of the first things he'd learned when he'd gone to school in Europe was to dress for success and that truly affected people's opinion of him.

In his college days he'd dressed in long flowing Muslim robes that had been made in Mogadishu, and many people treated him like a refugee or a poor Somali. After he'd earned enough money for his first suit, he was treated differently. And he took his time now, making sure he looked every inch the wealthy man that he was.

It worried Samatan Habeb hadn't checked in and the chopper wasn't on its way back here. He knew that men who were tortured would reveal much information.

He looked at himself in the mirror and made the decision to move the freighter. If they stayed put and Habeb was forced to give up their location, it could be dangerous. He'd come too far to let the mission fail at this point.

He picked up the handset that connected him to the bridge. "Take us north, Captain."

"At once, sir."

"Also I need you to keep your eyes out for any craft that is approaching the freighter. If you see anything, notify me right away."

"Yes, sir."

"I will be in the conference room," Samatan said before hanging up.

He picked up his satellite phone and called Laurent, who was one of his lieutenants like Habeb. He ordered the man to ready his men and get ready to retake the *Maersk Angus*. Samatan wasn't about to lose the ransom from the ship. Maersk always paid to have their ships returned and that kind of money wasn't something he was going to just walk away from.

He left his quarters and walked down the long hallway toward the conference room. Unlike the *Maersk Angus*, the

Liberty Sun wasn't an aging tanker. It was a fast ship and could outrun most ships in the ocean, but it was big and that took its toll on the ship. A lot of fuel was required to power it.

That was of no consequence to Samatan. His boss gave them whatever they needed provided he always was successful.

He entered the conference room to see Djimon sitting on the credenza watching the woman. He knew the bodyguard took his job very seriously. Samatan had brought him to the ship three years ago and not one time had he had any problems with the big man.

"Good job, Djimon," he said in Portuguese.

"Thank you, sir. Do you require that I stay?"

"No. You may go. I will ring for you when it is time to move the prisoner."

Djimon nodded at him and left.

Samatan turned to Bert, a young British Muslim who'd been working for him for just under eighteen months. The other man was an expert in computers and kept them connected to the people they needed to communicate with.

"I want to do a live feed, Bert," he said in English. He wanted Daphne to understand what was going on.

"Not a problem. I've contacted International Tankers and introduced myself as your spokesperson. I told them I was expecting a video file from you with news of the tanker and the hostages."

"Thank you, Bert. But we aren't going to be able to ransom the tanker anymore. I believe the crew has retaken it. This message will need to go to the U.S. government. So contact the state department."

"At once, Samatan."

While Bert worked at his computer, Samatan walked to the end of the table where Daphne sat. She'd been quiet since he entered the room, not even looking at him as he talked to his men.

"Are you ready to play your part?" he asked.

She shook her head. "I'll do what you ask, of course, but you should know that Paul's family will not pay any ransom for me. We're divorced."

"That is of no concern to me," Samatan said. "I am not looking for your family's money."

"Then what are you looking for?"

"Nothing for you to concern yourself with," he said. "My boss has his own plans for you."

"For me? Have you been after me the entire time?" she asked.

She was smart for a woman and he'd seen that she had a great heart when she'd comforted her friend and acted to save her. This woman was rare and he wondered why her husband had cast her aside. Perhaps she wasn't very good in bed. But she had qualities that Samatan's own fiancée had, and it made him realize that he had made a good choice when he'd asked Mare to be his wife.

"You are just one piece of the puzzle."

"Explain it to me," she said.

"I fear your woman's mind wouldn't be able to understand the complexities of it."

"I think I can do okay. I'm pretty smart."

"Then you should know when it is wise to shut your mouth," Samatan said.

"We are ready, sir," Bert said.

"Good."

Samatan walked behind Bert so he could see the video image they were sending.

"Ex Mrs. Paul Maxwell, you will say the date and the time and"—Samatan reached behind him for the *Guardian* newspaper, which had been delivered from London—"you will also read these headlines so they know you are alive right now."

"And if I don't?"

He raised his eyebrow at her. “Then we will hurt you and one of my men will talk for you. Don’t forget we just need your body in relatively healthy condition to get the ransom.”

“You disgust me. I thought when I spoke to you on the bridge of the *Maersk Angus* that you were a man of conviction. A man that was made into a bad guy by circumstances but that you had a soul. But I see now that you are nothing more than a money-grabbing psycho.”

Samatan shrugged. “Calling me names doesn’t bother me. I make decisions that I can live with and move on. You would do well to remember that.”

“Would I?”

“If you want to get off this freighter alive, then yes.”

He walked back down by Bert. “Are we ready?”

“Yes, sir. Both parties are on the line as you requested. Whenever you want to start broadcasting,” Bert said.

Samatan stepped back to make sure he was out of the camera’s view and signaled Bert to begin.

“Hello,” Bert said. “I am the negotiator for the pirates who have taken the wife of U.S. Senator Paul Maxwell hostage.”

“We don’t ransom U.S. citizens.”

“Should we kill her?” Bert asked.

“No. Don’t do that,” a young deep voice said. “We will pay the ransom.”

Samatan glanced at Bert. He muted the sound and then turned to him. “I videoconferenced her children in. I thought that might make the government act.”

“Good thinking,” Samatan said.

And if it didn’t motivate the government into acting it would make a martyr out of Dr. Bennett and cause a lot of problems for the United States.

Laz and Mann were the two who were on the freighter first. Savage was docking their speedboat. “One moving.”

"Command will be two," Mann said.

"Affirmative," Savage said.

Laz tried to be just in soldier mode but after seeing the state Franny had been in, it was just a little bit harder. He knew he was going to rescue Daphne; he just didn't know what kind of state she'd be in.

"This is Four. The girl will likely be in a conference room on deck three," Van said.

"Copy that," Laz said.

He glanced at Mann. And the other man nodded. They moved forward in the pattern he'd used with Wenz earlier. Both of them kept their weapons drawn and moved carefully.

They encountered a soldier at the base of the stairs on deck three. The man was tall and built like a brick wall. Mann tangled with the pirate, signaling Laz to keep moving. He did.

"Four, what room?"

There was a pause and Laz was about to start opening doors randomly to find her.

"The third on the left," Van came back.

Laz moved to that door and cracked it open just a bit. Samatan was standing midway down the room. It was set up like a conference room in an executive office building. There was a nerdy guy operating a computer and videocamera at one end of the room and at the other end sat Daphne.

Laz started to move as he realized the men in the room were concentrating on the computer.

"We will pay the ransom," a young man's voice said.

"You have three million dollars?" the nerd asked.

"Let us see our mother and then we will discuss payment," the boy said.

Laz felt his heart clench as he saw the videocamera turned to Daphne. Tears were running down her face and she was so choked up she could barely speak. But he understood her words.

"Do not pay any ransom. I love you, Josh and Lucas. Don't ever forget that."

Samatan walked down the length of the room and Laz brought his gun into position, lifting it, sighting Samatan. "Permission to take out target."

"Denied. We need him alive," Savage said.

For a second Laz tightened his finger on the trigger and almost disobeyed orders. This man was evil—the kind of demon that shouldn't be allowed to live—but he knew that making that decision wasn't his responsibility. He holstered his gun, kicked open the door, and ran for Samatan.

Climbing up and over the table, he hit Samatan in the chest with a flying sidekick that knocked the other man back.

Samatan's head hit the credenza. The other man reached up inside his jacket and Laz knew he was going for his weapon. He didn't give the man a chance. He grabbed the lapels of his jacket and used that to swing the pirate king around. Laz used his upper body strength to slam Samatan's head and upper body against the table.

In the background he was aware of Mann entering the room and dealing with the nerdy guy but Laz didn't let up. He just beat on Samatan until the other man couldn't stand up. Then he pulled the chair out and dumped his body in it. He reached inside Samatan's coat and pulled out his weapon.

"Leave him," Mann said. "Take care of the woman."

Laz did. He turned to Daphne, who was looking at him with a mixture of relief and shock.

"I thought you weren't going to get here on time," she said. "I thought I was going to die."

"Not while I'm around to protect you," Laz said.

"I was afraid to believe in you," she said.

He bent down to untie her feet and then removed the other bands that held her in the chair. He lifted her out of the chair and into his arms, holding her close to him. She was sweaty and bloody and so was he, but in that moment he knew that he had found his home.

"Mom? Are you really okay?"

"That bastard videoconferenced my kids," Daphne said to him.

"Yes, honey. I'm fine. Can you still see me?"

"Yes. And that bad ass who saved you."

Laz didn't know if he wanted Daphne's kids to have witnessed what he did. He was pretty sure their father had never done anything that violent.

"I'm sorry—"

"Don't apologize. Another man couldn't have saved my life, Laz. You did."

She kissed him softly. "Can we try to see my boys?"

Laz nodded. Daphne took a step but her legs were weak and she was wobbly. He lifted her in his arms and carried her to the end of the table where the computer was.

There in a small window was a man in a suit and in the one next to it were two teenage boys. They were both standing over the computer and staring intently at it.

"Mom? We can't see you any more," the taller one said.

"I'm here, Josh."

Laz reached up and turned the videocamera to face her and her face appeared in a little window.

"There you are."

"Here I am, Lucas. Are you boys okay? I was so afraid—"

She started crying and Laz put his hand on her shoulder.

"Don't cry, Mom. We weren't going to let anything happen to you."

"Thanks, boys. I love you very much."

"We love you too," they both said in unison.

"One, this is team leader. We need to take control of the freighter. If you think Daphne is safe lock her in the conference room, but you need to move."

"Confirm that. We still have work to do, Daphne."

"I'll talk to my boys later," she said.

"Bye, Mom," they said and closed their video window.

They didn't say anything to the other man in the video screen, just shut down the computer.

Mann had tied up the two men they'd taken out and was ready to move.

"Do you want to stay here?" Laz asked.

"No."

Mann nodded at him over Daphne's head. Laz squeezed her hand and then let it drop. He still had a lot of work to do and he knew he couldn't forget that. They needed to take over this ship and then rendezvous with the authorities so that Samatan and his men could be taken into custody.

"Let's move out," Laz said. "We are going to take the bridge."

Daphne didn't say anything, just stayed between Laz and Mann as they moved through the ship. They had to pause once when someone was moving toward their location but Laz stepped forward and knocked the man unconscious. Mann took the lead position while Daphne took his weapon and stood guard until Laz was able to tuck the body out of the way.

They started to move again and Laz had never been so anxious for a mission to be over. He really needed to be alone with Daphne and make sure nothing had changed between them.

Chapter Eighteen

The two worst strategic mistakes to make are acting prematurely and letting an opportunity slip; to avoid this, the warrior treats each situation as if it were unique.
—PAULO COELHO

Daphne stayed with Laz and Mann until they reached the bridge, then he signaled her to stay out of the way. She took the weapon he offered her and stood tensely for less than ten minutes before Mann came back and signaled for her to join them on the bridge.

She was so tired she felt like she was bordering on exhaustion. She knew the signs of fatigue and had a feeling that she was going to collapse soon. She felt emotionally drained as well and wanted nothing more than to find a quiet place and curl up. She had a million questions but would ask them later. Laz was at the controls of the ship and on the radio talking to someone.

"Damn it. We are not in position for a chopper to land," Laz said.

"Make ready because we are on our way. ETA five minutes."

"What's going on?" Mann asked.

"A Marine Sea King chopper is requesting we hold position so that they can land," Laz said.

"Which government?"

"U.S." Laz said. "Savage?"

Laz listened to whatever his team leader said and Daphne just stared at him. She didn't have time to figure out what he meant to her. Right now she was in love with him but he wasn't the kind of man she could imagine spending a quiet Saturday running errands with or getting up early on Sunday to go to church.

Yet her heart was saying that he was the man for her.

"Sea King, you have permission to land," Laz said.

"What if it's a trap?" Daphne said.

"I'll take them out," Mann said.

He pulled a long sniper rifle from his pack and opened the window from the bridge that allowed them to see down to the entire deck. He leaned down low and took aim at the helipad.

"Where is your boss?" Daphne asked.

"Right here," Savage said, joining them on the deck. "Let the crew of the *Liberty Sun* know that we are in charge and order them to assemble on the deck."

"Mann, you are in charge of the chopper and deciding if it is a threat. Daphne, why don't you sit down?"

Savage was a commanding presence on the bridge and took control and gave orders easily. She walked to the battered looking chair in the corner and sat down.

Laz spoke to the ship via a loudspeaker system and Savage went to the deck and was joined by Wenz and Hamm.

"Where did they come from?" she asked Laz.

"After we pulled Franny from the water, Wenz took her back to the *Maersk Angus* and left her in Jerry's care. Then he and Hamm came to help us take this ship and deliver Samatan to our clients."

"Is Franny going to be okay?"

"I think so. I will find out after the chopper lands and the crew gets on board."

"How did you find me?" she asked Laz.

"Van was able to get the information from Habeb. He's really good at getting people to talk," Laz said.

"How?"

Laz looked at her. She ran her fingers through her hair and realized it was sticky. She imagined she looked the worse for wear right now. "Never mind. I don't want to know."

"He does what he needs to in order to get the job done," Laz said.

She nodded. "Thank you."

"For what?"

"Coming for me," she said.

"I gave you my word, Daph," Laz said. "I would never break it."

Suddenly she believed him. Trust wasn't just about what she felt inside about men in general and this one in specific. Trust was about the man who was giving his word and with Laz she'd always know where she stood. If he committed himself to her, he'd honor that commitment no matter what.

There was chatter on the radio and Laz turned back to that and concentrated on assisting the chopper to land.

After the rotating blades at the top stopped spinning, the door opened and a man in a three-piece suit stepped out.

"Who the hell is that?"

"Paul," she said. She stood up and walked over to Laz. "I can't believe he came here."

Laz didn't say anything. She had no idea what he was thinking but she realized that the power she'd always thought Paul had came from the way he used and commanded other people. She'd seen real power tonight in Laz.

"Why is he here?" she asked.

"I have no idea. You should go down there and talk to him."

She shook her head. "I don't know what to say to him. When I needed his help he wasn't there for me," she said. "Why is he here now?"

"Because he did let you down," Laz said. "He is trying to make up for that. And you are the mother of his children. He probably needs to make sure that you are okay if for no one else then for them."

That made sense to her. She wondered if he'd take her to the boys. But if she left with Paul, when would she see Laz again?

"I'm not sure where I'm going," she said. Then realized she sounded like a flake. "I mean if I go to Paul he might suggest going to the boys."

Laz looked at her. "Do what you have to do."

She thought long and hard and then looked at him. "I'm not ready to say good-bye to you yet, Laz. Will you . . . will you call me if I leave with Paul?"

He nodded. She looked around on the bridge and found a pen. She jotted her phone numbers and address and e-mail address on a piece of paper. "Here you go."

He took the paper. She glanced down at the deck and saw that Paul was talking to Savage. She looked back at Laz. Comparing the two men now was like comparing a Ken doll to G.I. Joe. It was so unfair to Ken because there was no way that a plastic man with great hair could compete with a battle-hardened warrior.

Daphne reached for Laz and wrapped her arms around him. His arms came up to enclose her and she felt for the first time since the night began that she was safe. She started to cry again because she didn't want to leave Laz. What if he decided that he didn't want to see her again?

She shook her head. She wasn't going to think that way. Life was a continuous journey and everything she encountered was to make her stronger. Hadn't she learned that the hard way tonight?

She cupped Laz's face, ran her fingers over the stubble on his jaw and the small cuts that were along his face and neck.

He'd fought hard to rescue her and she wasn't going to let him walk away. She had waited her entire life for a man like him.

She leaned up to kiss him and he took over the embrace in a second. His lips moving powerfully over hers, his tongue thrust deep into her mouth making a claim.

"Go. I will find you," he said when he lifted his mouth.

Reluctantly she did as he asked.

Laz watched Daphne and her ex reunite, and get on the Marine Sea King chopper. He knew that he might never see her again. He glanced down at the note where she jotted her contact information but he knew deep in his heart that once she got back to her real life a battle-scarred warrior like himself would have no place in it.

He remembered the tears on her face when he'd come in to rescue her and he wanted to go back down to that conference room and finish beating Samatan until the man no longer could draw a breath. But he wasn't a savage. Well, he wasn't today.

Because he really did hope to see Daphne again and he knew he couldn't go to her with blood on his hands. Not blood from a man who didn't need to be killed.

Savage entered the bridge. "We are late to meet with the client."

"I know," Laz said. "I didn't know if we should go with the Senator onboard."

"I've spoken to him and told him he must leave," Savage said.

Laz saw that Paul and Daphne were doing just that. He didn't feel any jealousy when he looked at them together because it was clear from their body language that Daphne and Paul weren't a couple. Paul walked ahead of her, leaving her behind while they went to the chopper.

But then she hesitated and he realized she wasn't going to

go with her ex. He wasn't sure how he knew it but he did. She looked up at the bridge and he felt . . . really felt . . . the love that had been growing in him since the first moment they'd met. He leaned out the window and pointed to the chopper.

She shook her head. But he shook his back. "I'll wait for you in Madrid."

He nodded once to acknowledge he heard her. Then she turned and walked back to the chopper. Laz focused on getting the chopper off the deck of the *Liberty Sun*.

"I guess you want some leave time after this mission is over," Savage said.

"Hell, yes," Laz said. There'd be time later to figure out the details, but he wasn't about to let Daphne walk out of his life.

He put that to the back of his mind as he concentrated on steering the ship to the rendezvous point. They were there for less than five minutes when they received word that another chopper was on its way and would be landing. Abdu Samatan and his "negotiator" Lambert Syles were brought on deck. Laz was needed on the bridge and stayed there as the men were loaded onto the helicopter. There was a second transport type chopper that landed next and collected the rest of the pirates on board.

They met up with the *Maersk Angus* and Laz took back his ship. The crew and the doctors were happy to see him. It took two more days for everything to be wrapped up. Tankers International sent another captain to take the *Maersk Angus* into port and Laz was happy to leave the ship behind. The Savage Seven missed capturing Samatan's boss but had a lead that they were tracing.

The doctors' group had all been flown back to Madrid, and Laz had heard from Rudy that Franny took Bob's body back to the United States. Jerry and Rudy apparently had spent the last two days drinking and trying to "forget their time on the ship."

No one had mentioned Daphne and Laz didn't ask about her. He waited until he was in Madrid. He had used his contacts to find out where she was staying and now he stood in the lobby of the very luxurious Hotel Orfila.

Standing here he realized he was outclassed by her. This wasn't the kind of place he'd ever choose to stay in. He could afford it because being a soldier for hire paid well. He had always figured it was because men who asked you to put your life on the line knew they had to pay you well.

But now he realized that bank accounts had nothing to do with the differences between them. He wondered why he'd even come here.

"You going to stand here all day or go and see your woman?" Mann asked him.

Laz shook his head. "Mind your own damned business. Aren't you supposed to be meeting Olivia here?"

"Yes. She said your lady has good taste in hotels."

"I'm not sure she's my lady," Laz said.

"Why not? I saw her face when we rescued her. She looked at you the way Olivia looks at me. It's something I can't describe because I'll sound like a mook but you'd be a fool to let that girl go."

Laz knew he wasn't a fool. "This life . . ."

"Is how she is coping with almost having died. I didn't understand that at first. But being married to Olivia has taught me that women cope in different ways than we do."

"Kirk!"

Laz and Mann turned at the sound of his name. Standing there was Kirk's lovely wife. Laz watched as Kirk tipped his head to the side and Olivia ran to him and threw herself in his arms. Olivia was dressed to the nines and Kirk wore his jeans and a black T-shirt. Looking at them together like this Laz knew that the outer trappings of men and women had nothing to do with why they were together.

He walked away from his friend and took out his cell phone. He dialed Daphne's number and waited until she answered his call.

"Hello?"

"It's Laz."

"Jean-Pierre, I've been waiting for your call. Where are you?"

"In the lobby of your hotel."

"Want to come up?" she asked. "My sons are here with me."

"I . . . I'm not sure," Laz said. He had always been very sure of himself but suddenly he didn't know. Loving Daphne was going to be the easy part. But she had kids. And they had seen him beat the hell out of another man.

"Maybe this is a mistake," he said.

"No. It's not. Stay there. I'll come down to you."

She hung up before he could agree or disagree. And Laz stood there in the lobby for five of the longest minutes of his life until Daphne stepped off the elevator.

Seeing her again made him realize that whatever he had to do to keep her, he was willing to do. He didn't want to live without this woman. He wasn't going to.

She wore a light and airy sundress and her hair hung in soft waves to her shoulders. She hurried her pace when she saw him and when she was close enough she reached out and drew him into her arms.

She hugged him so close to her and then put her hands in his hair and just stared up at his face. "I missed you. I've spent days in this hotel room wondering where you were and if you were okay."

He hugged her close to him and then kissed her. He couldn't say the words that he felt right now. They'd leave him too weak and too vulnerable and he wasn't prepared for that. Not now at any rate.

He used his kiss and his embrace to tell her how much he missed her. He tried to communicate with his body how very much he needed her and that he never wanted to let her go.

"Wow, Mom. That's some kiss."

Daphne laughed and pulled away from him. But kept hold of his hand. "J.P., these are my boys Josh and Lucas. Boys, this is J.P."

The older boy stepped forward first and held out his hand. "I'm Josh."

He looked a lot like Paul but had Daphne's eyes. His grip was strong when Laz shook his hand.

"I'm Lucas."

The younger boy looked exactly like Daphne and his grip was just as strong. "Thanks for saving our mom. We are going out to do the tourist thing. You two can talk upstairs."

"Yeah, we'll see you for dinner, okay?"

The boys walked away after hugging Daphne and she watched them go. "I told them all about you."

"Really? What did you say?"

She looked up at him and then stepped closer. "I told them I loved you and if there was any chance you felt the same way I wanted to try to make a life with you."

"I love you too, Daphne. But I'm not sure I'm cut out for life in suburbia."

She took his hand in hers and led him to the elevator. "We can figure that part out later. I didn't imagine you'd quit your job and stay at home with me."

"You didn't?"

"No. Do you want to?" she asked.

They were alone on the elevator and she pushed the button for her floor. As soon as they started to move he realized that this was real. That this woman was his.

He pulled her back into his arms. "I think I'd do whatever you asked me to."

"I'm not going to ask you to be anything other than the man you are. I love you very much, Jean-Pierre Lazarus. You brought me back to life and then saved me when I thought I'd die."

"That's just hero worship stuff, Daph. Are you sure you love me?"

"Yes."

"Make very sure because I realized when we were on the *Liberty Sun* that I'm not going to let you go. Once I claim you as my own, we are going to be together for the rest of our lives."

"Promise?" she asked.

"I do," he said.

He repeated those same words nine months later in a simple marriage ceremony on the beach in South Florida. The men of the Savage Seven were in attendance, as were Daphne's sons and Jerry, Rudy, and Franny.

They had figured out their lives the best they could. Laz continued to work with the Savage Seven and Daphne continued her practice. She no longer felt hemmed in and trapped by her routine because of Laz.

He was the man who had proven to her that promises were made to be kept and love didn't mean having to settle.

"You may kiss the bride."

Laz pulled her into his arms and kissed her long and deep and Daphne knew that the promises would last a lifetime in his embrace.

If you liked this book, go out and get Emma Lang's RUTHLESS HEART, out now . . .

Grady had never met a woman like Eliza, if that was even really her name. She talked like a professor, rode around with twenty pounds of books, and could build a campfire like nobody's business. Yet she was as innocent as a child, had a sad story about a dead husband he didn't believe for a second, and seemed to be waiting for him to invite her along for his hunt.

He snorted at the thought. Grady worked alone, always and for good. There sure as hell was no room for anyone, much less a woman like Eliza.

He had damn well tried his best to shake the woman, but the blue-eyed raven-haired fool wouldn't budge. Truth be told, he was impressed by her bravado, but disgusted by his inability to shake her off his tail the night before. Rather than risk having her do the same thing again, he decided to ride like hell and leave her behind. He should have felt guilty, but he'd left that emotion behind, along with most every other, a long time go. Grady had a job to complete and that was all that mattered to him.

The only thing he was concerned about was finding the two wayward wives he'd been hired to hunt and making sure they regretted leaving their husband, at least for the five seconds they live after he found them.

Grady learned as a young man just how much he couldn't trust the fairer sex. His mother had been his teacher, and he'd been a very astute pupil. No doubt if she hadn't drank herself to death, she'd still be out there somewhere taking advantage of and using men as she saw fit.

The cool morning air gave way to warm sunshine within a few hours. He refused to think about what the schoolmarm was doing, or if anything had been done to her. If she could take care of her horse and build a fire, she could take care of herself. Food could be gotten at any small town, but then again maybe she could hunt and fish too.

Somehow it wouldn't surprise him if she did. The woman seemed to have a library in her head. Against his will, the sight of her unbound black hair popped into his head. It had been long, past her waist to brush against the nicely curved backside. Grady preferred his women with some meat on her bones, better to hang onto when he had one beneath him, or riding him. He shifted in the saddle as his dick woke up at the thought of Eliza's dark curtain of hair brushing his bare skin.

Jesus Christ, he sure didn't need to be thinking about fucking the wayward Miss Eliza. If she was a widow, no doubt she'd had experience in bed with a man. It wasn't Grady's business of course, so he needed to stop his brain from getting into her bloomers, or any parts of her anatomy.

As the morning wore on, Grady's mind returned to the contents of her bags. The woman didn't have a lick of common sense and fell asleep, vulnerable and unprotected. Good thing he didn't have any bad thoughts on his mind or she wouldn't have been sleeping. She even snored a little, something he found highly amusing as he'd rifled through her things.

Her smaller bag had contained a hodgepodge of clothes, each uglier and frumpier than the last, a hairbrush, half a dozen biscuits in a tattered napkin and some hairpins. A measly collection of a woman's life, and quite pitiful if that was all she had. Perhaps she'd been at least partially truthful about taking everything she owned and hitting the trail. Her husband must have been a poor excuse for a provider if this collection of bags was all she had.

The bag of books was just that, a bag stuffed full of scientific texts ranging from medical topics to some titles he couldn't even pronounce. In the bottom of the bag was a battered copy of *Wuthering Heights*. He didn't know what it was but it was much smaller than the other books, likely a novel. She obviously put the spectacles to good use judging by the two dozen tomes she had in her bag. He wondered how she'd gotten it up on the saddle in the first place.

"Fool." He had to stop thinking about Eliza and what she was doing and why. Grady would never see her again.

As a child, Grady learned very early not to care or ask questions. It only bought him a cuff on the ear or a boot in the ass. A boy could only take so much of that before he learned to keep his mouth shut and simply sneak around to find out what he needed to know.

As a young man, it served him well and garnered the attention of the man who taught him how to hunt and kill people in the quickest, most efficient way. Grady had learned his lesson well, even better than his mentor expected. When the job was put before him to hunt and kill the man who had taught him those very skills, Grady hesitated only a minute before he said yes.

The devil rode on his back, a constant companion he'd come to accept. He didn't need a woman riding there too.

And try Cynthia Eden's latest, I'LL BE SLAYING YOU, out now from Brava!

The music was terrible, the food was shit, and the crowd of dancers were all but screwing on the floor.

Dee leaned against the bar, trying to ignore the throbbing in her temples and letting her gaze sweep past the throng inside Onyx.

This was the eighth club she'd been in since she'd hit the streets. Humans only. Well, mostly humans. Onyx catered to the unaware, and that made the place perfect for vamps. So much easier to pick up prey when the humans didn't realize the danger they faced.

They didn't realize it, not until their dates stopped seducing them and started feeding from them.

By then, it was too late to scream.

Her nails drummed on the bar. Zane lounged in the back corner, his emerald gaze sweeping over the room. Some big-breasted blonde was at his side. Typical.

Jude hadn't made an appearance yet. But he would soon. She'd use his nose to sniff out the place. See if he could detect the rot of the undead and—

"Let me buy you a drink."

She'd ignored the men beside her. Greeted the few come-ons she'd gotten with silence. But that voice—

Dee glanced to the left. Tall, Dark, and Sexy was back.

And he was smiling down at her. A big, wide grin that showed off a weird little dint in his right cheek. Not a dimple, too hard for that. She hadn't noticed that curve last night, now with the hunt and kill distracting her.

Shit, but he was hot.

Thanks to the spotlights over the bar, she could see him so much better tonight. No shadows to hide behind now.

Hard angles, strong jaw, sexy man.

She licked her lips. "Already got one." Dee held up her glass.

"Babe, that's water." He motioned to the bartender. "Let me get you something with bite."

She'd spent the night looking for a bite. Hadn't found it yet. Her fingers snagged his. "I'm working." Booze couldn't slow her down. Not with the one she hunted.

Black brows shot up. Then he leaned in close. So close that she caught the scent of his aftershave. "You gonna kill another woman tonight?" A whisper that blew against her.

Her lips tightened. "Vampire," she said quietly and dropped his hand.

He blinked. Those eyes of his were eerie. Like a smoky fog staring back at her.

"I hunted a vampire last night," Dee told him, keeping her voice hushed because in a place like this, you never knew who was listening. "And, technically, she'd already been killed once before I got to her."

His fingers locked around her upper arm. She'd yanked on a black T-shirt before heading out, and his fingertips skimmed her flesh. "Guess you're right," he murmured and leaned in even closer.

His lips were about two inches—maybe just one—away from hers.

What would he taste like?

Keep an eye out for BEDDING THE ENEMY
by Mary Wine, coming next month . . .

He was staring at her.

Helena looked through her lowered eyelashes at him. He was a Scot and no mistake about it. Held in place around his waist was a great kilt. Folded into pleats that fell longer in the back, his plaid was made up in heather, tan and green. She knew little of the different clans and their tartans but she could see how proud he was. The nobles she passed among scoffed at him but she didn't think he would even cringe if he were to hear their mutters. She didn't think the gossip would make an impact. He looked impenetrable. Strength radiating from him. There was nothing pompous about him, only pure brawn.

Her attention was captivated by him. She had seen other Scots wearing their kilts but there was something more about him. A warm ripple moved across her skin. His doublet had sleeves that were closed, making him look formal, in truth more formal than the brocade-clad men standing near her brother. There wasn't a single gold or silver bead sewn to that doublet but he looked ready to meet his king. It was the slant of his chin, the way he stood.

"You appear to have an admirer, Helena."

Edmund sounded conceited and his friends chuckled. Her

brother's words surfaced in her mind and she shifted her gaze to the men standing near her brother. They were poised in perfect poses that showed off their new clothing. One even had a lace-edged handkerchief dangling from one hand.

She suddenly noticed how much of a fiction it was. Edmund didn't believe them to be his friends but he stood jesting with them. Each one of them would sell the other out for the right amount. It was so very sad. Like a sickness you knew would claim their lives but could do nothing about.

"A Scot, no less."

Edmund eyed her. She stared back, unwilling to allow him to see into her thoughts. Annoyance flickered in his eyes when she remained calm. He waved his hands, dismissing her.

She turned quickly before he heard the soft sound of a gasp. She hadn't realized she was holding her breath. It was such a curious reaction. Peeking back across the hall she found the man responsible for invading her thoughts completely. He had a rugged look to him, his cheekbones high and defined. No paint decorated his face. His skin was a healthy tone she hadn't realized she missed so much. He was clean-shaven in contrast to the rumors she'd heard of Scotland's men. Of course, many Englishmen wore beards. But his hair was longer, touching his shoulders and full of curl. It was dark as midnight and she found it quite rakish.

He caught her staring at him. She froze, her heartbeat accelerating. His dark eyes seemed alive even from across the room. His lips twitched up, flashing her a glimpse of strong teeth. He reached up to lightly tug on the corner of his knitted bonnet. She felt connected to him. Her body strangely aware of his, even from so great a distance. Sensations rippled down her spine and into her belly. She sank into a tiny curtsy without thought or consideration. It was a response, pure and simple. Her heart was thumping against her chest and she felt every beat as if time had slowed down.

A woman crossed between them, interrupting her staring. It was enough time for her mind to begin questioning what she was doing. Fluttering her eyelashes, she lowered her gaze, forcing herself to move through the court on slow steps. She ordered herself to not look back. She was warm, warmer than the day warranted. The reaction fascinated her but it also struck a warning bell inside her mind. She should not look back.

But a part of her didn't care for that. It clamored for her to turn and find him again. His eyes were as dark as his hair but lit with some manner of flame. She wanted to know if he was still watching her, wanted to know if she glimpsed the same flames in his eyes that she felt in her cheeks.

Ah yes, but fire burns . . .

Helena smiled. She enjoyed the way she felt, a silly little sort of enjoyment that made her want to giggle. The reason was actually quite simple. The way he looked at her made her feel pretty. Court was full of poetry and lavish compliments, but none of it had touched her. His eyes did. The flicker of appreciation was genuine.

She had never felt such before.

"Good day to ye."

She froze. The man must be half specter to move so quickly. But she wasn't afraid of him. Quite the opposite. Her gaze sought his, curious to see if his eyes continued to fascinate her up close.

She was not disappointed. Her breath froze in her lungs, excitement twisting her belly. His gaze roamed over her face and a pleased expression entered his eyes. In fact it looked a bit like relief.

She was suddenly grateful to Raelin all over again for having freed her of the heavy makeup. The way he looked at her made her feel pretty for the first time in her life.